THE DELTA TANGO TRILOGY is an in-depth journey of one man as he threads his way through personal problems and the challenge of his harrowing career as a U. S. Border Patrol Agent. His life of trials and sorrows rivals any fiction story today.

–**Clive Cussler**, *New York Times* bestselling
author of the Dirk Pitt series

ESSENTIAL AND GRIPPING. *Delta Tango Trilogy* is a heartbreakingly honest tale of the lives that intersect and are forever changed along our bleak and dangerous southern border. This is an important set of novels, not to be missed or forgotten.

–**Margaret Coel**, *New York Times* bestselling
author of *Winter's Child.*

USING HIS OWN EXPERIENCE in the U.S. Border Patrol, Christopher LaGrone paints a detailed and intimidating picture of the physical and mental hardships that must be painstakingly endured in order to work as an agent.

–**U.S. Review of Books**

READER COMMENTS

I think those who read the trilogy will be sad that there isn't another Layne Sheppard novel forthcoming. Book Three: *Moments of Truth* is amazing!

I'm hooked! I know next to nothing about the life of a U.S. Border Patrol agent, so this is new reading territory for me.

After reading *Fleeing the Past*, I have a totally new respect for what it takes to become a Border Patrol officer. I'm looking forward to Book Two: *Felina's Spell* and Book Three: *Moments of Truth*."

After having read *Fleeing the Past*, I was anxious to read the next book in *The Delta Tango Trilogy.....Felina's Spell*. It did not disappoint! The author's descriptive language makes you feel like you are right there with Layne on his night patrols. I am impatiently waiting for the final chapters of *The Delta Tango Trilogy, Moments of Truth*.

In Book Two of the *Delta Tango Trilogy, Felina's Spell*, author Christopher LaGrone makes it clear that there are no easy answers to the turmoil the borders create. I am looking forward to the third book in the trilogy, which promises to be as engaging and thought-provoking as the first two.

DELTA TANGO TRILOGY

The *DELTA TANGO TRILOGY* by Christopher LaGrone follows Layne Sheppard from the day he applies to join the U.S. Border Patrol through the rigors of the Federal Law Enforcement Training Center (known as the Border Patrol Academy) and his alternating exhilaration, anxiety, and drudgery as a field trainee, to the often harrowing moments of shift work on the U.S.-Mexico border. Along the way he deals with his own insecurities, a serious drinking problem, the internal politics of Douglas Station in extreme southeast Arizona (where he's assigned) and, for him, the unimaginable: Falling in love with a beautiful girl who was brought over the border as an infant—one of those illegals known as a Dreamer. Through Layne's experiences, life in the U.S. Border Patrol comes alive in ways few Americans can even imagine.

In Book One—**Fleeing the Past**—Layne strives to prove, to himself and others, that his failures of the past are in the past. As he seeks self-respect and self-confidence, he endures the boot camp-like ordeal of the Border Patrol Academy in sweltering New Mexico—punishing long-distance runs and debilitating hand-to-hand combat. During precious free time he meets Felina Camarena Rivera. Both keep personal secrets and pursue plans for escaping them—plans they also keep to themselves, even as their attraction for each other deepens.

In Book Two—**Felina's Spell**—Layne struggles to overcome the politics of the BP's Douglas Station and advance from trainee to regular agent status—to succeed. As he rides with seasoned veterans, Layne gets a first-hand look at the challenges border agents face on a daily and nightly basis and learns realities that agents either accept begrudgingly or surrender to. Felina's clever plan to become Layne's wife seems headed for success, despite Layne's serious drinking problem, when Felina's brother is charged with DUI and deported.

In Book Three—**Moments of Truth**—Layne realizes the inevitable loneliness and fear of patrolling the border without a partner, and pressure from management mounts. While experiencing many "agent adventures," he faces several moments of truth, both personal and professional, among them dealing with secrets Felina has held. She, too, must come to grips with tough choices; can she rely on Layne? They undertake an audacious gamble, and their futures, individually and together, hang in the balance.

THE DELTA TANGO TRILOGY

BOOK THREE

Moments of Truth

THE DELTA TANGO TRILOGY

BOOK THREE

MOMENTS
OF
TRUTH

A Layne Sheppard Novel

CHRISTOPHER
LaGRONE

NEW YORK

LONDON • NASHVILLE • MELBOURNE • VANCOUVER

Moments of Truth

The Delta Tango Trilogy - Book Three / A Layne Sheppard Novel

© 2022 Christopher LaGrone

All rights reserved. No portion of this book may be reproduced, stored in a retrieval system, or transmitted in any form or by any means—electronic, mechanical, photocopy, recording, scanning, or other—except for brief quotations in critical reviews or articles, without the prior written permission of the publisher.

Publisher's Note: This novel is a work of fiction. Names, characters, places, and incidents are either products of the author's imagination or used fictitiously. All characters are fictional, and any similarity to people living or dead is purely coincidental.

Published in New York, New York, by Morgan James Publishing. Morgan James is a trademark of Morgan James, LLC. www.MorganJamesPublishing.com

Morgan James BOGO™

A **FREE** ebook edition is available for you or a friend with the purchase of this print book.

CLEARLY SIGN YOUR NAME ABOVE

Instructions to claim your free ebook edition:
1. Visit MorganJamesBOGO.com
2. Sign your name CLEARLY in the space above
3. Complete the form and submit a photo of this entire page
4. You or your friend can download the ebook to your preferred device

ISBN 9781631955495 paperback
ISBN 9781631955501 eBook
Library of Congress Control Number:
2021933922

Cover and Interior Design by:
Chris Treccani
www.3dogcreative.net

Morgan James is a proud partner of Habitat for Humanity Peninsula and Greater Williamsburg. Partners in building since 2006.

Get involved today! Visit
MorganJamesPublishing.com/giving-back

*To a dream realized
and a legacy preserved*

IN MEMORIAM

The unexpected phone call from Nancy came in mid-December 2018. "Denny, I have terrible news," she said. "Chris died."

And that's how the completion of The Delta Tango Trilogy began.

I had gotten to know Nancy as the person in charge of author events at the Barnes & Noble bookstore on Colorado Boulevard in Denver. Over several years she hosted me each time I had a new book, and we collaborated on several Colorado Authors' League events.

One day, I think it was in 2016, she asked if I would be willing to look at a manuscript written by a young guy who wanted very much to be an author; he needed a professional critique of what he had written.

Sure, I said. I enjoy working with aspiring writers.

Chris LaGrone (the brother of Nancy's sister-in-law, I later learned) was then in his late thirties. He had been an agent in the U.S. Border Patrol for a time and had written a novel based on his experiences.

I read it and was impressed with the quality of his writing and the content of his story. But I told him, "No publisher will ever publish this, Chris, because it's too linear. It's just your character's experiences getting into and going through the Border Patrol Academy, being a field trainee, and then becoming an actual agent." I thought it provided insights the public didn't have, but to make a compelling book it needed more.

"Novels," I told him, "have subplots—twists and turns that make the overall story more complex, and thus, more interesting."

I gave him an example: "You're writing about someone whose job is to catch illegal aliens trying to sneak into the United States. Why not have him fall in love with an illegal? That would complicate matters!" I suggested that he read Helen Thorpe's wonderful book *Just Like Us* to learn what a so-called "Dreamer" faces living in America without legal status.

I also told Chris his main character, Layne Sheppard, needed to have a personal issue to overcome—a demon to conquer. I left it to him to decide what that would be.

Chris proved to be the most coachable writer I've ever worked with. He came back to me some time later with a rewritten manuscript that contained love, conflict, and a demon for the main character. Again, I read it. And again, I was impressed. But again, I saw a problem.

"No publisher will publish this, Chris," I told him. "Two hundred fifty thousand words is too long."

But I offered a suggestion: "We could turn this into a trilogy," I said. "This would break nicely into three books."

Chris liked that idea and saw immediately how to divide his story into three parts. Thus began almost two years of rewriting and editing. Chris would send me chapters as he finished drafts. I'd edit them and send them back to him for revisions. He'd return them to me, and I'd add the finished versions to a growing manuscript file.

We had finished Book One this way and were halfway through the same process for Book Two when Chris informed me that he was going to Argentina in August 2018 to improve his already fluent Spanish and learn more about the Hispanic culture. From Argentina he was to travel to Chile and Peru.

Before Chris left Denver, he finished drafts of all of Book Two's chapters, and we discussed a rough outline for Book Three. His absence allowed me time to focus on a book of my own that I was finishing.

In late October I emailed Chris, asking when he would be returning. "We need to hit it once you are back in town," I wrote.

"I'm in South America for another few months," he wrote back. He was looking forward to visiting the Atacama Desert in Chile, where the thirty-three Chilean miners were trapped underground for sixty-nine days before their dramatic rescue in August 2010.

By early December 2018, Chris had made his way to Cusco, Peru (elevation 11,152 feet), via Lima (sea level). He was headed for Machu Picchu, the center of the Inca civilization of the fifteenth century, high in the Andes Mountains.

"Chris suffered from severe asthma his entire childhood," his mother Sherryl told me later. "It continued into his adult life. Changing altitude quickly when he flew from Lima to Cusco, his body was not able to adapt to the thin air quickly enough."

I can't begin to express how stunned I was when I received that startling phone call from Nancy in December 2018. But, somehow I knew right away what I wanted to do.

"This isn't the time," I began. "But when you think the time is right, please tell Chris's mom and sister (Aimee) that, if they'd like to have the trilogy finished as Chris's legacy, I'll volunteer to write Book Three. I have a good idea where Chris was going with it."

By then I had worked with Chris for more than two years. Over countless meetings I had coached him to develop the story as a three-book series. While Book Three wasn't yet in draft form, Chris and I had discussed it at length. I didn't know exactly how he planned to conclude, but he'd put all of the building blocks in place. And I'd edited enough of his writing to have a good feel for how he expressed things; I was confident that I could replicate his style.

I've never been in the Border Patrol, of course, and know virtually nothing about being an agent. Sustaining Chris's intimate knowledge of life in the Patrol would have been impossible for me. Luckily, I had a source who agreed to provide me with insights into Border Patrol policies and procedures and many examples of an agent's adventures. Thus, I knew I'd be able to fill Book Three with the kinds of true-life experiences Chris related so realistically in the first two books.

Just after the start of the new year, Nancy made sure I knew when and where Chris's memorial service would be held, and said she hoped I would attend. I didn't want to miss it, and afterwards I was thankful I hadn't, because, for as well as I had gotten to know Chris, I had no idea how important writing was to him until I listened to speaker after speaker talk about how badly he wanted to become a successful writer. It drove everything Chris did the last several years of his life.

I knew then what to expect, and a week or so after the service I received an email from Sherryl LaGrone that read, in part: "Aimee and I are very much interested in having you finish Chris's work." A week later his mother and I talked by phone, and in March I met her face to face for the first time, before a Colorado Rockies Spring Training game in Scottsdale, AZ.

The book I was finishing when Chris died was my tenth as an author, but all are non-fiction. I had tried writing fiction almost forty years earlier but decided that, as a career newspaper journalist trained in reporting facts accurately, I just wasn't good at making things up. But I'd edited many novels and had been working with Chris for two years. So, I was willing to take another crack at "making things up"—especially since Chris had done most of the hard fictionalizing: creating characters, setting scenes, and establishing the story arc.

My first step was to finish editing Book Two. I decided to end it five chapters earlier than Chris planned, and use those chapters in Book Three. I also had other material from Chris to build on, meaning at least a third of Book Three is his origination.

From there it was just a matter of answering the recurring question every novelist faces, though it was a new one for me: What happens next?

Chris inspired the answers.

I hope I've honored my friend Chris with the way I completed the story he created, and that my attempt to capture his storytelling style reads like the rest of this trilogy.

—Denny Dressman

ACKNOWLEDGMENTS

MY SON CHRISTOPHER was a successful high school and college baseball player, and like most athletes, most of his focus was on his sport. After graduating from college with a degree in marketing and working in various jobs, he discovered that his true passion was not athletics or marketing, but writing. After uncovering his passion, it became his goal to become a published author. Chris began pursuing his dream earnestly while serving as a U.S. Border Patrol agent.

His loving father Mark, my husband, was a high school teacher and Chris's baseball coach at Arvada West High. Mark, too, loved writing but kept it on a personal level. He encouraged Chris to write what became the *Delta Tango Trilogy*. The two of them would talk daily about their love of words, the challenges of working on the southern border, and the importance of pursuing one's dreams. Mark was Chris's rock.

When Mark died of cancer in 2014, the loss was tremendous for Chris, missing his daily visits with his dad. It was then that the LaGrone family's dear friend, Alan Olds, became Chris's confidant and mentor—and initial editor when Chris began writing his first *Delta Tango* manuscript. Retired from a full career as a highly respected and successful high school English teacher in Colorado, Alan guided and instructed Chris, who'd had no formal writing education. Our family is grateful for all the hours Alan spent with Chris, not only on his novel, but also as Chris's devoted and loving friend.

When expressing thanks, the first person who comes to mind is Denny Dressman, whose role is detailed in the *In Memoriam* section. Without Denny, there may never have been a *Delta Tango Trilogy*. For more than two years, he not only edited Chris's work and helped him develop his novel, ultimately into a trilogy; Denny also became a good friend to him during that time. Since Chris's unexpected death, Denny has become a good friend of mine, a mentor who has guided and instructed me throughout the process of bringing the trilogy to publication. I am eternally grateful for Denny Dressman, a true professional who is also kind and compassionate.

Thanks, also, to Nancy Hestera, wife of my son-in-law's brother, who first asked Denny if he would read Chris's original manuscript. And to Terry Whalin of Morgan James Publishing, and everyone in founder David Hancock's Morgan James family who helped produce this book and the entire trilogy.

It is with tremendous pride, as well as a heavy heart, that my daughter Aimee and I see Christopher's dream realized, and his legacy preserved, with publication of the *Delta Tango Trilogy*. We miss both Chris and his father deeply, but we know that they have been reunited in a better place.

—Sherryl LaGrone

Christopher LaGrone

MOMENTS
OF
TRUTH

IT WAS NEAR 5 A.M. but still as dark as midnight when Layne Sheppard walked wearily beneath the parking lot lights toward the Douglas Station entrance this early February morning. The stars were still visible, but his nerves repressed his usual admiration for them. *It's amazing how fast time goes by,* he thought. It was Friday morning already. His last exchange with Agent Tipton following Training Supervisor Escribano's most recent harangue, a mere twenty-four hours earlier, seemed like it had happened weeks ago. Worry over the threat posed by the Spanish Oral Board Exam could no longer be set aside for another time. He had no choice but to face the possibility his career would be over within a matter of hours.

The Spanish Oral Board Exam came at the end of a Border Patrol trainee's progression to agent. It tested each trainee's fluency in the language of the border but was subjective enough to enable management to discriminate regarding the personnel they would be dealing with during their tenure. It was management's last chance to get rid of trainees who weren't hard workers and any others they didn't want to keep around for whatever reason. This political dimension was what concerned Layne. He reminded himself that they'd have no choice but to advance him to regular agent status and assign him to a unit—if he cleared this hurdle—and that his Spanish had held up just fine when he lived in Mexico for a time years before.

Layne opened the door to the post-Academy classroom where the trainees who were to be tested this day mustered and realized he was the last to arrive. Everyone else was waiting quietly at their desks with their Smokeys resting on their desktops. Nine trainees, total, were scheduled to

1

make the trip to Tucson, where they'd take the exam.

The trainees weren't chatting sociably as they did before a normal day of class. Their anxiety was evident by their posture and the apprehensive expression they shared. Two of Layne's Border Patrol Academy classmates, Runyon and Carlos, said hello discreetly as he set his Academy backpack on the floor and prepared to take a seat at the desk nearest them. A third classmate, Melanie Schumer—who had given Layne a hard time throughout academy and field training and barbed him whenever an opportunity presented itself—for once had no snide comments to greet him. The others pretended Layne hadn't arrived. They had learned from months of observation that they were expected to disassociate themselves from those who didn't conform.

Layne swept off his desk chair and checked to make sure he didn't sit in gum or anything that would blemish his dress uniform. Everyone had spent additional time ironing and starching the creases in their pants and shirts to perfect folds. Likewise, each had taken care to pin their badges to the breast of their shirts to make sure the gold shield was perfectly vertical. Layne took off his Smokey and put it on the empty desk next to him, then removed his study materials from his backpack. Agent Cunningham, who taught them Spanish in post-Academy upon their arrival at Douglas Station, had not yet arrived. He was the lucky one who would transport them to their deliverance in Tucson. Layne recalled Melanie saying of Cunningham in the post-Academy classroom shortly after the trainees began Phase One: "I think he's kind of cute." He was certain she'd benefited in some way.

"I heard you got into it with a drive-through the other night," Runyon leaned over and whispered to Layne. Carlos grinned with interest and joined the huddle. Layne had grown to like Runyon, the Southerner who said he'd been in the military in Afghanistan before applying to the Border Patrol, even though he was always popping off. And steady Carlos Dos Santos—the polar opposite of Runyon—had become his best friend among the trainees. Carlos seemed secure. A *nativo,* he'd grown up speaking Spanish. And he seemed at ease in the Patrol's culture, though Layne had no idea why.

Layne resisted the urge to explain the event in detail because of the possibility the others could hear him. Someone like the irritating Melanie, the only female in Class 590, or her friend Greg would likely report what was overheard to a member of management. Layne could see peripherally that their ears had perked up, sensing secretive information was about to be shared.

"Dude, it was nuts," Layne whispered. "I'll tell you guys about it later—if, hopefully, I'm still here."

"Me, too," Runyon whispered back, the comment having straightened his grin.

"I hear ya, there," Carlos followed, even though he had the least reason for concern.

Layne felt like a marked man as he opened the page in his notebook that he had bookmarked with a stapled photocopy of the Voluntary Removal questions. The Spanish Oral Board Exam was no real danger to those who had been approved through the vetting process of Field Training, as long as they didn't freeze under pressure. But there were no guarantees for anyone except Melanie, who figured to sail through because no examiner would be willing to risk the hassle of an EEOC complaint if he flunked her. A trainee's ability to orate in Spanish was of little importance if he or she possessed management's stamp of approval, which came almost automatically for the females. With regard to white trainees who had been accepted into the brotherhood, as long as they demonstrated they had learned something in Spanish class they would be a regular agent by Monday.

Runyon was doomed but couldn't grasp how much danger he was in; he remained in denial. His pretentious behavior merely irritated his fellow trainees, but he frequently had gone too far and subjected superiors to it. His fellow trainees had watched in disbelief as he made pompous comments in inappropriate settings, such as lectures during post-Academy. He had an obnoxious tendency to correct Agent Ortega during a talking point at the white board, which was misconstrued as implying the instructor's knowledge was incomplete. Carlos had warned him to stop, but Runyon dismissed the advice and suggested that the instructors considered his interruptions to be class participation. At times, he had gone so far as to interject his expertise in the Fishbowl when an FOS and a supervisor were discussing procedure.

Rumors had begun circulating a month prior that Runyon was already on the hit list. He was the perfect victim due to his race and incompetency in Spanish. He was simply incapable of retaining vocabulary and understanding sentence structure, and his pronunciation was laughable despite considerable effort and time invested studying.

Layne wasn't much better off, though for vastly different reasons. He'd been called on the carpet for losing his notebook with all of his computer codes and passwords in it—and accused of lying about it even though he honestly didn't even realize it was missing. He'd been back in the hot seat for pursuing a Delta Tango—a drive-through pickup loaded with marijuana—in violation of policy because he wouldn't say that the veteran agent with whom he was riding had told him to chase the fleeing vehicle. And he'd been hung over more times than he could count when reporting for classes at the Academy and trainee shifts at Douglas Station, likely the reason the other incidents had resulted in disciplinary action. His performance on the Spanish Oral Board Exam would need to be nothing short of masterful to survive.

* * * *

LAYNE REACHED INTO HIS pocket to reassure himself that he had the prescription bottle containing the Valium that his aunt had sent him just for this day. He had claimed a window seat in the front-most bench of the van, directly behind Cunningham in the driver's seat. The ride to Tucson Headquarters was passing quickly—as traveling toward dread always did, Layne told himself. Agent Cunningham guided the van northwest on

State Route 80 with minimal commentary. He responded to questions about procedure with concise answers; preoccupation appeared to prevent him from elaborating as he usually did.

Layne resumed staring out the window with his chin on his palm. Sunlight sparkled on the early morning dew that glazed the desert shrubbery between Douglas and the Benson crossroads. It occurred to him once more that scenic beauty struck him most when trepidation prevented him from enjoying it. A vibration in his pocket notified him that a new text message had arrived. He removed his cellphone from his pocket and saw that the message was from Felina. It read, "Good Luck today. I'm proud of you." Layne smiled as he put his cellphone back in his pocket, then swallowed hard. The message served as a vivid reminder of what was at stake. If only he could have good news the next time he spoke to her. He couldn't think of anything he had ever wanted more.

Layne had met Felina Camarena Rivera at a graduation party for one of his Academy acquaintances, Ryan Danielson, who was in a class ahead of Layne. He fell for her almost instantly, though his insecurities had continually caused him to doubt that she could actually be attracted to him. Initially, he had sought to be a Border Patrol agent to put years of personal failure behind him and prove his self-worth. But after meeting Felina, his motivation expanded to include—as his top priority—achieving the prestigious position, which he convinced himself would win Felina's heart and hand.

But it wasn't a matter of prestige with Felina. While she found Layne funny and fun and wanted to be with him, she could put a lifetime of troubles behind her if he succeeded in becoming a Border Patrol agent, then married her. One of those illegal immigrants known as Dreamers, Felina had been brought across the border from Mexico as a baby by her parents. She had grown up in America, and her dream was to attend the University of Arizona and become a medical doctor. But first she needed the U.S. citizenship that marriage could bring, despite her illegal status. Her friend, Marianne, had told her at a pool party about Border Patrol agents who married Mexican women they'd caught trying to enter the U.S. illegally. She had conceived a plan that Layne was an essential part of, even though he didn't know it.

The van carrying the trainees to *el examen* was already on Interstate 10 after what seemed like only a brief period. The saguaros that dotted the desert as it streamed by and the Catalina Mountains that became visible in the distance to the right indicated the trainees were nearing Tucson.

Cunningham drove with his left hand on the bottom of the steering wheel and his right elbow on the armrest. He had been avoiding eye contact with Layne in the rearview mirror since they left Douglas. Layne had studied Cunningham every Friday in post-Academy for four hours since arriving in Douglas. Cunningham was tall and thin and had an intelligent, scholastic appearance. He looked like he would've worn glasses had he chosen any other profession. When he was teaching verb conjugation to the class, he resembled a white-collar inmate who had volunteered to teach his fellow prisoners in exchange for a reduced sentence.

Layne suspected the reason Cunningham was avoiding eye contact with him was because of the kill order he had been directed to communicate to headquarters regarding Layne. When they arrived, Cunningham was to meet with the kangaroo court of examiners in private to debrief them on Douglas management's wishes—such as the desire to forget what Runyon's voice sounded like. Each individual report that Instructor Cunningham was about to deliver to headquarters was momentous.

The dissonance remained perceptible in Cunningham's expression as Layne continued to glance at his reflection in the rearview mirror. Cunningham seemed to have been willing to teach Spanish but, Layne privately theorized, hadn't been aware of the dirty work involved with his chauffeuring duties until after he had agreed to perform the task. He had earned his day off from the field each week through intelligence rather than cronyism. Layne had a hunch Cunningham didn't approve of how management used the Oral Board to conduct its popularity contest. It was as if the trainees were pledging a fraternity. Cunningham didn't fit in either and seemed to disapprove of the informants and sycophants in the class.

* * * *

LAYNE STOOD IN LINE with the others and looked up at the menu board above the cashier, trying to decide what to order despite his lack of appetite. He felt people peering at him from the booths next to the window, and he watched his boots self-consciously until the gawkers concentrated on their food again. Cunningham had chosen to stop for breakfast at a McDonald's in east Tucson, being that they were slightly ahead of schedule. When in dress uniform, the trainees were required to wear the Smokey unless they were seated. This morning was only the third time Layne had worn the hat and polished green material of the ceremonial uniform. The pants wore like slacks and were decorated with a navy-blue stripe from the waist to the cuff. He didn't mind the stares while he was in rough gear. He thought the perception of him was more soldier-like. But the formal uniform drew a different ogle.

Half a cup of orange juice was required to wash down a bite of the dry sausage biscuit that molded itself to his palate. The cottonmouth had already set in. But the pharmaceutical ace up his sleeve kept him tolerably calm and reassured. He had transferred the precious contents of Aunt Teri's envelope to one of his prescription bottles labeled with an innocuous medication.

The crucial variable was the timing of when to take a Valium—the effects only lasted a few hours. He was not scheduled for a specific time to take the test. He knew only that he would be called sometime during a four-hour window. His timing was going to have to be determined by intuition. He was attempting to coordinate the drug's effect so that it peaked at the most beneficial period. But considering the intensity of the circumstances, he was uncertain of the dose required to remain calm. He had only three pills. If he needed all three, it would be difficult to determine when to take them. If he took them too early, they would wear off before he needed them. But if he took them just as the examiners called him, the drug wouldn't take effect until after the stress was over.

He decided to gamble that he wouldn't be among the first trainees to be called. He wouldn't take one until they arrived and he had a chance to gauge the procedure. He reasoned that calling him first would make the examiners' biased intentions too pronounced. He had gathered from experience that management was diligent about camouflaging collusion. Calling him somewhere in the middle would maintain the exam's fair and objective appearance.

* * * *

THE POST-ACADEMY CLASSROOM at Tucson Headquarters felt unusually cold, and despite the reunion of Academy classmates, it remained still and muted. Layne and his fellow Douglas Station trainees were the last to arrive. His classmates from other stations nodded and grinned at their friends as they filed through the doorway, and each chose an empty desk. Once they sat down, Layne counted twenty-five trainees waiting to take the exam. After modestly greeting one another, they became quiet again. The magnitude of the final exam's significance prevented the group from socializing.

Layne found a desk next to Fleming, his twenty-year-old friend from the Academy who was sitting directly behind Schneider, one of his old roommates.

Fleming was looking at his study materials as if it were just another day in class. He was able to stay calm no matter the situation. It was a skill Layne wished he could teach his nervous system. He considered perhaps it was because Fleming was so young; he knew he had plenty of time to correct his life's mistakes. It was well-known that his Spanish was as inadequate as Runyon's.

Schneider, who passed his free time at the Academy reading bodybuilding and health magazines, was a study in consistency. Everything fell neatly into place for him, as if securing a career in the Border Patrol were a letter he was mailing. His mood had never fluctuated throughout the four months that Layne had lived with him, even throughout the trials of Stacking and OC Training. Layne, meanwhile, could never decide which was worse, getting pummeled by four guys at once in Stacking or being blinded by pepper spray in OC. He still wondered how he had survived them—much less passed.

As soon as the Douglas Station trainees found seats, Cunningham made an immediate 180-degree turn and went directly back into the hallway to meet with the examiners. Speculation about what was being said behind closed doors increased Layne's anxiety, and his knee began to bounce. After five minutes, the doorknob turned, and like a hangman, a Tucson Station supervisor opened the door and came halfway into the classroom. He propped the door open with his back and read from a clipboard, "Danielson."

The fiancé of Felina's close friend Marianne, the one responsible for the "graduation" party where Layne met the girl of his dreams, put his Smokey on as he stood up and followed the supervisor out of the room. The sound of the door closing behind them was impactful in the stillness.

"Well, they're not going in alphabetical order," Melanie commented aloud.

Word was passed along that the examiners intended to place the trainees in the Muster Room after they finished the exam. It ensured that trainees who were finished couldn't share any test information with trainees who hadn't yet been examined.

Just under a minute later a different supervisor opened the door with paperwork in hand, "Fleming, you're up." Fleming took his time getting up from his seat, put on his Smokey, and carefully adjusted the strap in the back. He calmly looked around at his companions in the class as if to form a memory. His expression was downcast, like he was looking at each of them for the last time.

After the door closed behind him, Melanie said, "They're doing two at a time. They must be in a hurry to get done." Layne took notice with alarm. He hadn't anticipated multiple exams being administered simultaneously. The succession was much more rapid than it had been during the hiring process oral boards in Denver. He realized he had dodged a bullet by not being a part of the first round. Then he realized there might be more than two examiners, and he felt the blood rush to his face with panic. He stared at his desk in critical deliberation while his heart vibrated in his chest.

"Fleming's girlfriend is pregnant. He's getting married in a few months. Talk about pressure," Schneider said.

Layne was too overcome by his own dilemma to respond.

The trainees spent every last available minute cramming. The tension in the room didn't allow for any sustained conversation. Layne retrieved his Voluntary Removal questions from his notebook and pretended to review them for a moment. Then he stood up and mumbled that he had to use the bathroom. The others barely glanced away from their notebooks at him as he left the room as casually as adrenaline would allow.

The spacious hallways resembled what Layne imagined the hallways in the Pentagon would feel like. They were vacantly quiet, and the squeaks from his polished roper boots echoed the length of the corridor while he hastened for signs of a bathroom. Tucson Sector Headquarters was at least three times the size of Douglas Station. Concertina wire enveloped several hundred green and white vehicles in a complex that resembled a military compound. Day-shift agents were in the field, leaving the hallways abandoned except for a few agents busy with administrative duties. They carried paperwork and glanced at him, nodding in salute as he passed, oblivious to his derelict status in Douglas.

He ducked into a bathroom and breathed a sigh of relief that his intuition had been correct about the chosen order. The only sensible move to make now would be to take one tablet, hoping it would be enough and his turn would come in a half-hour or more. He looked in the mirror above the sink and straightened his collar, then adjusted the tilt of his

Smokey. He felt like he had slipped away to the bathroom to do drugs at a costume party. The feeling that he had succeeded as an infiltrator came over him again. He removed the prescription bottle from his pocket while he leaned sideways to look and make sure there were no feet beneath the stall doors. He had to be overly cautious; being seen taking prescription pills under these circumstances would become gossip that would spread like wildfire. He placed a tablet under his tongue, and it began dissolving into a chalky paste that he washed down at a hallway drinking fountain on the way back to the classroom.

After twenty minutes of trying to remain still, he began to feel the tension in his chest release to a more tolerable plateau, and the pace of his knee bouncing declined. The first supervisor, who had come to get Danielson, returned and again held the door open with his back, clipboard in hand. He was about forty years old and appeared to be accustomed to wearing the dress uniform every day by the way he carried himself in it. Layne held his breath as he studied him. The supervisor lifted a page on his clipboard and said, "Schneider."

Schneider put on his Smokey as he rose from his seat and walked to the door with purpose. The other examiner would most likely arrive within a matter of minutes. Layne's intuition told him he would be next. Only ten milligrams of Valium were merely taking the edge off the agitation; the dosage wasn't sufficient. He stood up and headed for the door again, saying nothing. This time eyes followed him. He reassured himself that if anyone questioned him, he would tell them he had to vomit.

He stood in front of the bathroom mirror again, unsure of how much to take. He was afraid the second pill wouldn't be enough and that he might not have a suitable opportunity to take the third without someone noticing. He couldn't make three trips to the bathroom. But three tablets total, thirty milligrams of Valium, might be too much. He might strike the examiners as being inebriated. Nevertheless, he took both pills, reasoning that the approaching turbulence would balance the drug's effect. He returned to the classroom and sat down at his desk as inconspicuously as he could manage. The other trainees watched him, and Melanie leaned over to whisper something in Greg's ear. Layne pretended not to notice.

After fifteen minutes the second examiner opened the door. Layne knew intuitively while the doorknob was turning that his time had come.

"Sheppard, you're up," the examiner said as he verified the name on his clipboard. He took a long look at Layne as he rose from his seat and donned his Smokey. The examiner held the door open and fell in next to Layne as the door shut behind them. They said nothing to one another while they walked the long hallway, as if Layne were under arrest.

Layne's mouth was bone dry from fear, but he was holding himself together. Just as they turned a corner and slowed near the examination room, he felt the added twenty milligrams of Valium enter his bloodstream. The fear in the core of his chest was melting with each step, replaced with a warm, loving feeling. His movements and speech began decelerating to slow motion, and he found himself enjoying the situation he was in. They came to an office with the door closed, and the examiner said, "Wait here. I need to meet with my partner, then I'll come get you."

"Okay," Layne said. He stood waiting comfortably, as if he were waiting in line to deposit a check with a bank teller. The slowing sensation made him wonder why he couldn't maintain this frame of mind without substances. The drug didn't modify his surrounding circumstances to make them more bearable, only the way he perceived them. His confidence began to soar. He reminded himself he had once gone two lonely months speaking only Spanish in Mexico. He knew the examiners were going over their plan to thwart his attempt to pass, but it didn't concern him.

The same examiner opened the door and said, "We're ready for you. Come on in."

The office was small with a large desk and two cushioned chairs facing it. The office didn't seem to belong to anyone. It hadn't been personalized with photographs and desk trinkets. A female agent in her late thirties was sitting behind the desk. "Good morning. I'm Agent Sedillo, and this is Agent Kendrick."

"Nice to meet you," Layne said. Neither one of them offered to shake hands with him. He took a seat as Agent Kendrick sat down beside Agent Sedillo. Layne interlaced his fingers on his lap and smiled. Agent Sedillo did a confused double take at his grin. As Layne looked her over, he realized she was a supervisor by the bars on the collar of her dress uniform. She was Caucasian with a Spanish last name but wasn't wearing a wedding ring. She had blue eyes and sandy blonde hair that was situated in a tight bun in the back, below the rim of her Smokey. Agent Kendrick was blond and overweight. He was a foot shorter than Layne and appeared to be in his early to mid-forties. He looked like he was a lifetime employee of the government, beginning with the Army after high school. Both of them wore deceptive expressions that seemed to say to Layne there was much he didn't know about the situation, and he was naive to presume the test was fair.

Agent Sedillo pointed to a pencil and several sheets of notebook paper near the edge of the desk on Layne's side. "You have three sheets of scratch paper there."

Layne could tell they had been anticipating his exam. They behaved as if they had just finished talking bad about him behind his back and unexpectedly had to face him. Agent Sedillo seemed intrigued by his appearance. He didn't fit the image she had established in her mind. She said, "We'll start with the Voluntary Removal questions. Then we're going to trade off reading sentences in English, and you need to translate them and read them back to us in Spanish."

"Yes, ma'am," Layne said confidently.

"Go ahead and start with the VR questions when you're ready," Agent Sedillo said.

He recited the Voluntary Removal questions in Spanish effortlessly, without touching the pencil and paper. His primary concern was to mimic the Mexican accent as accurately as possible. Agent Sedillo was charmed by his pronunciation and fluency. She suppressed a flirty smile when she asked him questions. Agent Kendrick was surprised and impressed. Once

Layne completed the VR questions, they moved on to the improvised English to Spanish translations.

"You'll have two minutes to respond with your translation of each English sentence. Let me know when you're ready to begin," Agent Kendrick instructed.

"I'm ready now," Layne said without hesitation.

The examiners attempted to confuse him with every tense possible, and Layne returned the sentences to them as quickly as they could read them. He had ascended to an unassailable drug-induced zone. He felt incapable of making a mistake or forgetting anything he had ever learned. While in this state, a challenge only made what he was involved in more entertaining. He began to challenge himself by responding more instantaneously with each subsequent response until the examiners ran out of material to try to stump or trick him. By the end of the exam, Agent Sedillo looked fascinated and Agent Kendrick dumbstruck.

Agent Kendrick escorted him to the Muster Room, opened the door, and said, "Go ahead and have a seat in here." One by one, trainees entered the Muster Room, looking more anxious than they did before they had taken the exam. They tried to read the expression on others' faces as they entered the room and considered where to sit.

Layne had calmly sat down at a table next to Fleming. "I heard from guys who already took it that the examiners will call the people who failed into the hallway," Fleming said. "Then they'll tell the rest as a whole they passed. It's no big deal; it's just my life on the line," he added with gallows humor.

Layne remained silent.

"How'd you do?" Fleming asked Layne.

"Good. There was only one word I forgot, tools, *las herramientas.*"

"That's *all* you forgot? I didn't know squat. I'm screwed if I don't pass. I got a kid on the way," Fleming said.

The last two trainees finished their exams and were led to the Muster Room where they sat down to join whispering conversations. Trainees like

Fleming who had difficulty with Spanish waited in silent agony to learn the results. Layne yawned with fatigue; the Valium was beginning to wear off.

An hour went by until the door finally opened again. Everyone in the room held their breath. Agent Sedillo came into the room with a clipboard and announced, "We need to speak with Mr. Runyon and Mr. Fleming."

Layne looked to see Fleming turn white. He wouldn't look at Layne or make eye contact with anyone as he rose grimly and put his Smokey on. Layne glanced over his shoulder to the rear of the room where Runyon was sitting. Runyon put on his Smokey and leveled the tilt of the brim once he stood erect. The color disappeared from his cheeks and forehead as he pushed his chair in. Fleming stood behind his chair with a pallid face and waited for Runyon to pass by to fall in behind him. No one made a sound. Runyon remained looking straight ahead as he lumbered toward the door. It was as if he were walking to the scaffold for his execution. Agent Sedillo waited for them with a sympathetic frown.

As Runyon passed by, Fleming took his first step to follow him, and his knee buckled. His body went limp, and he fell sideways and crashed into the floor like a statue falling over. Layne watched in dazed disbelief as everyone in the room rushed to his aid. Then Layne rose to stand in the huddle that surrounded Fleming and watch dispassionately. The Valium dulled the effect of any kind of emotion. Agent Sedillo rolled Fleming onto his side and repeatedly told him he was okay as his eyes tried to open. As he observed the scene, Layne came to a difficult realization: He couldn't handle life's roulette-wheel spins without chemical assistance.

Carlos and Schneider helped Fleming to his feet, and Agent Kendrick led him out of the room and down the hall to receive medical attention. Agent Sedillo escorted Runyon to a room in the opposite direction. The rest of the trainees returned to their seats, and conversations began until the room was buzzing. Layne sat staring blankly at the whiteboard on the front wall. *What will my fate be?* he fretted.

Suddenly, the door opened once more, and the talking instantly ceased. Agent Sedillo stood in the doorway and beckoned Layne with her pointer finger. What was left of the Valium in his blood prevented his heart from jumping out of his chest. He was satisfied that there was nothing more he could've done to save himself. The room fell silent. He stood up and put on his Smokey as if he had been expecting to be summoned.

Agent Kendrick shut the door behind them as they entered the hallway and said, "We decided to pass you. You obviously know the language. Just make sure you do what you're told from here on out."

"Yessir."

"How did you learn to speak Spanish so well?" Sedillo asked.

"I lived in Mexico for four months in a house with a Mexican family, and they didn't speak English."

"What were you doing there?"

"Preparing for this," Layne said. "I've been planning this for a long time."

2

"OH! HI, MOM!" LAYNE SAID. The phone call came as he was opening the door to his little house in Bisbee. "Yeah, I just got back to my place. The test was in Tucson, so it's been a pretty long day. We left Douglas Station before six this morning. What? It's about two hours each way." Layne wanted to sound glad to hear from his mother and happy with the outcome. But he was tired and knew he'd be starting another two-hour drive back to see Felina as soon as he finished the call and changed out of his Border Patrol uniform. He did his best to sound engaged and eager to talk.

"It wasn't as bad I thought it might be," he said in response to a question. "I actually shocked the agents who administered the test. They couldn't believe how good my Spanish is."

He listened intently as his mom spoke, then said, "Yes. I passed. I'm now a full-fledged U.S. Border Patrol agent."

Being able to say those words—full-fledged Border Patrol agent—didn't leave Layne euphoric, as he expected they would when he dreamed up this gambit. All he could think about was the complications he dared not share with his parents and how new problems replaced old ones as life unfolded. He was sure they would not be pleased, would not understand.

"Congratulations! Your father and I are very proud of you!" Layne heard his mother exclaim.

"Thank you. I'm relieved," Layne admitted. He didn't want to get into his troubles with Escribano, and he hadn't yet mentioned that he was in a serious relationship, or at least a relationship he hoped was serious. His mom wanted to set up a visit right away. His parents were eager to make the trip from Denver to celebrate with him.

"Oh, I think it would better if you and Dad waited a little while longer before visiting me here," Layne demurred. "We can celebrate once I've had a little time as an agent on my own. Right now, I need to focus on doing a good job and getting off to a good start." *The last thing I need at this moment is a party to celebrate anything,* Layne thought. "I've worked all three shifts at different times the last four months, and I don't know yet when I'll be scheduled or how long I'll be on whichever shift I get to start."

Layne's mother didn't give in easily. His father really wanted to come down, she told him, and show him how pleased he was that Layne had succeeded. Layne was near panic. He had to think of something that would convince his mom and dad to wait.

"Sure, I'd love to talk to him for a minute," Layne said. "Put him on."

After listening to his dad tell him how proud he was and that he knew he could do it, Layne said, "I know you were hoping to visit now. But I don't want you to come here and me be working the overnight shift and sleeping during the day. And I don't want to not be able to spend time together because of something that happens while I'm on duty. I really need to settle into being an agent on my own before I entertain any visitors, especially family."

What Layne really wanted was a little more time for his relationship with Felina to progress, which he was sure it would now that he had achieved his goal of a full-time government job. He also was hoping that Escribano would let up on him now that he had qualified to be a regular agent. It was even possible that Layne could outwait his nemesis, and he'd go to the Academy as an instructor. Layne suggested his parents wait until late April or early May. He knew that his mother would be okay with whatever his father agreed to. He reiterated the logic in allowing him a little time to get established as an agent.

"Thank you," he finally was able to say. "I think that will be much better—well worth the wait."

Layne was ready to end the call, but his dad said something else.

"Love you, too, Dad," Layne said. Then: "Love you, too, Mom."

* * * *

LAYNE BEGAN BITING HIS NAILS as soon as he activated his car's turn signal to exit Interstate 10 a few miles from Felina's apartment. He had left Bisbee fifteen minutes after the call with his parents ended. He didn't feel great about persuading them to delay their visit, but he felt it had to be. *Too many loose ends right now,* he'd told himself. The coal grey clouds of a storm front were building in the west over the panorama of mountains he had come to associate with sanctuary. *Symbolic of what awaited?* he wondered.

He realized he had forgotten to turn the radio on and had been driving in silence for two hours. What should have been a day of triumph was instead fraught with unease—jubilation replaced with foreboding. Felina hadn't sounded as excited as he anticipated she would when he called from Douglas to tell her he passed. She drearily offered to come to Bisbee, but Layne had long planned to celebrate in Tucson. Something was wrong.

Wild speculation came to mind about the explanation for her change in attitude since the arrest of her brother Eduardo. Felina had told Layne that Eduardo, her younger brother, had been pulled over by a Pima County Sheriff's deputy at two in the morning. She'd said he was driving the wrong way on Ina Road. Layne feared the story about the arrest was a stopgap. He feared perhaps she had a child she was hiding from him. Or maybe she was secretly married . . . or both. He was afraid she planned to confess to cheating. Or something worse; perhaps she had appeared in a pornographic movie in the past. The thought nearly made him nauseous.

As he climbed the stairs to her apartment, he decided he would pretend he didn't suspect that anything was wrong and hope whatever it was blew over. He knocked three times, and when she answered, he was once again taken aback by her beauty. She was wearing tight jeans that gorgeously accentuated her hips. She had on a white camisole with a white sweater over it, buttoned part-way, exposing her bosom. Her olive skin was darker than the last time he had seen her. It made him wonder what she had been doing to become tan. Her hair was behind her ears, his second favorite way she wore it. But she was wearing a grim look that she was attempting to mask.

He smiled, and she responded with a grin that seemed to transcend the circumstances momentarily. It was the look they shared with each other that only they were aware of. It was as if their souls were winking at one another. He approached slowly to embrace her. Once she was in his arms, he lifted her off her feet and whirled her around in celebration. His hands remained holding her waist when he returned her to her feet. Her attempt to reciprocate his cheer appeared to be stagecraft. He could feel a forthcoming conversation of the sort he dreaded most. He followed her through the doorway, and she shut the door and locked the deadbolt behind him.

"So how does it feel to be a Border Patrol agent?" Felina asked him as they entered the kitchen.

"I don't feel any different than I did before," Layne said as he opened the refrigerator door and selected a diet pop. In his imagination, he was about to take a sip from a flute of cold champagne; he could taste the carbonation on the back of his tongue as it traveled his throat. The thought crossed his mind that Felina might allow him to drink just this one night, being he had proven himself and earned it. He would just have to lead into the question tactfully.

"So, was the exam as hard as you thought it was gonna be?" Felina was leaning with her backside against the dishwasher and her hands gripping the countertop behind her. It was a posture that was unnatural to her.

"No, it was easy. But I realized on the way up here it was just like a bookend that separates my old group of worries from the new ones I know I'm gonna have. Ever since I got the call to go to the Academy, I've been visualizing this day, and I thought there'd be marching bands and ticker-tape parades," Layne said.

"I know what you mean. I've felt like that before, too. I've just never been able to experience what victory is like," Felina responded.

The drunken bathtub incident still lingered in the atmosphere. It had occurred during a weekend visit a while back; Layne had been sneaking shots of vodka from shooter bottles and collapsed into Felina's bathtub, where she found him unconscious. He vowed then to stop drinking and had done his best. But it was hard, and Layne knew Felina remained concerned.

Layne cracked the top to his can of soda and slurped the foam from the rim, then said, "Runyon didn't make it. They got Fleming, too."

"Oh, no. Were those the only two that didn't pass?" Felina asked.

"Yeah. Fleming fainted when they called his name to tell him. They took him to the emergency room. I guess his fiancée is pregnant, and he was under a lot of pressure."

"Oh, those poor guys. Have you talked to them?" Felina said.

"I'm gonna call Fleming later. I talked to Runyon in the van on the way back to Douglas. He was pretty down in the dumps. He said he's moving back to Kentucky, but he signed a six-month lease on his house."

"I hope he's okay."

"He said he's concentrating on damage control," Layne said.

Felina looked at the floor, and Layne could tell she was trying to gather courage to say something. He said the first thing he could think of to interrupt her train of thought.

"How have you been holding up—with the brother situation, I mean?"

"I'm doing better. We're dealing with it. It's all you can do, you know?" Felina brought her hands together and looked down at the fingernails on her right hand.

"Yep, you just gotta pay the fines and forget about it," Layne said to try to continue the conversation.

Felina said abruptly, "Layne, there's something I gotta tell you about that."

A hair-raising shockwave of panic radiated up and down his spine that caused his scalp to tingle. He skipped a breath and resisted the urge to swallow dryly while she was watching him.

"What's wrong?" Layne said. It was no use trying to appear indifferent; he knew he looked desperate.

She looked down and began to fidget with her hands again. "Maybe we should sit down."

Layne didn't respond, and his mouth became instantly dry. He followed her from the kitchen to the living room as if he were facing a firing squad. His heart was beating like a snare drum as he quietly sat next to her on the couch. Flashbacks from sweaty nightmares overcame him, and it was difficult to look her in the eye. Felina took a deep breath while Layne waited with terror.

"I don't know how to say this; it's really hard for me," Felina said.

Layne froze in silence, expecting the worst.

"After my brother got arrested for DUI, some agents from ICE came and got him and deported him to Mexico," Felina forced herself to say.

"Deported? What do you mean?"

"When I was a little kid, my brother and I were in serious trouble . . . my whole family was," Felina said. She took another deep breath and seemed to all at once muster the strength to tell him. "We used to live in Mexico, and my mom and dad couldn't make enough money to take care of me and my brothers. So, we had to take a chance and come here so my parents could find a way to afford to feed us and buy us clothes. They were desperate."

A confused expression came over Layne's eyes and brow as he listened.

"We came over when I was about two. My dad came here first to find us a place to stay, and my mom brought me and my brothers to meet him here."

Layne's eyes became wide when she finished the sentence. He felt his heart arrest and start back up. In a state of shock, he whispered, "You were born in Mexico?"

Felina's strength collapsed when he spoke, and she began to cry. "Yes, in Guadalajara. My mom used her life savings to pay a coyote to bring us over the border. We came with a group of about twenty people. I can only remember bits and pieces of it."

Layne didn't respond. He turned away from her. He was stunned to such an extent that he felt incapable of speaking. *I've just become a Border Patrol agent, and I find out I'm in love with an illegal—the very type I'm trained to apprehend,* he thought. He stared at the coffee table in front of them. His neck and face turned blood red, and he wiped the perspiration from his forehead with the back of his hand.

"I'm so sorry, Layne. I didn't mean to mislead you in any way," Felina sobbed.

"And you've never gotten documentation?"

"No, I can't. If I tell them how I got here, I'm disqualified. I couldn't tell you when I met you. You're still the only other person besides Marianne who knows."

Layne couldn't speak, his head low as he tried to take in what he had just heard. Felina reached over with both hands and clutched his hand as she cried. Layne gently pulled his hand away and stood up slowly while Felina remained on the couch. She watched him as he walked toward the dining table between the kitchen bar and living room. He grabbed his jacket off the chair and put it on as he walked slowly to the door.

"I couldn't tell you. I had no choice," Felina pleaded as tears ran down her face. She stood up from the couch to follow him.

Layne unlocked the deadbolt and turned the knob to open the door without saying anything. Felina was sobbing uncontrollably. His reaction was worse than she ever imagined it would be.

"Layne, I'm sorry. Don't go. Please, talk to me."

But he opened the door and shut it behind him as he headed down the stairs. He hurried to his car and began backing out as soon as the engine started. He could see Felina watching him from the landing as he exited the parking lot.

* * * *

LAYNE WAS EXHAUSTED AND running on auxiliary power as he drove. His shoulders slumped; he was in an unstable state of disbelief. He had to remind himself that what had just happened was real, even as he wished it were just another dream. The sky was becoming dark, and he was the last one on the road to realize it was time for headlights. This time he chose to leave the radio off. Inevitably, the theme of being smitten with a woman would arise in a song. It would only compound the suffering.

The rhythmic tone of his turn signal blinking seemed to denote the ticking time bomb his emotional state had become. He quickly ducked into a gas station on the side of Ina Road and hurriedly parked next to the air pump for tires. He opened his door just in time to vomit on the smooth cement without making a mess on the car's interior. He kept the door propped open while excruciating dry heaves repeated themselves. When he felt it was over, he looked around to see if anyone was watching. There was a middle-aged man who glanced at him from one of the gas pumps while he was filling his truck. But the man returned the pump's nozzle to its hook and replaced his gas tank cap without looking in Layne's direction again. Layne wiped his mouth with his forearm and returned to the road. His phone began playing Felina's incoming ring tone. When the sound eventually stopped, there was a pause while his voicemail message intervened, then the tone resumed. He reached in his pocket, found the power button with his thumb, and turned it off.

He drove in a trance-like state on Interstate 10 and didn't stop in Benson the way he customarily did for gas and beef jerky. All he wanted was to get home, and he turned south onto State Route 80 with just enough gas to get there.

When he arrived home, he went to his room and sat on the edge of the bed to remove his shoes. He decided he would put away the clothes in his backpack later, when he felt better. "I don't know what to do with myself," he mumbled. He decided he would take a shower and try to go to bed. As far as what to do next, he was at a loss. He was thankful he had convinced his mom and dad that they should delay their visit for a while.

He had forgotten to open the bathtub drain and the water was pooling above his feet as he shampooed his hair in the shower. He opened the drain lever with his toes and stared for an extended period at the swirling water as it drained the soap lather from the tub. When he was a boy, he liked to watch the water drain from the tub. He thought the water funnel that developed looked like a tornado. He began staring at nothing while he thought deeply about it. Back then, he thought he would grow up to be married on time, with kids that hugged his legs and a job that required a tie and briefcase. He had visualized kissing his wife on the cheek as she was drying dishes, wearing an apron. It had been a feather in the wind—as difficult as achieving self-respect. Perpetually falling short left him feeling inadequate; he thought he wasn't worth as much as people who lived a traditional lifestyle.

He turned off the water and dried off, still staring at objects and spots on the wall. He put on a pair of boxer shorts and got under the covers while his back was still wet. The heater hadn't been on long enough to make his room comfortable to be wet in. He climbed out of bed and opened his closet to find a T-shirt. As he browsed through the hangers, he came across a beige blouse. Its presence suddenly made everything seem to smell like her. He lay in bed and tried to close his eyes, but racing thoughts caused his eyelids to spring back open. He turned on his side, then turned to face the other way. He was so run down from the day's events that he slowly drifted off.

Sleep was worse than consciousness. He seemed to be lucid and aware he was dreaming. A scene came along that required him to search a female alien for weapons in the field, and he was horrified when she turned around, and he realized it was Felina. He woke up cold, with a layer of sweat on his neck and face. The sheets were damp. He looked at the digital alarm clock on his nightstand. It was 10:30. He had been asleep for only an hour. He decided to watch one of the movies he kept on DVD, even though he had seen all of them at least twice. He needed something to get his mind off of what had happened.

He turned on the television and played a random DVD. But he watched for only ten minutes before he sat on the edge of his bed and put his face in his palms. Everything he touched turned to dust.

He cursed at the ceiling.

Suddenly Layne jumped up from his bed and scoured the house for Valium. He searched all the drawers and the pockets of all his coats. Then he realized there was a remote possibility there was a Xanax for emergencies in the shaving kit he had set aside long ago and forgotten about. He removed the shaving kit from his backpack and rummaged through it on the bathroom countertop without success. He searched below the sink, also without success, and kicked a cupboard door shut in growing frustration. He avoided looking at himself in the mirror as he looked in the medicine cabinet. Finally, he was on his knees looking on the floor under the bed.

He leveled with himself; he had never once overlooked the location of such a drug. He felt tears begin to well, then one ran down his cheek. Deep down, he had always known that eventually, his greatest fear would come to life again. It was a miracle he had made it this far.

$$\textbf{3}$$

LAYNE WAS THE ONLY customer in the liquor store. The middle-aged woman in a flannel shirt behind the counter looked like she was probably the owner's wife or close relative. She seemed concerned as he approached to pay. He had seen her once before when he was buying a twelve-pack from her while still in his rough gear uniform after work. She was hesitant to sell Layne the bottle as she made change from the cash register drawer. It was obvious he had been crying, but she was unsure of what to say. He focused on the register to avoid eye contact with her while she put the bottle in a brown paper bag for him. He told himself to get it over with. He would never have to return to this store and never have to be face to face with her again. He took his receipt and the bag but was unable to say thank you. He felt her watching him empathetically as he opened the door to leave and the entrance alert chimed.

He had decided to wait until he made it home to imbibe. But he changed his mind on the way there and glanced in every direction to make certain there weren't any cops observing him. He took into account his number one rule—never take a pull at a stoplight. He steered using his elbows while he broke the seal and unscrewed the plastic cap. The first swig burned his tonsils; the room temperature liquor felt cold as it evaporated in seconds from his tongue and the inside of his cheeks. It was sinfully gratifying to feel the warmth of the liquor settling in his stomach, smothering the pain. He checked his rearview mirror again. He drove cautiously and waited a few minutes to have another. He arrived home and pulled his parking brake, already feeling more accepting of his situation.

* * * *

LAYNE AWOKE UPSIDE DOWN on his bed. He was lying on his back looking at the ceiling, his feet touching the headboard. For the first few seconds, he didn't remember what had happened, but it all came back in a rush. He realized he didn't get to enjoy the initial five seconds after waking up when he was unaware of what had happened. It seemed like it had only been a few hours since he decided to go to the liquor store before it closed.

Once he oriented himself, a disheveled bedroom came into focus. He sat up and saw an empty fifth of vodka on the carpeted floor next to the bed. His heart jumped with panic. He contemplated that he had promised himself he wouldn't do this anymore, yet here he was again. It was frightening to realize he couldn't enforce his own rules. The anguish he had attempted to drown returned, along with guilt about capitulating to the bottle. He had failed to take into consideration the horror of time that he couldn't account for before he started drinking. It was like an alien abduction. The only feeling more miserable was someone witnessing it and later telling him about unsavory things he had done.

He remembered buying the bottle around 11:00 p.m. Friday night. But it was dark now, and he was certain he had been asleep long enough to wake in the morning. He checked his watch: 8:19 p.m. He checked his phone to read with horror that it was Saturday evening. He told himself he was okay. He hadn't been a no-call, no-show the very first day after becoming a full-fledged Border Patrol agent. He could taper off by tomorrow afternoon and report for duty Monday.

He forced himself up from the bed and tottered around the house in fear of what he might find. A lamp was broken on the floor in the living room, but the bulb was still functioning and could have caused a fire. There were empty liquor bottles and beer cans on the floor in every room. He looked in the kitchen and found that he had left the refrigerator door open. There was an eighteen-pack on the second shelf with roughly half the cans missing. He reached in and grabbed a room temperature can and cracked the top.

He did his best to avoid remembering what had happened. But his mind slowly assembled the jigsaw puzzle of memories after he began drinking. He didn't have even a vague memory of buying the beer or additional liquor. He shuddered to think he had driven again after the first trip to the liquor store. It made him fearful of seeing his car. His heart palpitated when he realized he could have run over somebody in a trance and killed them without knowing it.

The thought of leaving the house was terrifying. There was a sense of loss that he had missed a whole day. It was as if he had been possessed by a demon spirit that had assumed control of his consciousness. He pulled out debit card receipts from his pockets and wadded them into the wastebasket. He was afraid to look at the items and time of sale. He didn't want to see his checking account or learn about anything else he didn't remember. He recoiled at the thought of what he might have said or done in such a state.

The lenses of his eyeballs were sensitive to air, and it stung to blink. It occurred to him he had unknowingly made up for every night he had gone without drinking in one bender, as if he had been starving and gorged himself. His empty shaving kit was in the tub, and toiletries were scattered all over the bathroom floor. He put his mouth sideways under the kitchen faucet for a long drink to wet his dry tongue. He took several long gulps, then ran back to the bathroom and vomited every ounce of the water into the toilet. Nothing but time would allow him to feel better.

* * * *

BY SUNDAY EVENING HE WAS still too sick to go outside. He hesitated to press the last number to allow the phone to dial, and he considered hanging up while it rang. There were three rings before a voice on the other end answered, "Douglas Station, Fishbowl." It hurt to speak; he hadn't heard a voice in several days except his own within his head.

"Yes, this is Layne Sheppard, requesting sick leave." His voice didn't sound like his own.

"What's your Star Number?"

"Delta-328."

There was a pause. "Eight hours sick leave?" the voice in the Fishbowl asked.

"Yes, please."

"You got it," the voice said and hung up.

He felt a few seconds of relief at not having to go to work, then pain of every kind returned. He knew what he had done to himself would take a week to recover from. But, at that moment, it seemed he would feel this way indefinitely. He couldn't call in sick more than two days in a row without a doctor's note. He didn't know how many hours of sick leave he had left. He was afraid to know, the way he was afraid to know his checking account balance.

He was still too ill and weak to take a shower. He picked up one of the pillows from the floor and lay on his bed in a fetal position to resume staring at the wall. A little light looked through the bedroom window. He had lain in this position seemingly without moving or blinking from sunrise to sunset. He imagined being crucified, enduring the adrenaline of panic while immobilized with sick pain and the hopelessness of black depression. It was incomprehensible that even a touch of prior experience with such suffering hadn't dissuaded him. He had known for a long time that whenever he started drinking, disaster often followed. He was honest with himself. Once he got started, he couldn't stop. And what was worse was, he couldn't keep from starting.

His next thought was one he had never focused on before, but it felt more obvious and clearer than ever before. There was undeniably something wrong with him; he could pinpoint what it was now. After an alcohol-related disaster, he swore never to drink again. Then at some point, within a matter of weeks, he convinced himself nothing bad would happen this time because he was only planning to have a few beers. To behave in the way that he did when he was drunk seemed like a fluke or an accident because his thinking was so much different sober. That moment between calamities, when he dismissed what happened the last time, was the source of the illness. He learned from his mistakes the first time with everything else. There was a malfunction in his thinking when it came to booze. His will was strong in every other aspect of his life.

He stared at the same spot on the wall through another sunrise and sunset, barely blinking. He drifted in and out of consciousness with aching despair. Being in this condition was doing hard time.

On Tuesday at 5:00 a.m., he forced himself out of bed, his legs still wobbly. He paced around the house, stalling to call the Fishbowl. Finally, he forced himself to dial.

"This is Layne Sheppard, requesting eight hours sick leave."

"Can you speak up a little bit?" the voice said.

"This is Layne Sheppard, requesting sick leave," he repeated.

"Do you have the time on the books?" the voice questioned. It was the voice of a different supervisor, but he sounded like he knew that Layne had been absent the day before. Layne was certain everyone at the station had been talking about him.

"Yes, I think so," Layne said, as his voice cracked in the middle of the last word.

"You need to talk to your Supe'," the voice said.

"I need the time, please," he pleaded.

There was a pause, and then the voice said, "I'm going to mark you down, but you need to talk to your Supe'."

"Thank you, sir. I will."

* * * *

FELINA'S PHONE CALL HAD REACHED its fourth fruitless ring, and she had almost reached the conclusion that she wouldn't be able to reach Marianne at the moment. *I can't get Layne to answer me, and now I can't even get through to* *my best friend.* She frowned in her mind. Then, suddenly, someone picked up on the other end of the line.

"Hello, honey," came Marianne's voice. Her Caller ID had told her it was Felina. "Sorry I couldn't get to the phone faster. I was just finishing my shower; I'm dripping all over—"

"Oh, Marianne," Felina blurted, cutting her off before she could finish 'the floor.' In a flood of words and emotion, Felina tearfully told Marianne what had happened with Layne and what she'd been through since.

"I know I told you I wouldn't blame him if he didn't want anything to do with me once he learned the truth about me," Felina sputtered. "And I know I said I'd understand if he turned me into ICE for deceiving him. But so much has changed since then."

Felina paused to wipe her nose. Marianne knew she needed to let her distraught friend unburden herself, so she waited in silence for Felina to continue.

"When I came up with this plan," she resumed, "my idea was to find a guy who I could use to accomplish my goal of becoming a citizen so I could go to college and become a doctor. I'm ashamed to say that I wasn't really looking to fall in love with someone. But that's what happened. And now I'm afraid I've lost him.

"I still want to become a doctor. And I still need to be a citizen to get into college and eventually go to medical school. But Layne is more important. He won't even respond to my text messages or answer the phone when I call. I know he knows it's me calling. I don't know what to do."

Marianne was thankful that Felina couldn't see her grimace as Felina's anguish poured out. She knew she needed to find words of consolation and hope—in a hurry.

"Honey, don't give up," she began. "This doesn't mean Layne has dumped you. More likely, it shows how much he cares for you. He couldn't be this hurt if you weren't very important to him. You have to give him time to get over the shock of being a Border Patrol agent who fell in love with an illegal. As much as it hurts right now to have him reject your attempts to communicate with him, you have to try to understand what he's trying to get his head around."

There was silence on the call after Marianne finished. Privately, Marianne was thinking that Layne was a jerk for reacting the way he did. But she knew better than to say that to Felina. She knew her friend was sincerely hurt by Layne's reaction to what Marianne knew was a humiliating and agonizing admission on Felina's part. She knew Felina could only be this distraught and devastated if Layne was really important to her. After a long pause, Felina finally spoke, and it caused Marianne to gasp. She wasn't expecting what she heard, and she was sure it was emotion talking.

"Forgiving me may be hard for him," Felina said. "But forgiving him will be just as hard for me."

4

AGENTS WERE POURING OUT OF the Muster Room on their way to the field, but Layne wasn't one of them. He hadn't slept more than a few hours; there were dark circles under his eyes for all to see. He hadn't eaten in days. He felt hollow and tremulous; his duty belt was too big and needed to be tightened a notch. He noticed people glancing at him then looking away before eyes met. He tried to avoid looking at anyone as he walked the hallway toward the computer room. He was certain it wasn't paranoia. He suspected everyone had been talking about him while he was gone.

He took a second look at the G426 that had been distributed in Muster. He was assigned to Processing, separate from the agents listed under their supervisors and units. He had not been assigned to a unit yet. Next to Sheppard, it read in parentheses: "See supervisor." The events involving Felina had left him feeling apathetic. He merely headed toward Escribano's office in a state of numbness without anticipation of any kind. He opened the door and poked his head in to ask, "You wanted to see me, sir?"

Escribano looked up from his paperwork. This time he looked Layne directly in the eye. "Mr. Sheppard, you are to meet me in PAIC Kramer's office in fifteen minutes. You'll be permitted union representation, ten-four?"

"Ten-four," Layne said, then shut the door.

He headed straight to the union steward office. Ortiz was looking at police dash camera videos from the Internet on the computer at his desk. He acknowledged Layne after finishing the last of the video he was watching. "What's up?"

"I'm supposed to meet with Escribano in the PAIC's office in ten minutes." Layne stood in the doorway, waiting for a response. No further explanation was necessary. Ortiz's confidence became absent from his face all of a sudden, and he stalled to respond. He seemed to be reconstructing their previous dealings with Escribano. After a moment he asked, "Well, what's the meeting about? What are the allegations?"

"I assume they're gonna to try to intimidate me into quitting," Layne said.

"No," Ortiz said, backing his chair away from the desk, as if getting ready to rise. "They don't want you to quit. It's probably a new course of action."

"Are you coming with me?" Layne asked.

Ortiz got up from his chair slowly, hesitating after he'd gotten to his feet. He had no choice but to go. The union dues were deducted from Layne's paycheck every two weeks. The lack of focus in his eyes displayed vividly the level to which PAIC Kramer was exalted by everyone at the station. Layne and Ortiz walked side-by-side down the hallway to a door that led to an outdoor walkway made of concrete. They passed by a picnic table and into a separate part of the building, which was exclusively for administration.

As they walked, Ortiz appeared to be rehearsing to himself what he would say to the PAIC. Layne knew where the indecision lay: Ortiz and Escribano were friends. Escribano had been a union steward at one time. He was the one exception to Ortiz's anti-management attitude and allegiance to the union, which Ortiz occasionally demonstrated in Muster by taunting members of management during a presentation. It was routine and predictable: A supervisor would tell the agents to do a certain thing, and Ortiz would stand up and say, "Nobody has to do that. That's against the rules." Management was always trying to get the most out of the Agents, and the union guy, Ortiz or whoever it might be, was just trying to rock the boat.

As he and Ortiz entered the large office together, Layne realized he hadn't seen PAIC Kramer since the orientation, almost a year before. Kramer was standing behind his desk. Layne was struck by twenty years of trophy pictures Kramer had covering the walls. In the pictures, he was young and amongst groups wearing the old uniforms, kneeling with M-16s by mountains of dope and smiling for important handshakes. But it was obvious by the look on Kramer's face now that the pictures were there merely because he had to put them somewhere. He wasn't interested in such things anymore. He was interested in overseeing a smooth operation with low maintenance. Layne felt like they were in a junior high principal's office.

"Have a seat Mr. Sheppard," Kramer said with annoyance. "In all my years at this station, I don't recall what happened with you ever happening before."

"What's that?" Layne responded. He sincerely wasn't sure what Kramer was referring to, but the PAIC took the comment as a show of insolence.

"What's that! It's calling in sick the first two days after you've reached regular agent status," Kramer exploded. "That's what!"

Layne swallowed hard. He wasn't expecting this. And he still felt lousy.

"Do you think that now that you're no longer a trainee you can immediately start slacking off? Is that what missing your first two days of work means?" Kramer was indignant. "Are you going to be one of those slugs who wants the prestige of the uniform and the title but doesn't want any of the burden of cutting sign and catching illegals?"

"Sir, I was truly ill," Layne said without further explanation.

Escribano was standing to the left of Kramer's big desk. He had assembled a compendium of petty infractions for Layne's dictionary-sized file, and he passed it to Kramer. Kramer slammed it on his desk for effect.

"Impressive file you've got here," Kramer said. He rubbed the back of his neck as if he had a headache.

"I've done the best I can, sir," Layne said.

"Your absences on top of the documentation in here raises serious questions about your future dependability as a Border Patrol agent," Kramer said.

Layne sat down and examined the unfamiliar flower ornament on the collar of Kramer's rough gear uniform as he waited for the PAIC to continue. Kramer was wearing the cargo pants and shirt but no duty belt. He was an inch taller than Layne and bald, with a blond Highway Patrol mustache. Layne guessed he was approximately fifty years old. Ortiz appeared to be psychologically intimidated by Kramer, a feat Layne hadn't believed possible.

Unexpectedly changing his tone, Kramer said in a fatherly manner, "You know, son, this job's not for everyone. To tell you the truth, if I wasn't able to get out of the field way back when, I don't think I'd be wearing this uniform right now."

"I've heard that several times before, sir," Layne responded, "and to be honest, I think that phrase applies to me. I'm meant for something else. But I've left my home, moved to two different states, and invested a lot of time in the Service." Layne sounded as if he were speaking his last words before being executed. Kramer's face flushed with indignation. He was expecting someone more submissive.

"With what's in this file, I can have you separated from service," Kramer said.

"I understand that, sir." Layne sat up as straight as he could in his chair. "But I'm never gonna quit."

"I'm not telling you to quit," Kramer said, irritation evident in his tone.

"I don't understand what you're telling me then, sir." Layne forced himself to maintain eye contact with the PAIC.

Kramer gnashed his teeth and turned to Ortiz. "Mr. Ortiz, do you have any suggestions?"

Ortiz fumbled and turned to Layne. "Why don't you go back to the Academy? If you resign, you're SF-51 will be clean, and you can start over at a different station."

"I don't wanna retread at the Academy. I couldn't get back in with that file," Layne said.

"I'll throw the file away," Kramer said.

"I don't think I can make it through four more months in Artesia," Layne said.

"Well, I guess we'll just have to see how it goes. You'll be assigned to a unit and receive your new schedule on Monday. How does that sound to you, Mr. Escribano?" Kramer said.

"That sounds like a good plan," Escribano said with frustration. Exposing Layne's case to the patrol agent in charge had demonstrated Escribano's desperation to wash his hands of it. Layne's refusal to go away was foiling Escribano's plan to tie up loose ends in order to move on with his promotion as a law instructor at the Academy.

"I need a doctor's note from you for the days you missed," Escribano added.

"Okay," Layne said.

"That'll be all, gentlemen," said Kramer picking up the manila folder and handing it back to Escribano.

Layne and Ortiz left the office while Kramer and Escribano remained behind. Once the door closed behind them, Ortiz turned to Layne and said, "You can't talk to him like that."

"I've been submissive since I got here," Layne said, "and it's brought me to this. He's going to fire me anyway. He needs to know I'm not playing ball with him and the boys." Layne smiled at the image. "They can send me packing, but I won't quit."

Ortiz looked ready to erupt, but he caught himself then said, "Just study your maps and your sensor list. There's gonna be a lot of eyes watching you so watch your step." Then he peeled off in the direction of his office, and Layne made his way to the Processing floor to start his shift.

* * * *

ALL WEEK WHILE LAYNE WAS assigned to Processing, the text messages kept showing up on his cell phone. "You're not answering your phone. Should

I stop calling?" And, "I'm sorry. Please call me." And, "I miss you. Will I ever hear from you?" The pleading transmissions were all from Felina. Still recovering from his whopper bender, Layne didn't respond—didn't *feel* like responding.

Entering detained migrants' information into the ENFORCE system was like driving through the desolate stretch of New Mexico on I-25—virtually mindless. Layne couldn't decide what upset him more, finding out that the girl he had fallen in love with was, in principle, the same as those he was processing, or failing—again—to live up to the promise he'd made to stop drinking. He knew that, in the past, he didn't really mean it when he said he wouldn't drink ever again. But this time, he was sincere and determined, or so he thought. But along came a huge disappointment, and he backslid. Backslid! It was one of the worst drunken binges of his life.

Is any of this even worth it now? he asked himself over and over as he plodded through monotonous shift after monotonous shift. *Why put up with the politics here, all the games they play just to make me miserable? Maybe I* should *do what they want me to do and just walk away.*

But no sooner had Layne, in his consummate despair, considered giving up than another of Felina's text messages popped up on his phone.

"Please give us a chance," she pleaded.

That was it. No reasoning. No persuasive argument or excuses. And, no promises. Just, "Please give us a chance."

For some reason—Layne couldn't explain why, even to himself—that one stopped him cold. It was like a slap in the face. It made him stop thinking about himself and begin to ponder *them* . . . the life together he'd pictured if he could make it in the Border Patrol . . . Felina, with her luscious, long black hair and her striking figure—all his . . . proving to her he could stop drinking . . . gaining the self-respect he had wondered if he could ever feel when he began this outlandish journey.

The past week had been a blur. Layne was still reeling, physically and emotionally, and he couldn't quite conceive how he would make it to the end of today's shift. Despite the breakup being a week in the past, he saw trails of Felina everywhere he looked. He wondered how long the process of separation would last. It was the routine of her that he missed—the little things, like watching her in the mirror as she finished getting ready for a night out.

I need time to think, Layne told himself as his final shift in the purgatory of Processing came to an end. *Next week, I'll be in the field, by myself. All alone . . . maybe I'll be able to figure this out.*

* * * *

THE DARKNESS OF THE DESERT wasn't a surprise to Layne as his first solo shift in the field stretched into the night. He had sensed the desolate silence while driving from Douglas back to Bisbee when he was working Mids in field training. But this was different. He was alone beneath the starry expanse. He wasn't an avid reader, but one of the books he had read was about Charles Lindberg flying across the Atlantic Ocean in that small single-engine plane and how lonely he was during the night, knowing that if he went down, no one would even know where to look. At least Layne could radio the LECA ladies, as cold and distant as they could be.

Layne recalled Agent Cruz during field training, telling him and the others on the ride that night:

"You will learn the area, and you will know every turn, every mile-marker, and every hill and saddle. The reason why you learn this stuff is if something bad happens to an agent, you will know where he's at, and you will be able to get to him. If you guys decide you want to be slugs and never catch a body, I don't care. But if I'm hurt, you better know where I'm at and find me."

Layne hoped the agents working Swings with him this night had heeded Cruz's dire warning. His mind flashed back to Lindberg, then to his own situation. He calculated the time it would take for rescuers from Fort Huachuca to reach him.

Douglas is about a thirty-minute life flight from the military base near

Sierra Vista. So, it'll be more like forty minutes for the helicopter to get to me out here—if they can land where I'm at. Then it's probably another hour to the Level One Trauma Center in Tucson after they help me, get me loaded, and turn around to head back.

I'm really on my own, Layne realized.

A picture formed in his mind of the nights he'd spent with Launius, Tipton, Darmody, and other agents, hiding in some deserted spot, waiting for a Delta Tango or a call to action on the radio. The difference then was that he was with somebody. He heard a sound and immediately tensed, preparing for some kind of encounter. Was it a forty-five, a group of Tonks trying to sneak across the border to find work? Or a forty-six, mules smuggling a load of dope into the U.S.? He heard another sound, and then . . .

A stray javelina burst into view, careening its way in search of the squadron of desert boars from which it had been separated.

It's scary, Layne thought, his relief apparent to only himself because there was no one else around. *Six months ago, I was at the Academy, in a safe spot. People were teaching us things, and we were learning. PT was hard and Stacking and OC were brutal. I worried about everything.*

But compared to this, I was fine. Safe.

Layne shifted in the driver's seat of his Kilo, and another sensation got his attention, though it hardly diverted his focus from the unease he was feeling. Driving to Douglas Station for his first shift as a field trainee after graduating from the Academy, Layne had been uncomfortable in his Kevlar bulletproof vest. But that was because he had fastened the Velcro straps too tightly and they were impeding his breathing. This was different. All of a sudden, the vest felt noticeably heavy, and another realization swept over him.

What have I gotten myself into?

* * * *

AS LAYNE'S FIRST NIGHT ALONE in the field dragged on, his thoughts shifted to the predicament in which he found himself with Felina. Yes, his primary purpose when he devised his plan more than a decade ago was to attain an irrevocable sense of self-respect, a psychological watermark he would always be able to reference that would keep his mental health stable during doldrums. He had spent the past seven years in search of a way to recapture the self-concept of his youth.

But there was another dimension that drove him. He wasn't sure if it was patriotism or prejudice. "If I make it into the Border Patrol, I'm gonna kick some butt," Layne had spouted to Fabiola, his prop of a girlfriend, months before when he was awaiting the background check that was a key to acceptance into the Border Patrol Academy. "I'm tired of these cheaters coming across the border and making themselves at home—waving Mexican flags," he'd said then. "They left Mexico because they couldn't earn a living there, yet they're so dang proud of it? It makes no sense. And all the lousy construction workers—there's so many of them that they're not even trying to keep a low profile anymore. Every time I get gas, one of them is filling up his truck loaded with landscaping equipment."

Such bravado was tempered greatly when Felina entered the picture.

That stunning Hispanic beauty didn't completely change Layne's fervor when she swept him off his feet the first time that he saw her. But she did cause him to view . . . *Mexicans* . . . differently.

Thank goodness she's legal, he'd often thought as he felt himself falling in love and simultaneously struggled to reconcile his affections with what he viewed as his mission as a Border Patrol agent. *She's exceptional,* he'd told himself many times.

During the countless conversations that took place in vehicles during field training, Layne had learned that quite a few Border Patrol agents had wives who were from Mexico. So why couldn't he? Layne and Felina hadn't reached the point of even bringing up the subject of marriage, but it had crossed his mind. He hoped it had occurred to her, too. Once he had passed field training and secured a regular agent position, he had thought—once he had achieved the security and stability of a government job—he would bring it up . . . and hope it wouldn't be yet another disappointment in his life.

But then Eduardo got busted for DUI, and all of Layne's dreams were derailed by a disappointment the likes of which he had never imagined. He had been betrayed, misled—even lied to? Felina wasn't a legal immigrant from Mexico. Because of her parents' law-breaking actions when she was barely walking, she represented what Layne had sworn to prevent when he took the U.S. Uniformed Services Oath of Office on his first day as a Border Patrol recruit:

"I, Layne Sheppard, do solemnly swear that I will support and defend the Constitution of the United States against all enemies, foreign and domestic," was the very first part of that oath.

Layne wondered: Was Felina really an enemy? Or was she a victim? *The politicians can't even agree,* he muttered to himself.

Suddenly the LECA's voice rang out over the radio: "Delta-328, 866, ten-eighteen."

Security check, Layne realized. "866, Delta-328, ten-nineteen."

Having confirmed that he indeed was on the job, as well as verifying his safe existence, Layne returned to mentally arm-wrestling the conundrum of Felina's immigration status and his place in her life—their future. How could he rationalize being a Border Patrol agent and doing nothing about a particular known illegal? Could he possibly have a girlfriend who didn't belong in this country? Was there any way he could be married to someone who was not a citizen and keep his self-respect as an agent charged with protecting the nation's border? How could he live up to the oath he had taken? How could he keep his job?

What if Felina doesn't really share my feelings? Layne abruptly asked himself. *"What if she just wanted to use me in some way once I became a Border Patrol agent?"* These thoughts frightened him worse than being alone in the desert in the dark of night. He had to stop and attack this more logically. He had to trust her. He began reconstructing what he knew.

Felina was two years old when her mother smuggled her and her brothers across the border. At that age, Felina had no idea of right or wrong, the law, borders, or of the United States or Mexico. Only recently had she learned to walk. She grew up as American as Layne, going to public schools, learning English, learning the customs of the only home she ever knew. She had aspirations—just like Layne: a college degree, a career, a family. But she faced insurmountable obstacles beyond her control. *I've encountered hurdles,* Layne admitted to himself, *but they were of my own making. Felina started out at the bottom of a lifelong hill the day her mom brought her here illegally.*

But that didn't ease Layne's confusion; it didn't answer the question: Why did Felina hide her status from Layne? He would not be satisfied, would not be able to decide what he should do, where he should go from here, without knowing what she was thinking in keeping such an important fact from him.

I have to ask her, he resolved.

Instantly, he felt ashamed of himself for walking out on Felina and for his spectacular crash after he got back to Bisbee. Selfishly, he had hurt her and had broken his promise to her and to himself. He wouldn't quit the Border Patrol, even though he had begun doubting whether it was right for him long-term. And he wouldn't give in to drinking again—at least not without a fight. He finally understood that he needed help.

5

LAYNE SAT WITH A CLIPBOARD in his lap, choosing answers to a series of multiple-choice questions about symptoms. His knee bounced. The jitters and paranoia were waning, but the feeling of being indisposed carried on. He was still incapable of smiling; it was painful to speak in complete sentences. He attempted to be honest as he filled in the lettered bubbles with a dull pencil that was tethered to the clipboard. He realized he had never in his life told a medical professional the whole truth in regard to any non-physical issue that tormented him. In times past, the purpose of scheduling an appointment like this was often to obtain a prescription drug by feigning symptoms. But today, he was fearful of having no place left to which he could retreat and, thus, was genuinely seeking help.

He glanced up from his evaluation periodically to look around. There were metal chairs with red fabric cushions around the perimeter of the waiting room. The only other people there for an appointment were a woman and her teenage son, sitting in the opposite corner of the room near the reception desk. Layne looked at the wall clock above their heads so he could glance at them discretely; luckily, he didn't recognize them. He wished he could wear a mask in case an acquaintance saw him leaving the office. It was difficult to be confident he wouldn't encounter someone he knew when he went out in public here because of Sierra Vista's small population.

He stood up to return the assessment with a shamefaced look while avoiding eye contact with the woman and her son in his periphery. He reasoned they were likewise there for an embarrassing purpose, which should have counterbalanced his feelings of awkwardness. Regardless, he was anxious to be out of their field of vision. The trip to the receptionist's desk and back seemed everlasting. When he finally reached the window where the receptionist was reading a computer monitor, he placed the clipboard on the counter, and she took it, saying, "Doctor Ballinger will call you shortly."

Layne's chin remained low as he snatched an outdated *Time* magazine from a table on the way back to his seat. The magazine sat in his lap for a few minutes as he stared at tall, green, potted plants, then prints of famous landscape and abstract paintings on the walls. He opened the magazine and read the captions of colorful pictures for ten minutes before the door next to the receptionist's desk opened. A middle-aged white man, wearing a dress shirt and slacks, looked directly at him and said, "Layne?"

Layne nodded as he put the magazine on the chair next to him and stood up to follow him. The man was slightly balding and wore glasses, and he looked at Layne without expression as Layne approached him sheepishly. The man was holding Layne's self-assessment. He reached out to shake hands with Layne and introduced himself. "I'm Doctor Ballinger."

"Nice to meet you," Layne said.

Dr. Ballinger held the door open for him with a sense of routine and followed him down the hallway. They walked side by side until they reached an open door that displayed Ballinger's nameplate. He gestured for Layne to enter and instructed him to have a seat at the chair in front of his desk as he shut the door. Layne sat down and examined the degrees in frames on the wall to his left. Then he moved on to stare, for longer than he should have, at a cheerful picture on Dr. Ballinger's desk of him with his wife and children that was professionally taken in a sort of picnic setting. The picture reinforced Layne's perspective as an outlier; life seemed so effortless and natural to others. The discomfort of becoming acquainted with someone under these circumstances caused Layne to pick at his fingernails and readjust himself in his seat several times. He seemed to continually find himself in this position—required to discuss his shortcomings with some kind of authority figure in an office setting.

He was growing tired of himself.

Dr. Ballinger sat down in his chair and sighed as he put the clipboard on his desk. Layne wasn't sure what to do with his hands while he waited for the doctor to say the first word. Ballinger pushed the clipboard aside and looked Layne in the eye for five long seconds. Layne struggled to avoid looking away. Ballinger folded his hands together as he leaned back in his chair and said, "Have you had enough?"

Layne turned to face the wall on his right side in an attempt to hide his reaction to the question. His lips frowned, and he couldn't prevent himself from crying. It had been like a rock in his shoe for almost a third of his life, and this was the first time he had acknowledged the problem to someone. It had scarcely been put into words before now; somehow it hadn't seemed completely real because it wasn't spoken aloud. For the most part, it had only existed as a dilemma in the form of thoughts in his mind. He sniveled and replied, "Yes."

"Alright, we can get started then. 'Cuz if you're coming in here to appease someone, then we're just wasting our time. I'm not even gonna read the rest of this crap you wrote down. I don't want a drunkalogue. I can imagine the lies you've told and the games you've played from what I've heard from others like you. I need you to be honest with me. If you don't get mad, this isn't gonna work."

The statement caught Layne off-guard, and his eyes widened. He reached for a tissue from a box on the desk. After wiping his nose, he said, "Okay."

"I saw in the paperwork that you're employed by Customs as a Border Patrol agent?" Ballinger said.

"Yes, I just finished training, but I missed my first two regular days on duty because of a problem I had with my girlfriend. I was hoping you could write me a doctor's note for work," Layne said.

"You mean you made yourself sick drinking and you had to call in sick?"

"Yes," Layne said.

"I'll write you a note, don't worry about that. The questionnaire also said you have a bachelor's degree?" Ballinger said.

"Yes, I have a business degree," Layne said.

"So, tell me what you're doing here," Ballinger said.

"I've known for a long time that I had a problem, but I just figured I'd deal with it when things slowed down, and I had a chance. Over the years, I've just learned to live with it like a disease. I thought I'd eventually find my way back to the way I was before if I could succeed at something."

Ballinger folded his hands together and rested his elbows on the desk. He nodded and Layne continued. "But it's getting to the point where I'm causing problems for myself that I can't handle. I've tried to quit a dozen times, but I end up convincing myself I'm a hypochondriac and that it's unrealistic to quit permanently. I quit for a while, just recently before this happened. I was planning to quit for good. I was dead set on it because of a girl. Then I did it again, and when I woke up, I realized I couldn't stop, and it scared me. I promised myself I wouldn't do that anymore."

"Are you afraid of something?" Ballinger said.

"I've been afraid my whole life. It just changes from one thing to the next," Layne said.

"Why didn't you ask for help earlier?"

"My parents wanted me to get help about four years ago, but I denied anything was wrong. I was too proud. I still had a high opinion of myself because I'd been so successful athletically before that. But the little bit of pride that was left when I got to the Academy is gone now," Layne said. Simply talking about it caused a sense of relief to wash over him, and he was able to speak unhindered.

"Have you told your parents what's going on?" Ballinger said.

"I don't want to worry them when there's nothing they can do about it," Layne said.

"You're probably used to hiding things from them. Don't you think they should know what's going on with their son? Even if it's painful for them?" Ballinger said.

"I don't know; I think deep down they know the truth. They found me drunk about five years ago and took me to the hospital. A couple weeks later, they found out I was drinking again, and they did sort of an intervention and took my car keys. They made me stay with them for a few weeks, and I stayed sober the whole time. I think they thought it was a phase, and I was past it. After that, I decided I was only gonna drink on Friday and Saturday nights. I always felt like I wasted the opportunity to get drunk if I didn't get hammered on nights when I didn't have work the next day," Layne said.

"And how'd just drinking on the weekends work out for you?" Ballinger asked.

"I'd get drunk on Friday night, then drink beer all day Saturday and do it again Saturday night. Then I'd end up drinking red beers or bloody Marys on Sunday morning and try to taper off by bedtime. I don't even like watching football, but I used to love NFL for that . . . because it was an excuse to drink during the day. That's why I love Las Vegas and Mexico—where you can do what you want without having to hide it," Layne said.

"Alcohol is different than other drugs," Ballinger said. "If you took thirty people and forced them to drink every day for a month, twenty-six of them would never wanna drink again. There might be four that wanna keep drinking. If you did the experiment with heroin, thirty out of thirty would keep going."

Layne nodded.

"Do you know why you drink?" Ballinger said.

"I don't wanna be drunk all the time. It's just that every day is such a drag. It's like a list of chores that never ends. I hate the routine of having to wake up for work every day with only two days off. I'm so unsatisfied with everyday life that I need a way to get my kicks to break the monotony. I just need to be able to look forward to enjoying something," Layne said.

Ballinger paused for a moment as if to consider something before he responded.

"You know, you're lucky you came in when you did—before something happened that's unforgivable. I had a patient that had a wife and two kids and a good job. He was holding it all together, but he was hiding the same problem from everyone. He was trying to cut back, but one night, he stopped by a bar after work with the intention of having only one or two beers. He remembered drinking at the bar, and the next thing he knew, he woke up in a jail cell. He thought it was a prank or something, and he yelled for a guard. He asked the guard what he was doing in there, and the guard told him he had been driving drunk and sideswiped a car. Two cops had pulled over a car on the shoulder of the road, talking to the driver, and this guy slid into the car and killed both cops. The guy had no memory of it at all."

The story was so disturbing that Layne felt sick to his stomach, and a ringing headache set in. All he could manage to say was, "Oh, my . . ."

"Yeah, you think you've got problems? Imagine being that guy?" Ballinger said.

Layne looked at his hands and didn't say anything.

"I want you to think about something. If you could observe someone with a gambling problem, and you watched him mortgage his house and lose all the money in one night—I mean lose everything he had, his wife, his family, everything. If you saw that guy in the casino the following week, what would you think?" Ballinger said.

"I would think it's a bad idea," Layne said. He had an idea where Ballinger was going with the question.

"Now, what if you could observe a guy drink until he pissed in his pants and nearly killed someone in a wreck. Then the following Friday you saw that same guy sit down at a bar and order a beer. What would you think of that guy?" Ballinger said.

Layne didn't say anything.

"You'd think he's insane. If a film crew followed you around twenty-four hours a day for a few weeks, and you could see yourself, would you like who you saw?" Ballinger said.

"I don't like myself," Layne said.

Ballinger nodded his head. "Alright. Now, you're gonna learn how to start doing things that you'd respect if you saw someone else doing them."

Layne nodded with study.

"Are you desperate?"

"Yes," Layne said shamefully.

"That's okay; desperation is a door that needs to be opened. It won't make sense now, but one day, you'll be glad you were in this position. Let me ask you something. Do you believe in a Supreme Being?" Ballinger said.

Layne was watching his hands clutch one another. The question was unexpected; it confounded him. He looked up to meet eyes with Ballinger and paused for a moment. "Yes, I always have, deep down. I just thought He created the earth and me, then left me alone after that."

"Maybe He doesn't acknowledge you because you're not doing what He intended you to do. There's something you've got to understand if you're serious about getting free of this. There's an unseen force that determines how your life transpires. Call it whatever you want; you just need to acknowledge that it exists. Everything you do matters and has consequences, even when nobody knows about it but you. And it's got nothing to do with going to church. A lot of guys spend three hours at church on Sunday morning, then go home and bang their neighbor's wife in the afternoon. The Creator doesn't care if you go to church. He wants to see if you walk the walk. Up to this point, you've been a checkered soul. But when you sacrifice to do the right thing, you'll notice that the things you really need will start falling in your lap. Once you witness it, you'll start to lose the compulsion to drink, and the dawn will arrive, so to speak," Ballinger said.

Layne listened with consternation then said, "I have a strong conscience, but a lot of times, I don't know what's right and what's wrong."

"To simplify it, all you need to do is treat people the way you'd prefer to be treated. You probably haven't heard that since kindergarten. It sounds like a cliché, but very few people actually handle all their affairs that way,"

Ballinger said.

"You're right. I haven't heard that since kindergarten," Layne said.

"I don't just mean telling a cashier at a grocery store when you get too much change back. I mean doing what's right even when it's inconvenient or time-consuming or expensive, even when it's scary—especially then. And never benefit from the misery of others," Ballinger said.

Layne nodded.

Ballinger leaned back in his chair again and folded his hands. "Tell me what you're doing here in southern Arizona. I mean, you don't seem like the typical law enforcement type. A lot of these guys are the tattletale types that enjoy having power over people. A lot of times it's to make up for things that happened to them in the past. Are you trying to prove something to someone, maybe yourself?"

"I came here to begin my education and get a fresh start somewhere new. I didn't feel like I learned anything in college that applies to reality, nothing useful in the real world, I mean."

"I think you're trying to learn something about yourself."

"I am, in a way. I thought if I could make it through all the tests, I'd feel so proud of myself that I'd be able to talk myself out of depression just by looking at my badge. And, I wanted the security of a federal job, so I'd feel like I'm being taken care of. I wanted to make some decent money and do something glamorous so I could attract a good-looking woman and get married.

"I wanted to be a respectable adult in society for once," Layne said.

"Are you passionate about being an agent? Because it doesn't seem like your heart's in it. Nothing will make you want to drink more than doing something you weren't meant to do—pretending to be somebody you're not," Ballinger said.

"I think it was the status I was passionate about," Layne said.

"The universe rewards those who follow their passion at all costs," Ballinger said. "Even if it leaves you a pauper, you've got to be true to yourself and pursue your labor of love, or you'll be miserable the rest of your life."

Layne stared at a file cabinet behind Dr. Ballinger. He was in deep thought momentarily then said, "I know what you mean. But I'd be afraid of running out of money. I need guarantees so I feel secure in life, like a union and a pension."

"There are no guarantees. But if you start doing the right thing all the time, you won't have to worry. Once you get to the point where you trust that force, that's when things will really change for you. It's called reaching the Fourth Dimension," Ballinger said.

"I've always felt like I'm treading water," Layne said as he blushed slightly and looked at his lap again. He was revealing the depths of himself against his will. It had always seemed emasculating to discuss his feelings, especially with a man. But the need to express himself was overwhelming, and he was helpless to withhold his thoughts, as if a levee had fractured.

"The problem that causes you to drink is in your head. You most likely have always had it. Drinking is just a late-stage symptom of a lifelong psychological condition. Do you see yourself as being selfish?

"I've always thought I was generous," Layne said.

"I bet a lot of the people you've known in your life would disagree with you. Did you feel inferior as a child, unworthy?" Ballinger said.

"I've always felt inadequate and inferior, like I didn't belong. It started when I was about junior high-age. It's like a weight tied to my waist." Layne looked at his hands again.

"Have you ever in your life been satisfied with yourself?"

"I was pretty close when I was twenty years old. It was because I was a college athlete; I'd reached a goal I'd set for myself. That's where my ego came from. I've been trying to recreate that feeling ever since. But it's strange—I'm an egomaniac, but I have an inferiority complex at the same time," Layne said.

"You felt fulfilled because you knew who you were back then—because you had agency. You were passionate about what you were doing."

"I thought I could put up with hating a job if I had money and a hot wife," Layne said.

"That's one of the lessons that takes the longest to learn," Ballinger said.

"I really thought I'd like BP work. But now that I've been here for a while, I've learned things are not what they seem. The way it truly is on the border isn't the way it's portrayed in the media. It's inverted reality," Layne said.

"What do you mean?"

"We just fingerprint the aliens and put them back in Mexico, even when they've got sexual assaults on women in the U.S. and other bad stuff. There's no punishment to deter them; it's called voluntary removal. It doesn't make sense. I mean, in most foreign countries, they don't have border patrol; they just use their army. They consider border crossing an invasion, and they shoot them on sight. But there's corruption everywhere in our government," Layne said.

Ballinger had become somewhat wide-eyed. He said, "I understand, I've heard some pretty amazing stories about the military, too."

"There's a group of Hispanic agents at my station that are dirty, and everyone knows it," Layne said.

"It must be a paradigm shift for you," Ballinger said as he adjusted his posture.

"It's automatic. Agents come out of the Academy gung-ho, then they lose morale when they see that the aliens they catch are being set free to try again, without even a slap on the wrist. After an agent's been in about four years, he completely stops trying to catch anybody if he has any brains," Layne said. He thwarted himself from the use of Agent Launius' theory as a corollary to avoid the skeptical response he anticipated.

"Let's move on, for the sake of time. Now, as far as this girlfriend you have. Is she someone you'll want to marry?" Ballinger said.

"I was planning to try. She was the one I've been looking for since I was sixteen. Ever since the night I met her, I've had this vision of a fairytale life with her where I come home, and she's taking cookies out of the oven.

But I just found out something unacceptable about her," Layne said.

"Was this unacceptable thing what caused you to start drinking again?"

"Yes. Everything we talk about is confidential right?" Layne said with a hushed voice.

"Absolutely. In addition to the law, you have my word."

"We've been dating for over four months now. She's Hispanic, but she has no accent. She just told me she came here illegally when she was two and has been living here illegally ever since. I don't have to explain to you the bad position that puts me in," Layne said.

"How does that make you feel?"

"I feel betrayed and deceived. I can't marry her now," Layne said.

"Why can't you?"

Layne looked puzzled.

"I try to exclude politics as best I can, but what would you have done if you were her?" Ballinger said.

That was the one question Layne had not asked himself as he sat, alone in his Kilo, during his first night in the dark desert. He replayed the discussion he'd had within himself that night on Swings. Finally, he answered, "I don't know."

"I think you're afraid to fail with her," Ballinger said. "I think you've experienced unrequited love in the past, so you're using her status as an excuse to give in. I think you want to assure yourself that it wasn't you that caused the relationship to fail."

Layne stared at the file cabinet again, and Ballinger allowed him time to ponder until he said, "Maybe you're right." Layne had planned on keeping Felina and his feelings about her to himself. But it felt as if a weight had been lifted from his shoulders; he felt a bond growing with Ballinger.

"I don't wanna tell you what to do," Ballinger said, "especially because it involves the law. But as someone older, I'll tell you this: A woman like that won't come along more than once or twice in your lifetime. If I were you, I'd try to find a way to make it work. I say that because I can tell how you feel about her by the look in your eye when you talk about her."

Layne stared at the file cabinet again without responding.

"I don't wanna give you the impression that what you're going through isn't serious. You're in danger of losing your federal employment, not to mention the love of your life. What are you gonna do if everything you're hanging onto all falls apart?" Ballinger said.

Layne frowned as he was nearly brought to tears again. "I don't know. I told myself this was my last chance when I was on my way to the Academy. This problem has brought me to my knees so many times . . ."

Ballinger rolled backward in his chair and opened his desk drawer to retrieve a pen from his desk and click it. He put a notepad on his desktop calendar and began writing something on it. As he wrote he said, "There's a support group I want you to attend. They meet every Thursday and Saturday night at 7:00 p.m. If you can't make it because of work, I'm sure there are other ones on different days and different times. I recommend this one just because it's in Bisbee." He finished writing down the group's address and meeting time and tore the note from the notepad and leaned across the desk to hand it to Layne. Layne reached to take the note then rotated it to read it.

"I'm afraid someone I work with might find out about me being there. I don't mean a member of the group; I mean someone seeing me go in a building or wherever it is," Layne said.

"No one's gonna see you unless they're a member of the group, and they're not gonna say anything—trust me. You realize there's an army base here, don't you? You're gonna see colonels and everything on up in the group. Nobody's gonna laugh at you," Ballinger said.

"Really?" Layne said with surprise.

"Yeah, it's behind closed doors, and you wouldn't know what it was for unless you sat down and listened. I know what a sewing circle your station is. Every law enforcement environment is buzzing with gossip like that," Ballinger said.

"Okay," Layne said reluctantly.

"Listen to me, son. None of this stuff you've done means you're a bad person. You can get better if you want to. I'll help you get through this; you've just gotta promise you'll give me one hundred percent effort," Ballinger said.

"I promise," Layne said.

6

LAYNE WAS STILL WEARING his uniform as he paced back and forth across his kitchen floor with his cellphone in hand. The anxiety was amplified by the sound of his boots tromping across the tile floor in concert with his inner voice rehearsing within his mind. Felina had given up trying to contact him at some point during the previous week because of his refusal to respond. After his session with Dr. Ballinger, he had spent several days reflecting on the quandary from her perspective and had come to the conclusion that he was the one at fault. But he feared that he had waited too long and allowed their embers to fade and burn out. He winced to imagine what he had put her through by ignoring her attempts to speak with him after she had risked everything by revealing herself.

Felina's number was ready to dial, but he lost his nerve every time he tried to push the button to send the call. He felt like he did when he was in high school and was calling a girl for the first time, months after he'd taken her out on a date and had said he'd call her the next week. There were nearly thirty voicemails and text messages from Felina that he hadn't acknowledged; they were a reminder of the state of mind he had been in the night when time went missing. He couldn't bear to revisit any part of that night for fear of discovering something he had done that he didn't want to be aware of. His conscience still ached from the ordeal, as did many of his internal organs.

He paced for thirty more minutes, deliberating about what to say and how to say it. Finally, he held his breath and forced himself to proceed. He nearly lost his nerve and hung up after the first ring but instead forced himself to keep the phone to his ear. The silent interval between rings seemed to linger; it caused him to wince in anticipation of hearing her voice. She didn't answer after three rings, and he questioned whether or not he should leave a message. After another ring, there was still no voice or machine, and concern grew that he may never speak to her again.

"Hello," Felina finally said. Her voice sounded as if she were surprised yet eager to answer his call.

"Hey, how are you doing?" Layne said, pretending to be confident.

"I'm hanging in there," Felina said with a runny nose.

"Have you heard from your brother?" Layne asked to bridge the conflict between them.

"Yes, he made it to my grandma's house in Magdalena. We wired him some money. He should be alright for a while." Felina sounded weary.

"I hope he's okay and makes it back safe," Layne said.

"Thanks," was all Felina said, and Layne was uncertain of what to say next. An awkward pause ensued. He could hear her breathing. Then she let him off the hook and cleared her throat as she prepared to speak.

"You know, I thought I might've heard from you earlier. You left me hanging. Do you have any consideration for my feelings at all?"

Layne was dumbstruck, and there was another pronounced pause while he struggled to respond.

"I'm sorry. It was really a blow. It took me this long to get over it."

"You couldn't even send me a text message saying that so I didn't have to wonder if you were okay?" Felina said.

Layne recognized the sincerity in her concern, which only intensified the guilt he felt over his behavior. "You're right, I should've texted you. It was inconsiderate of me." He felt the urge to confess his backslide and the breakdown that followed as an excuse for failing to return her messages. But he rethought the notion and realized it might cause her to lose additional respect for him. Another alcohol-related episode might be the last straw for her.

"Are you okay?" Felina relented.

"No—I miss you," Layne said instantly as he nearly broke down into tears.

"I miss you, too."

"I shouldn't have walked out on you," Layne said, "especially while you're going through this thing with your brother."

"Yeah, these past couple weeks have been unpleasant, to put it lightly," Felina said. "Do you realize how hard it was for me to tell you about myself? Do you think I'd tell you that just for kicks?"

"I was childish," Layne quickly conceded. "You were being an adult by telling me the truth. I was just in shock."

"Yeah, it was childish. I can't just go around telling that to everybody I meet," Felina said.

"I know you couldn't tell me earlier. Sometimes, I don't realize it when I'm being selfish. I'm trying to work on it. I went to see a counselor."

Layne could sense the smile that went along with the relief he heard in her reply.

"Well, I'm proud of you for that."

"I'm going to a support group as soon as I find out which shift I'm scheduled on next week."

"How have you been doing at work?" Felina asked.

Layne was still nervous and resumed pacing as he said, "It's going okay. I had to go talk to the PAIC the other day."

"Oh, really? Why?"

Layne made the fastest decision he could ever remember making. He wouldn't tell Felina that he missed his first two shifts after becoming a regular agent. He told himself it would be the last time he didn't tell Felina everything.

"He just wanted to make sure I was ready to be put on a unit," he told her. "They had me in Processing the first week. Then I went into the field on my own. What an experience it is to be in the desert, alone, at night."

Layne thought it best not to give her any additional information for the time being. He didn't want her to worry. After another momentary silent interlude, Layne said, "I have to ask you a question."

"Alright," Felina said.

"I was wondering if we could get together on Saturday. There's something important I want to talk to you about, and I think we should talk about it in person," Layne said.

"What do you wanna do?" Felina said.

"I remember you telling me we should go to Mount Lemmon sometime. Can we take a day trip up there?"

"I'm not sure, Layne; I'm not very happy with you right now," Felina sighed.

"I don't blame you, but you'll want to hear what I have to say. I promise."

"I suppose. It takes about an hour to drive up there from my place."

"I'm looking forward to seeing you," Layne said.

"I'm looking forward to seeing you, too."

* * * *

DESPITE THE HABIT HE DEVELOPED from Border Patrol policy that required him to wear one whenever he was in his Kilo or any other Patrol vehicle, Layne realized he had forgotten to buckle his seatbelt, which usually disturbed Felina when she was behind the wheel. The oversight was the result of his preoccupation with her as she drove away from her apartment right after he arrived from Bisbee. He liked the smell of the vanilla air freshener she used, and he admired the girly way she kept the car vacuumed and tidy. He liked every little thing she did, even when she was mad at him. She looked gorgeous this day despite having dressed down because of the activity they had planned. She was wearing a pink hooded sweatshirt with her hair in a ponytail; modest earrings dangled slightly beneath her earlobes.

Layne buckled up and observed Felina until she turned to face him. He smiled at her, and she smiled back. Their souls winked at one another again while they looked in each other's eyes, and Layne continued smiling as he returned to watching the road. He felt closer to her than ever before, the sense that they were keeping secrets from one another had lifted.

"Babe, I've been meaning to tell you about what I think is going on at the border," he cleared his throat to say.

"What do you mean?"

"You can't believe anything they tell you on the news about the border. The media is covering it up. Neither the TV news nor the newspaper will tell you the truth about what's going on. I think there's probably reporters who know, but they're not allowed to say anything about it, or they'll get fired."

"What do you mean? What's going on?" Felina asked, slightly intrigued.

"Well, I think I told you once before that I was suspicious about how we just fingerprint people and let 'em go, and they get unlimited tries to get away," Layne said.

"Yeah, you told me." Felina appeared to be slightly uncomfortable discussing the subject.

"I couldn't figure out why the government would do that. Not punishing people for it, I mean," Layne said. "Politics aside, it just makes no sense; it's like inviting them to come over. At first, I thought it was because of human rights or some reason I didn't think of or understand. Then an FTO told me it was because there were too many people, and we didn't have room in prison for all of them. But why wouldn't they just build more jails if that was really the problem? Like Sheriff Arpaio did in Phoenix? The government spends billions of dollars in Afghanistan and Iraq, and for what?"

"I guess I don't get it either," Felina agreed.

"Well, then a veteran agent told me it's because the people who are secretly in control of the U.S. Government want as many illegal immigrants as possible to get into the country. But they want them to be poor immigrants. They want the illegals to get on welfare so that it becomes a generational lifestyle. Isn't it strange how easy it is for illegals to vote and get a driver's license and public assistance? The people in charge don't care how much it costs. They'll just raise our taxes to pay for it."

"Yeah, that doesn't make sense, and it's really screwed up that people do that. It's not fair to people who work and only have stuff they can afford." Felina was thinking of her own situation as she spoke.

Layne said, "At first, I thought the guy was crazy, but everything he told me makes perfect sense compared to the news reports we see and hear about lack of budget."

"Why do they do it then?" Felina said. She sounded as though she was losing interest in the subject.

"Because they want to slowly condition the U.S. population to become dependent on government so they can gradually transform us into a socialist society," Layne said.

Felina looked at him with wide eyes and asked what seemed like an obvious question, a variation of one she had posed his first week of field training. The answer was extremely important to her.

"Do you think you can stick with it if nothing changes? Can you be a Border Patrol agent if they just let everybody go that you catch?"

The first time Felina asked about Layne's long-term commitment to the Border Patrol, he had said: "I have no choice. There's no turning back now. I have to make this work." Now, recalling what Dr. Ballinger had told him just days earlier, he said: "If that's what it takes to be with you, I will." This answer made her smile.

They were heading toward the Santa Catalina Mountains on a road that led to the small tourist town of Summerhaven, near the peak of Mount Lemmon. Summerhaven had been christened by those living in the surrounding desert who enjoyed the locale's clement weather when the summer heat became unbearable. The breeze-cooled pine trees and seventy-five-degree climate served as an oasis when the temperature in Tucson reached 115.

As Mount Lemmon grew larger in front of them, Layne said, "The mountains look like they've got stubble on them, like whiskers."

"They do, don't they!" Felina agreed.

When they drew near enough for a closer look, Layne realized the stubble was actually saguaros that covered the base of the mountain. Mount Lemmon Road was leading them through Sabino Canyon where there was an overabundance of desert vegetation despite no water in sight. Towering palm trees with slender trunks dotted the skyline and mountain backdrop of bare rock. Alongside the road were saguaros as tall as telephone poles and Joshua trees with branches that blossomed into needles like a porcupine. The Sonoran Desert that surrounded them was overgrown with yucca, prickly pear, and mesquite and cypress trees, as well as plants with every kind of spiked bulb imaginable.

Ahead in the distance sat houses so large they resembled small mountainside hotels in the foothills. Layne was using the scenery as an excuse to procrastinate over describing the plan he'd come up with and asking Felina the question burning inside of him. It felt strange to be afraid of a woman—it was the first time he had been in a relationship with someone who wasn't expendable.

The road looked like it had been carved into the base of the mountain where they began to enter a pass. They went past a brown wooden sign marking the beginning of the Coronado National Forest, where the scenery became so awe-inspiring that it further postponed the discussion. The road meandered as yellow road signs with black arrows warned of hairpin turns. All the bicyclists wore helmets, and their legs pumped with quick revolutions to climb the mountain in low gear. The road began ascending more quickly until they reached guardrails and a breathtaking view of the entire city of Tucson. Every square mile of Pima County appeared visible all the way to the horizon, where purple mountains met with boundless baby blue to create the desert skyline.

Layne was enjoying the scenery so much that he decided to put off the discussion with Felina until they sat down to have lunch. The rapid contrast in terrain piqued his interest, as it had in the past. Within a matter of minutes, they went from driving through the desert to entering a no-passing zone with road signs warning of falling rocks. The population of saguaros was thinning quickly when, at 4,000 feet, they ceased to exist, as if the elevation sign marked timberline for cacti. They passed rest areas with scenic overlooks where Asian tourists and families with small children took pictures of the majestic view.

Layne's ears began to pop like valves releasing pressure as the car reached an altitude where the contrails left by commercial jets lingered low overhead. The transparent clouds moved at a leisurely pace; the air was clean and fresh and smelled of pine trees and cedar firewood. At 5,000 feet the environment became lush with evergreens and coniferous shrubs, and the yellow road signs began to warn of deer wandering onto the road. The tiny cottages with rooftop solar panels in the lower elevations gave way to a log cabin ambiance as they reached their destination.

"Summerhaven is the southern-most ski resort in the United States—just a little factoid for ya," Felina said as she smiled. Layne fell head over heels for her every time he looked at her. She found a parking space along the road, and Layne climbed out to stretch his arms and legs while he yawned. Felina double-checked her jean pockets for her necessities and pulled the strap of her purse over her shoulder while she reminded Layne to make sure his door was locked.

"Are you hungry?" Felina said.

"Yes, are you?"

"Yeah. I'm gonna dominate a cheeseburger," Felina said.

Layne laughed. "Me too."

They checked both ways before crossing the road to a restaurant that reminded Layne of a mountain lodge with bear rugs. A high school-age girl at a hostess stand seated them on the balcony overlooking the road and thinning pine trees of the mountainside. Layne sat beside Felina at the umbrella-covered table, and they opened their menus while the waitress retrieved their drink orders. Layne felt better, but the calamity that had caused him to miss two important days of work was too recent for a beer to even sound possible. Besides, he had promised Felina he would quit drinking, and had told Dr. Ballinger he would. Instead, his eyes mulled over the menu while his mind devised the right way to resume the conversation they were having when they became absorbed in the scenery as they climbed toward Summerhaven.

"Anyway," Layne said as if he had been interrupted only momentarily, "the point I was trying to make earlier is that the autocrats that truly run the country are trying to let in as many illegals as possible by suspending the punishment. They wanna get rid of all borders in the world. The Border Patrol is just there for appearances—so it looks like the government is trying to stem the flow. It's bull. If they're gonna let people in to ruin the country, then I think you deserve to be a citizen. You know, someone who's self-sufficient instead of these breeders who are being used like cattle to accomplish an agenda. You're the opposite of what they wanna let in. You're a responsible American the way one's supposed to be. You're trying to contribute to society."

"I know, Layne, but that's the way it is," Felina said.

"What if we were married?" Layne blurted as his face turned blood red. He could hardly fathom that he had succeeded in saying it.

Felina suppressed a grin and tried to downplay the question as if it were part of a normal conversation. She couldn't believe that Layne had come up with the very idea that she'd been wondering how to propose to him—no pun intended. She made the snap decision to act as if it had never occurred to her. She told herself it would be the last time she didn't tell Layne everything.

Her eyes returned to the menu, but Layne could judge by the expression on her face that she was pleased with the proposition. Layne reached over and grasped her hand; her fingers were cold, and she looked in his eyes bashfully. Layne smiled and said, "I love you. I always have, since the moment I saw you."

"I love you, too," Felina said. But the way she said it made Layne think she had been ready to say something else. She leaned over and hugged him, but she seemed disappointed, as if she had expected him to say so much earlier.

"It's the only way you're gonna get into college and fulfill your dream," Layne said.

Felina kissed him and, with her arms still on his shoulders, said, "I don't want you to do anything illegal, Layne."

"I've been doing a lot of thinking about it the last few days. I swore an oath to defend the country against enemies, foreign and domestic. Well, we are actually serving the domestic enemies, and those of us who know it are breaking the oath every time we go to work. So, the way I see it, since there are no rules for them, there should be no rules for someone with brains like you."

"You're sweet," Felina said. "It's ridiculous. All I wanna do is go to college so I can get into medical school." She leaned back into her seat and stared down on the menu, lost in thought.

"I'm telling you. I think I've worked out a way to pull it off," Layne said earnestly. "You could go to Magdalena, and I could submit the paperwork for a K-1 fiancée visa. You would have to stay there while the paperwork is being processed. Surely your grandparents would be thrilled to have their granddaughter visit in person and stay for a while."

Felina was quiet, but he couldn't tell if she was considering the plan or if she was evaluating his mental health. *Unbelievable!* she was thinking.

"You've never been caught by Border Patrol or Customs, right?" Layne continued.

"No."

"I could submit the paperwork and claim that I met you while I was in Mexico living with that family. I have a record of being there. I could say that we have had a long-distance relationship the last couple of years, and now we want to be together. On paper, it would look like you've never even left Mexico. They'll never know the difference because there's no record showing otherwise. They'll have no choice but to approve it."

As Layne laid out his plan in words that sounded like a recording of what Felina had concocted, she initially felt guilty. But she knew her scheme was legal and could work just as Layne was saying so she convinced herself it was okay. *How can he think I used him if it was his idea?* she convinced herself. Sheepishly, she jumped in.

"I guess I could make tortillas with my grandma and help her sell them while I'm down there," Felina said pensively. But she didn't sound convinced.

"Yeah, and I could wire you money if you get low so you could get by while you're waiting for the visa to be processed. You could ride down there with someone who has a passport, and they could drop you off. Anyone can go *to* Mexico; Customs doesn't even stop the people headed south," Layne said.

"I don't know, Layne; it sounds crazy. It's a huge risk, and how do I know I can depend on you, and you won't change your mind?" Felina said.

She wanted to believe that Layne was changing, becoming more responsible and reliable. She wanted to believe that the idea—since both she and he had thought of it separately—could succeed. But this would be the mother of all gambles, worse than walking for miles through the desert in hopes of sneaking into America and making a new life, as so many migrants were doing.

She was roused to attention when Layne took her hand.

"You can count on me, I promise," he said. "It would feel weird going through with it while I'm working as an agent. But I guess I'd be just like the dirty agents who look the other way for dope and other stuff we're supposed to stop."

"What would the first step be?" Felina said.

"When is the lease on your apartment up?"

"In a few months."

"Are you sure your gramma would let you come live with her? I'm just guessing, but I'm thinking you'll need to stay there three to six months while the paperwork is being processed."

"Yeah, I'm sure I could stay there. But three to six months sounds rough," Felina said. "What if your plan doesn't work, and they deny your application? I'd be screwed."

Layne began to retort when the waitress returned and asked if they were ready to order. She looked as though she was accustomed to interrupting as she removed her pen and order pad from her apron. Layne's voice tailed off, and his eyes returned to his menu to quickly remind himself what the cheeseburger with fries was called. Felina ordered the same, then Layne gathered the menus and handed them to the waitress. He was in a hurry to continue his explanation before he lost his train of thought.

As soon as their server left, Layne said, "They won't deny it. They can't. It's automatic if you're going to marry an American, as long as you don't have an immigration record. If it was me, three to six months would be well worth the reward."

"I don't know, Layne. I'd have to quit my job and give up my apartment. What if something went wrong?" Felina said. She was trying to not sound overeager or like she had already given this a lot of thought.

"Nothing's gonna go wrong. Even if something didn't go as planned and you had to come back without documents, you could still cross illegally and get back. They'll give you unlimited tries to get away, and I could probably erase your file from ENFORCE when I'm in Processing if it came to that. You could always stay with me," Layne said.

The waitress returned with their plates on a tray, and it forced Layne to halt pleading his case again. By the expression the waitress wore as she put the plates on the table, Layne suspected she had heard part of the conversation and knew what was being discussed.

Layne sprinkled salt and pepper on his fries and reached for the ketchup bottle in the center of the table until she was out of hearing range. He chewed and watched Felina remove the onions from her hamburger and cut it into two equal parts. She took a tiny bite out of a half and waited until she finished chewing before she spoke. "I don't know if either of us would have the guts to go through with it."

Layne ignored her lack of confidence and continued without pausing. "What choice do you have? Do you want to retire from Jabba's office? You gotta take a shot," he said.

Felina nibbled on fries and said, "You've got me there. I don't know how much longer I can last at that job."

"And you were probably lucky to get that job. You're probably not gonna get one better than that," Layne said.

The comment appeared to upset her, and she looked down at her plate as she picked at what was left of her food. Layne realized she had already eaten the first half of her cheeseburger and part of the second half. He had been so busy talking that he had barely touched his. He took a few bites out of it without adding a comment. He realized that if it hadn't been for this last breakdown, she would've been more cooperative.

The check came, and Layne picked it up and reached in his back pocket for his wallet. Felina removed her wallet from her purse to contribute to the bill, but Layne dissuaded her and paid in cash and left a tip. They returned to the car, and Felina opened the driver's side door and unlocked Layne's side so he could climb in. They made their way down the mountain in silence as dusk approached.

Layne turned to her and said, "I just want you to consider it, Babe. I give you my word; I'll do anything in my power to make sure we're successful."

Felina continued steering and blocked the sun's glare as she reached for her sunglasses in the console to relieve her squinting eyes. She wasn't responding, and Layne put his hand up to block the glare in his eyes while he regrouped his thoughts. He was about to take another stab when Felina suddenly pointed to one of the scenic overlooks they had passed on the way up. "Hey, people are watching the sunset from there. Let's pull over and watch it. Wanna?"

"Okay," Layne said.

Felina put on her left turn signal and waited for an oncoming car to pass before she whipped into the pull-out and parked between a Jeep Wrangler and a Toyota truck. Layne put his jacket on as he climbed out, and Felina looked at him across the hood of the car while she pulled her sweatshirt back on. The mountain air took on a chill; the sun was departing as they made their way to the guardrails. Gravel crunched beneath their feet while the two of them found their own spot away from the sightseers at the other end of the lot. Layne and Felina could feel the warmth of the sun on their faces as it cast a heavenly orange light over Sabino Canyon. Layne put his arm around Felina, and she turned and kissed him.

"Wouldn't it be nice if you were here legally and about to graduate from medical school? I would take you to the best steakhouse in Phoenix to celebrate, then on a trip, like Hawaii," Layne said as he shaded his eyes from the light.

Felina said, "I'll talk to my grandma and try to work something out, and maybe I can sublet my apartment or something."

Layne turned to her with surprise and said, "So we're gonna do it?"

"This is the biggest decision of my life, Layne. I'm glad you're looking out for me, but I need time to figure things out."

Layne hugged her and lifted her off her feet. He spun her around like he had wanted to do after the Oral Board exam. Her willingness to simply consider the idea filled him with the exuberance he had fantasized about. He was confident that with time, he could talk her into following through to the end. But he was entering uncharted waters, and that was unsettling. He wasn't accustomed to anyone relying on him—for good reason.

Felina filled him with such a drive to help her that he was prepared to risk his life to do whatever it took. He began to envision her bringing him the happiness he had set out to finally achieve with his Border Patrol foray.

He let her down after another twirl, and they stood together at the railing, gazing upon the sunlit uplands, each with an arm around the other's waist. The sun was halfway below the horizon when Layne turned to look at Felina again. But she continued to stare straight ahead, lost in her own thoughts. The last rays of sunlight caused her dark eyes to gleam with what he interpreted as something that appeared to be similar to his own resolve to become fulfilled. They just might be able to pull this off.

LAYNE LOOKED CLOSELY at the posted schedule for the new pay period to find his name, and was relieved—even more, surprised—to see that he again was assigned to Swings, the 2:00 p.m. to 10:00 p.m. shift. He had expected to be moved to Mids, the overnight shift that ended at 6:00 a.m., as the latest step in Escribano's campaign to drive him to quit. He was pleased to see that, once again, he'd have his own Kilo and be working in the field, even if it was sure to be dark and lonely in the desert during the later hours of his shift. Then he noticed that he was supposed to be on the west side and wondered if that was some kind of a setup in itself.

Also checking the next schedule was an agent he hadn't yet met, an Okie named Thatch. He was not much older than Layne, lean and sunburned. He reminded Layne of a cowboy, thin-hipped and broad-shouldered, who moved with the easy grace of someone accustomed to being outdoors. Thatch spoke with a lazy drawl, saying "Ah" for "I" and putting extra emphasis on the first syllable of words that were pronounced otherwise.

"Processin', Swings," Thatch muttered as he found his name on the new schedule. "Figures."

Layne shot a glance at Thatch and couldn't restrain himself. "What do you mean?" he asked.

"Ah'm not on good terms with management raht now," he said.

Layne's interest piqued. He was always keen to hear that someone besides him had wrestled with the authorities. "What did you do?"

"Ah'm a-not gonna git inta it, but somethin' happened 'bout a year ago, and Ah din't play along. They been hasslin' me ever since. They make ev'r day a my life miserable as they possibly kin."

"What have they done to you?" Layne wanted to know.

"They make it look CO-incidental, but when they do mah schedule they give me split days off." Thatch rubbed the back of his neck. "In JU-lie, they'll assign me a KEE-low with no air-conditionin' and put me at JU-liet on the pavement where it's hundred ten degrees."

"That's so you just get slow-roasted for eight hours."

Figuring he had found a sympathetic ear, Layne launched into his personal history. "When I first got here, Escribano asked me if I needed a place to live 'til I got settled, and when I told him I already had a place in Bisbee, he gave me the 'this job's not for everybody' speech. You know how it works. The guys that he gives that speech to usually quit, or headquarters gets rid of them at the Oral Boards if they're white. But I speak Spanish, so they couldn't get rid of me that way."

Thatch looked like he was interested in the background so Layne continued.

"But it really started when I lost my notebook in the field, when I was with Ashlock. He wrote up a couple of memos about it, and Escribano has been pencil-whipping me ever since. He's had me sign probably ten corrective action forms. He tells me I need to shave every time I see him. I almost always come in clean-shaven. The beard he complains about is the one that's grown on my face during the eight hours I'm here. He wrote me up for that once. Anything he can think of."

Thatch started to respond, but Layne was on a roll. An incident he had forgotten came to mind—one he hadn't even mentioned to Felina.

"Actually, it started before I lost my notebook. Shortly after I started field training, our FTO told us we'd be going straight to the field this particular shift. Usually, we'd show up for Muster in our good uniforms, shined boots and everything, then change into field uniforms so we could run around in the desert and not worry about having to go home that night and clean and press our uniforms and shine our boots for the next day."

Thatch nodded as Layne continued. "So, I showed up in my field uniform. Escribano walked by and said, 'You're on FTU right now, aren't you?'

I said, 'Yessir.'

"He said, 'Why do you look like you do? Don't you know that the Border Patrol expects you to be presentable?'

"I said, 'They told us we were going straight to the field so I wore my field stuff. I have my other stuff; I can go change if you'd like.'"

"He said, 'You're not presentable. You're supposed to look presentable. If that's really what you're going to wear, I need you to write me a memo about how to iron pants, how to clean uniforms, and how to shine boots.'"

Thatch looked at him wide-eyed.

"I thought he was joking," Layne said. "I said, 'Sir, do you really want me to write a memo about how my boots aren't shined?' I was in disbelief.

"He said, 'That's exactly what I want you to do.'

I was like, 'Oh, man! This guy's serious!'

"I went out to meet up with my FTO, and I was ticked. I took one look at him and said, 'I have to write a silly memo about how my boots aren't shined, and you look like you just pulled your uniform out of a jockey box because it has so many wrinkles. And your boots look horrible!' I said, 'Really. We're worried about whether my boots are shined when we should be going to catch an alien?'"

"He said, 'That's the dumbest thing I ever heard of. But it's a supervisor so you have to do it.'"

Layne shook his head and said, "I think Escribano is going to fire me any day. I'm just waiting for the call."

"Why don't ya just quit then?" Thatch scratched his head, as if puzzling out the obvious.

"Because if I quit, it will make it easy for Escribano. I want to screw with him the way he's screwed with me." Layne could never overcome the impulse to get even. "I know it's a pain in the butt for them to fire anybody, even an intern," he said.

"True," said Thatch. "They fired a guy a few years back 'cause he was mentally ill, and it took forever. He din't do anythin' loco that DI-rectly; DIS-O-bayed orders, like sashayin' into Mexico on a shift. But he was seein' things and talkin' to hisself. They had to pile up paperwork on him for several years—spittin'-on-the-sidewalk type a stuff."

Thatch gave a slight shrug in recognition of their common experience. "Ah put in fer a TRANS-fer," he said. "Ah'm jes waitin' for the PAIC t' sign off on the paperwork. If they wanna get rid uh you, they sometimes allow ya t' transfer, or they'll PRO-mote ya outta here."

That sounded intriguing to Layne. He made a mental note to check that out, and they parted.

* * * *

THE NEXT DAY, LAYNE'S PARANOIA about being sent to an area known among his fellow agents for its concentration of drug smugglers receded as soon as he'd driven away from the station. As he settled into his routine, he recalled what he had learned about the area during the AOR tour led by Agent Schnabel. Nearby was the giant slag pile that served as a landmark for agents working the area west of the Walmart store.

"The Slag," as Schnabel said everyone in the Border Patrol called it, was a black mountain of mine waste in the middle of a dumping ground for rusted cars and decades of the Douglas area's other rubbish. "We reference it all the time so you need to orient yourself," Agent Schnabel had told Layne and the other trainees on the tour that time.

Beyond the overgrown junkyard were fields of desert sage and mesquite thickets, with washes that flooded during the epic thunderstorms that frightened even the area's regular inhabitants but, when they were dry creek beds, were handy hiding places for drug mules seeking shelter from the prying eyes of the National Guard women in the Camera Room.

"West of the junkyard, we need to catch them before they cross the desert between the fence and Highway 80," Layne remembered Schnabel saying. "It's about a mile to the highway from the fence right here. If they make it that far, a vehicle can pick them up on the shoulder, and the driver will take them east through Bisbee or north on Highway 191 to Pirtleville."

Layne hoped for a quiet last few hours to this shift. But not too long after a nearly full moon cast an almost supernatural light on the landscape before him, a voice from the Camera Room reported a sighting: two bodies, apparently carrying forty-six, just west of The Slag. Layne waited for an agent to respond that he was in pursuit. The last thing Layne wanted was to be responsible for apprehending two drug mules in the darkness of the desert. But the radio remained oddly—alarmingly—silent. With each passing minute, it seemed inevitable that he would be the one to chase them. He wondered if this was why they scheduled him here this time. Maybe they wanted him to fail. Maybe they told other agents to let him handle this one.

But how, he asked himself, *could they possibly have known in advance that drugs would be transported through here this night?*

The Camera Room voice came over the radio again, sounding impatient and annoyed this time. And it spoke directly to Layne.

"Delta-328—What's your twenty?"

"My twenty is a half-mile east of the Slag," Layne responded.

"Will you be responding to that traffic?"

"Ten-four, I'm thirteen, Delta-328." Layne swallowed hard, almost to the point of choking. As he prepared to exit his Kilo, he thought of Felina. But, for once, he wasn't imagining how impressed she would be when he told her of his derring-do. He worried, instead, that he might never see her again.

* * * *

USING HIS MAGLITE TO ILLUMINATE the trail, Layne found fresh sign in a wash that headed west before it turned in the direction of Highway 80. He was quite proud of himself; it made him feel like a real Border Patrol agent—

that maybe he could be good at this after all. He remembered Schnabel saying they had to keep the mules from reaching Highway 80 and began calculating how to do that in this situation. For the moment, he forgot that he was alone. He forgot to be scared.

Layne raced ahead, hoping to get in front of the two drug runners—if indeed there were only two. The thought occurred to him: *What if they are the last two in a larger group?*

He couldn't believe how much ground he was covering and with only the moon to light his path, no less! *Adrenaline is an amazing thing,* he thought. Sooner than he thought possible, Highway 80 was in sight. It seemed conceivable that he had cut them off, that his targets were still out there in the desert from whence he'd come. Now he had to find them.

Before venturing back into the vast unknown, Layne tried to call for help. He wasn't sure exactly what he should say in his radio transmission. *Fake it until you make it,* he recalled hearing someone say once. They weren't talking specifically about what to say on the radio, but he figured it applied to that, too. So, that's what he did.

"This is Delta-328. I'm north of The Slag at Highway 80. I'm tracking forty-six, two mules on foot."

The call drew only silence, and Layne wondered if he'd said the wrong thing. Or maybe no one wanted to help the new guy just because they knew he was on thin ice with management. But then, after what seemed like many minutes but probably was only a few, a male voice, most likely a supervisor, said:

"Shift is up. Mids will come out and help you. Stay with it."

Layne had lost track of time; momentarily, he was caught off guard. Quickly, his reaction changed; he could hardly believe his ears. *End of shift! Doesn't anybody put duty first?*

Suddenly a sound made the hairs on Layne's neck stand up. Instinctively, he knew this was no javelina. Wearing night vision goggles, he paused to adjust to the eerie picture they produced and marveled at the detail before his very eyes. He peered into the dim night and thought he saw the shape of a man, just standing in the open farther down the wash. Layne saw him, but he didn't see Layne. It was difficult, with the shadows, to tell how far away he was.

Layne watched the figure disappear into a mesquite thicket. He went scurrying after him, wondering: *Is he alone? Is his partner with him? Are there others?* He had no idea.

He watched the thicket from close range for maybe half a minute. The figure Layne had seen should have been right there. He looked. Nothing. *Did he see me? Is he hiding?*

Suddenly, Layne's head was on a swivel, looking in every direction, waiting for the first rock to hit him. It was the rocks, more than any other possibility, which unnerved even veteran agents. "Beware of guys throwing rocks," he had been told in the past; he couldn't remember who told him or when. "You never see them coming. You never hear them. You get beaned, and you're done. No gunfire or anything."

Layne decided the best thing he could do was just wait. Right where he was. And so, he did, until he heard voices in Spanish. *Where are these guys? How many are there?*

It's almost funny what practical stuff you remember when the time comes to use it, Layne thought as another piece of potentially life-saving information bubbled up within the limbic system of his brain: *There's almost always a scout with any large group, watching his load—watching his money.*

Again, Layne warily searched in the darkness for evidence of a larger group or any indication that someone, a scout, was monitoring his every step. He dared not use his Maglite. The light would make him an easy target to spot. He had to rely on the weird greenish images that came to him through his night vision goggles.

Another sound: movement in or just beyond the nearest thicket.

There's a knee moving back and forth. I see it! And there's a bundle. Oh, crap! Guns could come with drugs!

Layne crept closer, his nerve endings on edge, as alert as he could possibly make himself, barely remembering to breathe. He was too focused to have time for the usual doubts and insecurities he typically allowed to enter his consciousness. He grabbed his radio from his duty belt and tried to get someone's attention. Talking softly, in words he wasn't sure conformed to Border Patrol radio lingo, he gave his approximate location and said, "There's at least two bodies hiding in a mesquite thicket, and there's a bundle of forty-six laying near them. I'm going to jump them. Is anyone close?"

Layne crept forward, trying to figure out what his next move should be. He still didn't know if there were only two mules in the thicket or if they were armed. It was still dark, though the moon, he decided, was indeed a blessing from heaven. It was then that another piece of advice from the uncertain past made its way front and center in his memory:

When in doubt, get your gun out. Everybody understands the international language of gun.

But then what? Layne considered what he should do once he drew his sidearm. He tried to mentally rewind to when they covered this at the Academy but drew a blank. Was that one of the days when he was hung over from the previous weekend? An image of him on the firing range at the Academy flashed in his mind, a fleeting reminder that he had been shooting since he was a boy and was an expert marksman. But the thought that followed was another from the Academy range: He'd never fired at a human being.

He charged toward the figures he knew were in the thicket and shouted: "*¡Lavanta las manos!*" (Put your hands up!) To his surprise, he found that they had not two, but four, bundles of marijuana with them. And with relief, he determined that he had not cornered a larger group.

Two frightened young Mexicans did as they were told, and as they looked at him expectantly, Layne thought, *What do I do now?*

He decided on the truth: "*Éste es el trato. Estoy nervioso. Y si se mueven, los voy a matar a los dos.*" (Here's the deal. I'm nervous. And if you move, I'm going to kill you both.)

They were wide-eyed; obviously not doubting him or thinking, even for a second, that they could take advantage of his obvious discomfort.

Layne ordered them to the ground so he could handcuff them.

"No mames, wey. Nos vamos a ensuciar," one complained. (Come on, man. We're going to get dirty.)

At that moment, Layne was thankful for his fluency. He realized right then that the Academy class and the Oral Board exam dealt with formal Spanish. But in the field, face to face with people who risk their lives to sneak across the border in hopes of a better life or those who smuggle marijuana, it's street Spanish—slang and idiomatic talk—that carried the day.

"No me importa," (I don't care.) Layne told them. *"¡Bajen!"* (Get down!) As they complied, he said to the one who had objected: *"Si te mueves, wey, serás en recibir la primera bala."* (If you move, dude, you'll get the first bullet.) He could hardly believe what he was hearing. It sounded like his voice, but it didn't sound like him.

He was puzzling over how he was going to get two guys and four fifty-pound bundles out of the desert by himself when a face he recognized materialized out of the darkness.

"Darmody?"

"I heard you on the radio," said the agent known for finding trouble. "I got here as fast as I could after Muster broke. You were a little hard to find in the dark, you know."

Darmody had been the one veteran agent willing to show Layne the ropes in Processing and had even shared his lunch when he found out Layne had forgotten his that day. He was known as the guy who always found trouble, as well as one who caught a lot of mules and a lot of dope. Layne recalled the night when, while still a trainee, he was riding with Agent Cruz when the "shots fired" call came in, and they rushed to the scene of the incident. Darmody had stopped a load vehicle and shot the driver when the guy tried to drive off with Darmody's arm stuck in the chest restraint of his seatbelt. A lot of agents were critical of Darmody, but Layne didn't share their feelings. To him, Darmody was the kind of agent he hoped to be.

"I put out a call for help, and one guy—you—shows up?" Layne said. "Where's the teamwork, Adam?"

"You're going to learn that in the Border Patrol, some guys just don't want to tramp through the desert in the dark," Darmody said, "or do any of the other dirty work of catching mules or Tonks."

"But we're in law enforcement," Layne argued. "When I call, they're supposed to answer me; they have to come and help."

"No," Darmody corrected. "You have to prove yourself. Once you prove yourself, they'll always respond. But you have to prove yourself first."

Layne looked at the two disheveled illegals and the four bundles of marijuana. "How do we get them and these out of the desert?"

"By law, we can't make them carry any of it," Darmody said. "We have to walk them out, carry what we can, and kick the rest."

The eastern sky was beginning to brighten by the time Layne and Darmody reached his Kilo. Almost two full shifts had passed since he drove off the lot at Douglas Station not knowing what was in store.

* * * *

AS LAYNE EXPECTED, DARMODY eschewed the paperwork associated with catching the two mules with their load. Darmody was notorious among his peers for rounding up as many as fifty illegals in one try then dumping them in Processing without the G434 forms filled out for them. But Layne didn't resent being left with the necessary follow-through. He was thankful that Darmody responded in the field, and he appreciated the way Darmody had helped him in Processing when others didn't want to bother—especially considering how Darmody avoided that mundane chore whenever he could.

Besides a G434 for each mule, Layne had to get the bundles weighed and complete Drug Enforcement Administration paperwork. He was sure he'd reach a point when, like Darmody, he wished he could leave these details for others. But since this was his first interdiction, he was savoring this part, which made it official. He expected it to take another hour, at least.

As he prepared to start on the G434 for the first of his two captives, he recalled the time when his field training officer was that guy named Tipton, who later goaded him into a high-speed chase that was against Patrol policy. Layne and his group, which included his friends, Carlos and Runyon, and another trainee named Presussen, rounded up a large group of illegals before they could reach the safe haven of nearby Pirtleville. The trainees had to search them all then fill out a G434 on each one. "You guys know, don't you, that all of those IDs they give you are fake," Tipton had said. Layne wondered if his guys were carrying false IDs, too. He figured they were.

Before he asked his first question—name—he recalled something else Tipton had said that night. "Just write down whatever it says on the ID. They'll run fingerprints in Processing and find out who they are if they've been caught before."

Both mules had ID cards, but Layne assumed the information he entered on the G434 for each guy was worthless. He began to understand why Darmody felt the way he did about procedure after apprehension.

8

A FLOOD OF SURPRISES WASHED OVER Layne as he followed through on his promise to Dr. Ballinger. For starters, the support group in Bisbee met at a church. Well, not *in* the church, per se. But a place called The Annex was right next door to Covenant Presbyterian Church, and it was part of church property. It had been a hospital once upon a time, then Phelps Dodge, the big mining company, sold it to the church for a dollar. Now it was the site of numerous "educational and fellowship events" that the church supported in the small community. Covenant Presbyterian itself opened the year after the Copper Queen Hotel, which sat less than a hundred yards away on Howell Avenue. The church featured beautiful stained-glass windows and a spectacular pipe organ, both installed the year the church opened. The organ cost $2,500 in 1903.

Layne hadn't stopped marveling at the idea of drunks meeting in a church building when another assumption went kaput. "Hi, my name's Sylvia. I'm a recovering alcoholic," said the first person he saw upon entering The Annex. *I figured only men were alcoholics. Or at least that they were the only ones who would admit it.*

Others were arriving, and that made Layne self-conscious. He was sure this collection of strangers, even though it wasn't very large—or perhaps because it wasn't—would be as judgmental as almost everyone he'd encountered in the Border Patrol. His mind raced as his insecurities began to rage; he considered sneaking away. *One snide comment, and I'm outta here,* he thought as he spotted two more women and assumed at least one of them would be like Melanie Schumer, who hadn't backed off at all since advancing from trainee to agent.

But then:

"Hi, my name's Anthony, and I'm a recovering alcoholic," said a man who could have passed for Paul Bunyan. "Welcome to our group."

And then:

"Hi, my name's Seth, and I'm a recovering alcoholic. Welcome to our group."

Layne was reeling as people he didn't know, one after another, greeted him the same way. He'd never experienced such acceptance. He saw a man who appeared to be in his mid-fifties pouring a glass of water. He was dressed in military fatigues but different than Border Patrol-issue ones. He reminded Layne of General Lee at the Academy firing range. When the man turned back toward the circle of folding chairs that were filling up with support group regulars, Layne saw that his name was stenciled on his t-shirt. "Colonel Erickson," it said.

"Hello, sir," Layne said, stopping just short of saluting. *Dang it, Dr. Ballinger said there would be an Army colonel in the group.*

"Around here, just call me Cal," the officer said. "That's my name. I'm no different than everyone else in this group. We're all recovering alcoholics."

They're all so open about it, so matter-of-fact—nothing to hide. Amazing!

By the time Layne looked for a seat in the circle, the only vacant chair was next to the guy who had said his name was Seth. This time, Layne immediately noticed the long, grey ponytail; somehow, he had missed it in the flurry of introductions.

"You look familiar," Layne said. "Do I know you?"

"Hey," Seth said as the figurative light bulb went on. "Weren't you in my place back before Christmas, with that hot Hispanic chick? You bought her a pair of earrings."

"She's not a chick," Layne snapped. "She's my fiancée."

"Sorry, man," Seth responded quickly. "No offense."

Layne was taken aback by his uncharacteristic show of sensitivity. He realized immediately that he had looked at females in general, and

Hispanic girls in particular, as "hot chicks" himself. But now, after Felina, he was struck by how dehumanizing it sounded, how disrespectful. His sudden defense of her honor shocked him.

"No problem," he said to Seth. "I used to say the same things. Just sounded different when I heard somebody else refer to her that way; that's all."

Seth gave him an analytical look then asked: "Are you here because of her?"

Layne paused at such a personal question before concluding that no inquiry must be too personal in this setting. *Nothing is off-limits.*

"She asked me to stop drinking," he said, "but I'm here because I want to quit. I realize I need help."

"Good answer," Seth said with a faint smile.

Layne wanted to change subjects. "How long have you had your shop in town?"

"Almost since I moved to Bisbee," Seth answered, not really telling Layne what he wanted to know.

"When was that?"

"About eight years ago, I reckon. My memory's kinda bad. Too much whiskey for too many years."

Seth looked to be about fifty years old, but Layne was curious enough to ask. "How old are you, Seth?"

"Thirty-four."

It was Seth's turn to satisfy his curiosity. "You a Border agent?"

"Yep."

"I figured."

"Is that a problem?"

"Not for me; I'm legal."

Their conversation was interrupted by the man named Anthony, the apparent group leader, who for sure was at least fifty.

"We have a new member of our group with us tonight," he began. "His name is Layne. And, as is our custom whenever someone joins us, we'll start by reading, then discussing, our favorite quotation. Let's all read it together, aloud:

"The mentality and behavior of alcoholics
is wholly irrational
until you understand
that they are completely powerless over their addiction.
And unless they have structured help,
they have no hope."

"Who said that?" Layne whispered to Seth.

"I dunno; it coulda been any of us," he replied with a shrug. "It applies to all of us. That's why we're here."

"How long have you been in this group," Layne asked.

"My fifth year."

Layne fought to conceal his astonishment. *I thought this would take a couple months, at most.*

"Once an alcoholic, always an alcoholic," Seth continued. "Some people need maintenance, like a car, to keep running smoothly. I'm one of them."

Is that how it's going to be for me? Layne wondered. He wasn't yet ready to live with his illness for the rest of his life.

* * * *

"LET'S SUMMARIZE THE 12 STEPS," Anthony said to the group after each person of the regulars had taken a turn sharing the challenges they'd faced since the last meeting. A printed copy of the Alcoholics Anonymous 12-Step Program had been given to Layne when the meeting started, even though this technically wasn't an AA meeting. The summary was reinforcement for the members of the support group, he realized. He needed it more than any of the regulars, who by now had memorized the message, if not

86

the words verbatim.

"The 12 steps to recovery," Anthony began, "involve:

"Admitting that no one can control his or her alcoholism;

"Recognizing that a Supreme Being can give strength;

"Acknowledging past errors with the help of a sponsor who is an experienced member;

"Making amends for those errors;

"Changing behavior and learning to live a new life without alcohol; and

"Helping others who suffer from the same illness."

Hearing others talk openly about their temptations and struggles was eye-opening for Layne. He'd hidden, or had tried to hide, his failures from everyone for so long. He figured every alcoholic was in denial the way he was and thought they were smart enough, clever enough, to be able to fool everyone else into not seeing how they really were. And, of course, at one time, they did. But, no more.

To hear men—and women—put their years of alcohol abuse into context and admit how strong the pull was for them—still, after years of assisted sobriety—was perhaps Layne's biggest surprise on a night full of them.

It was uncomfortable hearing how similar the stories of the members of the group were to his own, but Layne used the parallels to reflect on the main points embodied in the 12-Step summary and how they applied to him. For several minutes he tuned out Seth, Anthony and everyone else, and flashed back to:

. . . all the times he'd "promised" himself he wouldn't drink on the weekend . . . how he vowed he would be "all business" starting on Sunday . . . telling himself that once he was at the Border Patrol Academy, he would "walk the line" . . . when he embarrassed himself on the Academy firing range, resolving that *I'm never gonna drink again* and declaring to himself that, if he made to the next Friday, "I will remember this day forever when I'm tempted" . . . as he picked up a pint to calm himself and be able to sleep, telling himself that "starting tomorrow, I'm done" . . . the night he realized he had been driving without headlights for who knew how long . . . and, worst of all, hearing Felina tell him, "Don't make promises you can't keep."

The summary of the 12 Steps played back in his head:

"Admitting that no one can control his or her alcoholism;

"Recognizing that a Supreme Being can give strength;

"Acknowledging past errors with the help of a sponsor who is an experienced member;

"Making amends for those errors;

"Changing behavior and learning to live a new life without alcohol; and

"Helping others who suffer from the same illness."

I'm living proof that an alcoholic can't control himself, he thought. *God, have I made errors. . . God! I can't say He's been much of a presence in my life, the way I've lived it up to now . . . How do I make it up to the people who matter? I'm so ashamed . . . The only way is to show them, to really change— and stick with it . . . A sponsor—yes, I need a sponsor, someone I can talk to and not worry about what they think of me because they've been there.*

"Layne! Layne!" It was Seth softly calling his name and nudging him with an elbow. "You still with us, man?"

Only then did Layne realize that Anthony had asked him if he'd tell the group about himself. Baring your soul was part of the first-night ritual.

"Sorry," Layne began. "I guess I was in my own world there, going over some of my failures and applying the Steps to what I've done."

"Why don't you tell us about you," Anthony said. "You'll find that it's actually therapeutic."

And so, Layne began, haltingly at first, gauging just how far he could go in telling his story—the whole truth, as he'd told it—for the first time ever—to Dr. Ballinger.

"I started drinking after high school," he began. "In college, actually. I'd been a big success in high school as an athlete—got drafted and played a couple years in the minor leagues. I couldn't handle it when I got hurt and that ended.

"When I started, I said I was only gonna drink on Friday and Saturday nights. Pretty soon, I always felt like I wasted the opportunity to get drunk if I didn't get hammered on nights when I didn't have work the next day. I'd get drunk on Friday night, then drink beer all day Saturday, and do it again Saturday night. Then I'd end up drinking red beers or bloody Marys on Sunday morning and try to taper-off by bedtime. I started buying those little bottles of vodka for a quickie whenever I needed it; kept some in my car, which was dumb.

"I worried about getting picked up for DUI. But somehow, I managed to avoid that. Lucky, I guess. Or maybe unlucky. Maybe that would have forced me to change sooner.

"I've known for a long time that I have a problem, but I just figured I'd deal with it when things slowed down, and I had a chance. Over the years, I've just learned to live with it like a disease. I thought I'd eventually find my way back to the way I was before if I could succeed at something.

"I came up with this plan that I thought would restore my self-esteem and be what I needed to be to stop drinking. I believed that, if I could become a Border Patrol agent, I'd be so proud of myself and be so important, that I wouldn't need to drink anymore. But it didn't work out that way. Those guys all drink worse than I do. Well, not all but a lot."

The colonel, Cal, interjected, "It's the same in the Army, son." No one reacted; they all knew his story already.

"I got crossways with management at Douglas Station," Layne continued, "because I was hung over so often when I came to work. I don't think they knew that, exactly. Maybe they did, and I'm so out of it I just think they didn't. Whatever . . . they started a disciplinary file on me. I'm under a lot of pressure to not screw up anymore. I'm like under a microscope.

"And then there's this girl I met." Layne decided that her name wasn't important in this situation. Why drag her into it by name? "I wound up driving to Tucson every weekend to be with her. We'd go out, and I'd tell myself to drink only in moderation. But one beer led to another and another. Pretty soon, I was sneaking off to the bar for tequila shots. I'd wake up the next morning at her place, and I couldn't remember what happened the night before. I convinced myself that I'd been cool with her, that she thought nothing of it."

Everyone in the circle looked to others and nodded knowingly as Layne continued. It all sounded so familiar to them.

"We were watching television one night at her place, and I had been drinking, though again, I didn't think she had noticed enough to think anything of it. I excused myself to go into her bathroom. I had some little bottles of vodka with me, and I popped a couple. Next thing I know, she's standing over me, crying and shouting my name. I had passed out and fallen into her bathtub. She was afraid I was dead. I was afraid I'd lost her."

Layne paused then said, "Do I need to go on?"

"I think we know the rest of the story," Anthony answered.

"I apologized and told her I was going to stop drinking. She said, 'Don't make promises you can't keep.'"

* * * *

WHEN THE MEETING ENDED (*at last!*), Layne asked Anthony about finding a sponsor. The big man looked him in the eye and said, "Seemed like you hit it off pretty good with Seth. Why don't you ask him? I think you and him would be a good fit, and I'm bettin' he'll do it." Seth had not left the room yet; he was having an animated conversation with the first person Layne had met, the lady named Sylvia. Layne waited until they finished then caught Seth before he could head out.

"Hey, Seth!" he called.

"Yo, bro," he shot back. Layne laughed at how different this guy was from the hippie he'd seen in the jewelry shop when he and Felina wandered in a couple of months ago.

"I need a sponsor—you know, somebody I can talk to when I'm having a hard time. Anthony suggested you, said we'd be a good fit." Layne fumbled and mumbled, self-conscious. "So, I, uh, so I'm . . ."

"That's one of the Steps, remember?" Seth interrupted. "You'll help me as much as I help you. That's how it works."

Another surprise! I expected to have to talk him into it.

Layne stuck out his hand, indicating he wanted to shake on it. "Thank you!" he said, the relief in his voice not lost on Seth.

"Why don't we stop for a soda and get to know each other a little better?" he said. They walked out of The Annex together. Anthony smiled, proudly.

Sitting across the table from Layne in a hole-in-the-wall on Main Street, Seth was first to speak. "So, what's it like to be a Border Patrol agent?"

Layne frowned.

"It's not glamorous; that's for sure," was the first thing that came to mind. "The general public really has no idea what it's like to be a line agent. Their image of the Border Patrol is what they see on television, what they read in the newspapers, the way the politicians oversimplify things."

The look on Layne's face as he spoke told Seth more than Layne's words.

"First of all, the Border Patrol Academy is as bad as Marine Boot Camp. You go through two grueling months of training that includes running for miles, tracking faint footprints in the dirt of the desert, getting nearly blinded by pepper spray, and defending yourself against a bunch of guys who beat the crap out of you for kicks. All under the blazing sun. Plus, you have to become fluent in Spanish, learn immigration law like a lawyer, and be able to hit the center of a target with a variety of guns.

"If you pass that gauntlet, you go through four phases of field training at the station where you'll be assigned as an agent, if you make it. You work three different shifts—your body clock never adjusts. You go to Swings, no more friends. You get off; nobody's awake. So, you're like, 'What do I do?' So, you go to sleep. You get up, and you've missed the morning, and then you're right back at work. You're like, I didn't see anybody today, and I'm right back here, doing the same cruddy thing, dealing with the same guys. And people are all over me about losing a notebook or not looking clean-shaven at the end of the shift; I'm getting nitpicked for everything. Nobody helps.

"You have to get to know a lot of wide-open spaces," Layne continued, "as if there were landmarks to go by, master the processing of the illegals who get caught. and actually track, catch, search, handcuff, and transport everybody from drug mules to mothers with their children. And you have to deal with the politics of supervisors who may be out to get you and some agents who don't want to be bothered with the actual work. After all that, you have to pass an oral exam in Spanish that is rigged to wash you out if management doesn't want you around.

"Once you make it—if you make it—it's incredibly lonely and scary, especially at night. It's really dark out in the desert, and it's just you and whomever you run across. When you catch people trying to sneak across the border, you know they'll be sent back to Mexico and probably come sneaking back within days. Some guys have caught the same illegals a half-dozen times or more. Catching people in the desert is putting a Band-Aid on it. It's not fixing the problem of illegal immigration.

"And if you nail some mules bringing drugs into the country, you can't even charge them unless you catch them carrying the stuff. Finding evidence on their clothes that suggests they had been carrying the bundles just before they were caught or catching them hiding with the bundles alongside them is not enough to charge them because they won't be prosecuted on that basis.

"There's this sea of people coming; we can't catch them all, and it doesn't seem like management wants to catch them. You'll be following a load vehicle, and they tell you, 'Cease and desist. You're driving too fast, and you're entering the city.' And we say, 'But he's right there.' It's all pretty frustrating. It's insane."

Seth marveled at what he'd just heard. "If people only knew. The politicians and the media are really out of touch with reality, aren't they!"

Layne didn't bite on that comment. Instead, he wanted to know more about Seth.

"You heard my story in the meeting," Layne said. "Seems like I should know yours if we're going to lean on each other. What got you to stop drinking?"

"I had a kid," Seth began. Layne realized immediately that this would not be a short answer.

"My old lady, her mom, drank almost as much as I did. We met in a bar and started looking for each other there. Pretty soon we were shackin' up and along came our kid. The poor thing didn't have much of a home life her first five years. Then her mom got real sick—too much liquor. Pretty quick, we knew she was dyin'.

"My little girl was about six by then, and she came to me one day and said, 'Daddy, will you take care of me if Mommy dies? I don't have anybody else.'

"Right there, I knew I had to do something about myself. I hadn't been much of a dad to that day. But somethin' in her question got to me. I couldn't let her down. So, I called Anthony and asked him how the support group worked.

"My kid's eleven now. Growin' up. Nice young lady, despite her parents. We're closer than I ever thought possible. I'd do anything for her."

Layne was speechless. *You never know about people,* he thought. *I'll learn more another time.* They talked for a few more minutes then exchanged phone numbers.

"Call me anytime," Seth said.

Layne went home to call Felina. It had been quite a night.

9

SKIPPING THE USUAL GREETING when Marianne answered her phone, Felina blurted impulsively: "I have to tell you the latest! Can I come over?"

"Where's Layne?" Marianne asked, caught off guard. "This is Sunday; aren't you with him?" She worried that some kind of calamity had occurred, though Felina sounded enthused, not alarmed. Layne and Felina had been spending every weekend together, usually in Tucson. Marianne couldn't fathom why this one would be any different.

"He's staying in Bisbee," Felina said, almost breathless. "There's so much I need to tell you about."

"How soon can you be here?" Marianne said excitedly. Her curiosity was overcoming the initial sense of apprehension.

"I'm on my way."

Fifteen minutes later, Felina pulled up in front of Marianne's house in the used car she had bought with her life's savings. The old Corolla had proven to be a questionable investment; it needed repairs that weren't apparent when she chose it. But it had gotten her and Layne to Summerhaven and her to Marianne's. At the moment, that was all that mattered. She locked the driver's side door and scurried to Marianne's front porch, ringing the doorbell the second she reached the stoop.

"Come in, sweetie! I can't wait to hear your news," Marianne said. She had a pitcher of lemonade ready and waiting. "Let's go out back by the pool."

They went through the house and walked outside. Being there again reminded Felina of the day she met Layne at the party Marianne threw for her fiancé Ryan's graduation from the Border Patrol Academy. For a moment, she relived that night—going out with Marianne, Ryan, and Layne, how funny she thought he was and how much she enjoyed being with him and letting him spend the night with her then wondering if she'd been too easy. She returned to the present as Marianne handed her a glass of lemonade.

"I don't know where to begin," Felina said anxiously. That only heightened Marianne's eager anticipation of what she expected Felina to tell her.

"Why don't you start by telling me why Layne's not with you this weekend."

Layne's phone call from the night before was fresh in Felina's mind. She was proud of him for actually following through and attending his first support group meeting, and even prouder after she heard him relate events of the evening. It had been hard to give up seeing him on Saturday, but it was definitely worth it once she found out how things went.

"He stayed in Bisbee Saturday so he could attend his first support group meeting. It meets on Saturday nights," Felina said. "I think he's really serious this time about getting his drinking under control."

Marianne stammered, "That's . . .that's . . . oh, sweetie, I'm so . . . that's . . . GREAT NEWS! What does this mean for the two of you?"

Felina wanted to tell Marianne about Layne's first meeting. The words spilled out in rapid-fire without her taking a breath.

"He-told-me-they-all-read-aloud-this-quote-about-alcoholism," she gasped. Marianne struggled to decipher. "He-talked-about-himself-and-his-problem. I-wasn't-sure-he-could-talk-about-himself-that-way . . . especially-in-front-of-strangers. And-he-met-a-guy-named-Seth-who-is-going-to-be-his-sponsor."

Marianne tried to slow her down enough to make sure she was understanding and taking in everything Felina was telling her. "That's awesome," she said. "How did he find out about the support group? How did he decide to get help? Tell me . . . *slowly*."

"He went to see this counselor, Dr. Ballinger, in Sierra Vista," Felina explained, trying hard to calm herself. "They talked for a long time, and Layne got some things out that I was sure he needed to tell someone. From what he told me, he opened up like he never opened up to anyone, even me. Dr. Ballinger sounds like a really wise man, someone who has worked with a lot of people with problems. He told Layne he would help him get through this, if he promised to do his part. Layne said he promised, and this time, I think he meant it.

"Dr. Ballinger recommended that Layne become part of the support group in Bisbee. So, Layne went. He said it was one surprise after another—from alcoholics being women as well as men, to how open everyone was about their problems, to how friendly and welcoming they were. The guy who is going to be Layne's sponsor, a guy named Seth, runs his own little jewelry shop in town. Layne bought me a pair of earrings there. He didn't seem so friendly that day, but he and Layne seem to have hit it off. That was one of Layne's biggest surprises, seeing the guy who ran that shop and finding out he had a past, too."

Marianne was doing her best to manage the deluge of information without quashing Felina's eagerness to bring her up to date or seeming impatient with any detail.

"I gather he came around regarding your admission to him about your brother and you and your family's status," she said.

"I guess I have Dr. Ballinger to thank for that, too," Felina acknowledged. "Layne called me after his meeting with Dr. Ballinger and told me he was sorry, that it was all his fault, that he reacted childishly. At first, I didn't know what I should say or do. He begged me to let him come to Tucson and make it up to me. He said he wanted to take me to Mount Lemmon. He said he had something important to tell me. I was skeptical—the way he walked out then ignored my calls and text messages really hurt. But I couldn't say no."

Felina proceeded to recount the drive up the mountain to Summerhaven and lunch there.

"You won't believe what happened next," she said, eyes wide. Clearly, she was relishing this part most of all.

"I can't wait!" Marianne gushed.

"He basically pitched our idea to me! I hadn't said a word to him about any of it, but he suggested that I go to Mexico and come back on a fiancée visa! He laid out every detail, just the way I had dreamed it up. I couldn't believe my ears!"

"So, what did you say to him?"

"I sure didn't tell him I was thinking the same thing, that I was plotting the same scheme. I told him I needed time to think about it, that it was the biggest decision of my life—which it is—and that I had to be able to count on him so that I didn't wind up stuck in Mexico.

"He said he wouldn't let me down. Then he said that if something unexpected went wrong, he'd help me sneak back across the border, and I'd be in the same situation I'm in now."

"Some reassurance," Marianne said. "So, what are you going to do?"

"We talked about it at lunch that day and decided we're gonna give it a try."

* * * *

"WHAT ARE YOU GOING TO TELL your parents?" Marianne had asked. With that question she pinpointed the first hurdle confronting Felina as she moved forward with her audacious plan. Her mom and dad hadn't even met Layne; they didn't even know their daughter was seeing him, much less how serious the relationship was. So, it would be touchy telling them she was in love with him enough to go back to Mexico and try to re-enter as a bride-to-be. She knew that her father, in particular, would disapprove because Layne wasn't Hispanic. To make matters worse, Layne was an agent in the U.S. Border Patrol, which both her parents distrusted. Felina conceded to herself that Eduardo's predicament would influence their thinking, too.

Over the next week, she put a lot of thought into how she'd approach them and discussed it with Layne as well as Marianne. With their help, she had broken it down into parts, like acts in a play. In the opening act, she would have to tell them all about Layne: where he's from, when they met, how their relationship developed, why she loves him, and what it's really like to be a Border Patrol agent. Next would come her feelings about growing up an illegal in America; her desire to break away from what she saw as the inevitable cycle of her culture—getting pregnant, marrying a guy who didn't love her, and living in poverty after he left her; her aspirations to attend the University of Arizona and become a doctor, and the obstacles she faces and the frustration she feels. Finally, she would have to explain the plan: return to Mexico through the Nogales Port of Entry as any other Mexican returning home and make her way to Magdalena; live with her grandparents and earn money however she could; have Layne apply for a fiancée visa, spinning the tale about meeting while he was living in La Paz; and eventually return to the U.S. and become a citizen by marrying Layne.

She knew she'd have to be strong enough to withstand her parents' predictably hysterical objections. And Layne would have to meet them and, hopefully, win them over. She, Marianne, and Layne all concluded that it was worth a try.

It took days for her to build up the nerve to face her parents. She dreaded the confrontation she was sure would ensue, but every time she considered that obviously high probability and wavered even a little, she looked around at her life as it was. *Whatever it takes,* she sighed.

Her parents lived in the city of South Tucson, a roughly square-mile enclave where more than eighty percent of the almost 6,000 residents had some Hispanic or Latino heritage. No one knew for sure how many were citizens and how many were illegals. The median income for a family was under $20,000, only slightly above the poverty level for a family of two. Gang and drug activity and alcohol-related crimes were declining because of neighborhood and local law enforcement efforts, but larceny, theft, and aggravated assault were four times the national average. The colorful buildings and murals and several popular Mexican restaurants along South Fourth Avenue belied the reality of life for almost everyone in South Tucson, including Felina's mother and father, Alba and Federico. As she drove to their house, Felina saw why she had to do this. It was all around her.

Even though it was her parents' house and had been her home growing up, Felina wasn't comfortable just barging in—even if the front door wasn't locked, as most were in the tough neighborhood. She knew that intruders were fairly common in the area, so she knocked rather than startle her mom or dad. Alba greeted her, quizzically.

"¿*Que te trae aqui hoy?* said her mother. She wanted to know why Felina had come to visit.

"I need to talk to you and Dad; it's important," she said. "In English; I know you speak it well enough to understand me. If Dad needs help, please translate for him." Felina was sorry if she sounded harsh. But she knew that, as anxious as she was, she needed to be in charge of this conversation from the start. It was going to be hard enough; if she were to let them set the tone, she'd have no chance.

"*Federico, ven aca,*" called Alba, looking a little scared. "*Felina quiere hablar con nosotros.*"

Federico came from the kitchen, sat down, and folded his arms to listen without saying hello. "Go ahead," said Alba, and Felina launched into Act One.

"I've met this guy," she began slowly. Her mother put a hand to her lips, as if this were bad news. "He's from Denver. We met back in September at a party my friend Marianne had for her fiancé, who was graduating from the Border Patrol Academy." She decided not to go into what happened that night.

"What is his name?" Alba asked. Federico nodded in agreement.

"Layne," Felina responded. "Layne Sheppard."

"That doesn't sound Hispanic," Alba said abruptly in Spanish. Federico nodded again.

Felina switched to her rudimentary Spanish, hoping both of her parents would understand. "He isn't Hispanic," she said, "but that doesn't matter to me. I've been seeing him on weekends since last Labor Day, and I like him a lot. Actually, I love him."

Federico muttered, "No," and Alba's hand returned to her lips.

"Why only on weekends?" she asked warily. It was obvious to Felina that the rest of this meeting would have to be conducted in Spanish so her father could follow along.

"He lives in Bisbee, so he has to drive to Tucson, or I have to drive there when he's not on duty."

"On duty?" Alba asked, frowning. "What does that mean?"

"He's a Border Patrol agent, stationed at—"

"NO!" Federico thundered.

"Oh, Felina," Alba said. "How could you?"

"He's funny . . . and fun," she began. "He makes me feel good. He cares about me. He's brave and a good person."

"Why couldn't you find a good boy from the neighborhood?" Alba challenged.

Felina was tempted to say, "Because there aren't any," but held her tongue. Then she almost said, "I don't want to wind up a single mother with a guy who cheats on me and leaves me at home, alone, with my child." But she knew that would only provoke an argument and hurt her parents. She didn't want that. So, she just said, "I don't live in this neighborhood anymore, and I hadn't dated anyone for a long time before he just happened to come to Marianne's party."

The Border Patrol was considered the enemy, especially since Eduardo was arrested for DUI and deported.

"Does he know you are not a citizen?" Alba asked.

"Yes," Felina answered, her head bowed. She wasn't ready to jump to Act Three just yet.

Federico questioned her for the first time. "Is he going to arrest you?"

"No. I'm already here. The Border Patrol catches people trying to sneak across the border, often trying to bring marijuana into the U.S. for the Mexican cartels. Being a Border Patrol agent is nothing like you hear on television or read in the newspapers. It's a dangerous, thankless job. At times, it's heart-wrenching." Felina could sense Act Two about to begin.

"What is heart-wrenching about stopping people who just want a better life and forcing them to go back to Mexico?" Alba questioned.

"First of all, not every situation is heart-wrenching. But a lot are, like whenever a mother is cowering under some mesquite tree, alone with her child, unable to understand English. Second, they're *illegal*."

"So are you," Federico retorted.

"That's not my fault," Felina snapped. "It wasn't my choice to come here."

She regretted saying it as soon as she saw her mother's face. Would Alba break into tears or lash out at her daughter? Felina wasn't sure. But the deed was done. And maybe it had to be.

"I understand why you brought me here as a baby," she said, hoping to soften the blow of her previous words. "I realize you were trying to provide me with a better life. But now, I'm stuck in a No-Man's Land. I want to go to college; I know I can succeed there. I want to become a doctor. But I can't even apply to community college because I'm not a citizen. I can't do anything but work dead-end jobs. I don't want that."

Felina decided to address the culture that was so obvious at her cousin's *Quinceañera*.

"I'm not going to marry just anyone and have a bunch of kids and hope the guy is responsible enough to stay with me," she said. "I don't want to wind up living in poverty as a single mom or settle for some other guy just because he'll stay with me and try to provide for my kids. That might be the way it is in Mexico and with Mexican girls here. But I grew up an American, even if I'm not yet a citizen. You made sure of that. And I'm very grateful. I want to live the American Dream."

"But how can you do that?" Alba asked. It was obvious that she felt guilty about putting Felina in such a hopeless situation. Federico, meanwhile, looked angry. Act Three was here.

"Layne and I have a plan," Felina began. "It requires me to leave here and go back to Mexico . . ."

Alba gasped and cried, "NO! You'll never come back."

". . . through Nogales," Felina continued, "then make my way to grandma's house in Magdalena and live with her for a while. Eduardo is already there, isn't he? Layne says he can apply for a fiancée visa after I'm there a while; he'll just say that we met while I was on vacation and he was living with a Mexican family in La Paz."

"Fiancée visa?" Alba interrupted again. "Does that mean you're going to marry this . . . this, Layne?"

"Yes! Eventually," Felina said with a smile.

"We haven't even met this Layne," Federico objected. "You can't marry someone we haven't even met!"

"I plan to bring him to meet you before I leave for Mexico," Felina assured.

"What if he lets you down?" Alba resisted. "You could be stuck in Mexico."

"That won't happen," Felina assured. "Layne promised me. But if something goes wrong that's beyond our control, he said he would help me sneak back across the border, and I could resume living as I am now. Of course, I don't want that."

Federico got up and left the room without saying another word. He had been criticizing his daughter for several years because she hadn't yet gotten engaged or married. But this wasn't what he wanted her to do. He needed a beer.

The distress was evident in Alba's body language as she watched her husband walk out without saying a word. She wasn't ready to give her blessing, but she had run out of arguments to toss at her strong-willed daughter.

"When will we meet this Layne?" she asked.

LAYNE SAT IN THE SAME SEAT he'd occupied the first time he met with Dr. Ballinger. But this time, the apprehension he felt that day was gone. In its place was a sense of excitement at the personal progress he was making, along with an awareness of the clock. Until he met with Dr. Ballinger and attended his first support group meeting, Layne admitted to himself, he had tried to conquer his drinking problem entirely on his own. He'd always thought he could beat it with sheer willpower. But, of course, going it alone didn't work. That would never work, he now knew. Finally, he realized he needed others' help. And luckily for him, he'd found it.

Layne wanted to update his counselor on his first support group meeting, tell him about Seth, and share with him that, for the first time since high school, he felt self-respect and optimism about the future. But he didn't have unlimited time. The drive from Sierra Vista to Douglas Station awaited, along with his next shift as a Border Patrol agent, solo in the field. He was again assigned to Swings and wondered what the night held in store.

Dr. Ballinger entered the room and invited Layne to begin telling him about his new circle of friends.

"You already know," Layne began. "It was one surprise after another. I've never been around a group of people who were as accepting and non-judgmental as they were. I expected them to have cliques and think bad of me when they heard my story. But I didn't get any of that!"

Quickly, Ballinger assumed his counselor's persona. "What did you tell them about yourself?"

"Pretty much everything I told you," Layne said.

"What did you withhold?"

"Nothing that I can recall."

"How did that make you feel?"

Layne looked at Ballinger and realized the doc was back in clinical mode.

"It felt good when they didn't show any disapproval. Some even said something encouraging. I was waiting for the kind of snide comments I've heard all the time at the Academy."

Ballinger smiled knowingly. He wasn't surprised. He already knew the answer to his next question but wanted to hear how Layne answered it.

"Did you line up someone to be your sponsor?"

"Talk about surprising," Layne began. "A while back, Felina spent a weekend with me in Bisbee, and we walked Main Street. I wanted to surprise her with a present. We walked into this shop that sold jewelry and leather. The guy who ran it looked like an old-time hippie—gaunt, a ponytail down to his belt. He wasn't very friendly. I figured he sensed that I was in the Border Patrol, and he didn't like anybody who worked for the government. It wasn't anything he said, just his unfriendly manner.

"I saw a pair of earrings that I thought would look great on Felina. She tried them on and looked terrific, as she always does. I bought them on the spot and didn't think another second about the guy in the shop.

"I walk into the support group meeting, and who's one of the first people to greet me? That hippie."

"You mean Seth," Dr. Ballinger interjected.

"Yeah! I should have known you knew who I was talking about," Layne continued. "We wound up sitting next to each other during the meeting, and when it ended, Anthony—I'm sure you know Anthony—suggested I ask Seth if he'd be my sponsor. We went out after that and got to know each other."

"Have you called him since that night?"

"Not yet. But I plan to."

"Don't wait until you're in crisis."

Layne made a mental note to check in with Seth the next morning, after his upcoming shift. Then he checked his watch and told Dr. Ballinger he'd better get on the road to Douglas Station. He couldn't dare be late for Muster.

"Drive safely," Dr. Ballinger said as Layne hurried off.

As Layne passed Lavender Pit and drove through the tunnel on the route to work, he replayed his recent call to Felina. He had listened anxiously as she recounted her visit with her parents, worried about having to meet her father and mother. He was sure they'd disapprove of him and find a dozen reasons why their daughter should not put her trust in a *gringo*, especially one who is a Border Patrol agent. He wondered how he could win their acceptance, what he could say or do to convince them that he was worthy of Felina's love and that he would make sure she realized her dream of U.S. citizenship. *Did they even want her to be a U.S. citizen?* He realized he didn't know how they felt about that.

The Muster Room was already half-filled by the time he arrived. No one acknowledged him, and he kept his head down. In truth, he had no idea who else was in the room, and he didn't much care.

The FOS thumbed through his stack of documents and began speaking. But Layne didn't hear him. He had sunken into one of his body-tingling fantasies. He imagined Linda, the LECA, and the military women in the Camera Room plotting his position on a large map table using croupier sticks like the Battle of Britain. In the dream, he was in and out of communication with them while leading a rogue squadron that was struggling to stop a drive-through. The top personnel at the Station held their breath as he prevailed, like Luke Skywalker saving the nation in an epic climax. He saw himself high-fiveing all of the agents, who were lined up to greet him as he returned to the station.

Reality was quite different. As soon as the FOS finished, Muster broke and agents fled the room to check out their Kilos and hit the road. Layne held his breath, expecting the FOS or Escribano himself to tell him to go down the hall for another specious "corrective action" meeting. But this time, nothing of the sort transpired. He caught up with the end of the line of agents at the checkout desk, and after a few minutes, was headed for his assigned Kilo, keys in hand.

The daylight part of the Swing Shift was routine, quiet, as usual. Darkness would bring border crossings, which meant chases and apprehensions. Layne fidgeted behind the steering wheel of his Kilo and noticed the same thing that occurred to him every time he was driving. He was armed, but his pistol was holstered on his duty belt. *How am I supposed to draw this weapon while I'm in the driver's seat?* he thought. He could barely reach it while sitting; pulling it out of its sheath was next to impossible. And agents were strictly forbidden from placing a loaded gun on the passenger seat. With as many ruts and holes as they drove through during a shift, a gun could easily bounce and discharge or fall onto the passenger-side floor then go off. And if an agent had to exit his vehicle suddenly, he wouldn't have it with him if he needed it. *The definition of catch-22,* Layne sighed.

When nightfall came, Layne found himself patrolling a stretch of fence near Brennan Ranch. He wondered if he'd see the overweight cowboy-wannabe in his pickup truck with a twelve-pack, and if he'd already be half in the bag. He was driving about two miles an hour, within a foot or two of the fence, lights off. He'd heard of agents running into the fence while doing this kind of sign-cutting. He was doing everything he could to not become one of them. He could just imagine Escribano's delight if he were calling Layne to task for something like that.

It was as dark as the night when he caught the two drug runners, but this time, his cutting light illuminated the ground alongside and to the front driver-side fender of his Kilo as he prowled along the fence. The window was down, and he was hanging his head out, scanning for anything that looked like a footprint or disturbed ground. Unless he found something to track, he could wind up doing this for the rest of his shift.

It was mesmerizing, and the longer he hung his head out of the open window of the driver-side door, the more he began to think he was seeing things. When that happened, he'd look away for a second to break his stare. It was like trying to fight off sleep, even though he wasn't drowsy.

Then, just after looking away, he thought he saw a pair of feet in dirty tennis shoes straight down from the side of his door. His eyes trailed upward, and he saw what looked like legs attached to the feet. The mind works in fractions of seconds in a situation like this. Quickly he continued up the legs, which looked as real as the feet. And there, in the dark, he was face to face with a disheveled Mexican, who looked at him blankly. *If he'd had a gun, I'd be dead now,* Layne thought.

Layne swallowed hard. He thought about the gun he couldn't get out of its holster as he sat behind the wheel. He recalled what some FTO—he couldn't recall which one—had told him and others when discussing a situation when they were endangered and couldn't get at that their weapon quickly: "The best thing you can do is gun it. Drive away." But something told Layne he didn't need to do that in this instance.

"*¿Estás bien?*" he asked. (Are you okay?)

"*No. Necesito ayuda,*" the man answered, saying he needed help.

"*¿Qué necesitas?*" (What do you need?)

"*Agua. No he tenido agua por dos días.*" The man was desperate for a drink of water.

Layne knew he was supposed to remain detached and not let sympathy for any poor soul cloud his judgment. He was a Border Patrol agent. This man was trying to enter the United States illegally. That made him a criminal under the law. But compassion gnawed at Layne's conscience. The man was pathetic, helpless. Without assistance, he would probably die. Layne decided he couldn't be that cold-hearted.

Before Layne gave the man his first water in two days—*how did he survive?* Layne marveled—he handcuffed him then told him to get in the truck. The man was cooperative . . . docile . . . almost thankful to be *rescued.*

"*Soy agente de la frontera. Estás detenido,*" Layne said, explaining that he was a Border Patrol agent and telling the man he was under arrest.

107

By now, it was time to return to the station so Layne just drove the man back to be processed. He didn't put his captive in the holding cell in the back end of his truck, even though that was procedure—no exceptions. *He had his chance to hurt me or hide from me,* Layne reasoned. *He's harmless.*

* * * *

IT WAS ALMOST LUNCHTIME when Layne awoke after his bizarre apprehension of the "Mexican in the Night," as he decided to call the migrant he stumbled upon the night before. He was deciding whom to call first, Seth or Felina. He thought she would be pleased that he was even considering calling his support group sponsor before her. In the end, though, he went with his heart.

"Hey, Babe," he began as soon as Felina accepted the call on her cellphone.

"Layne! I'm so glad it's you. I was starting to worry when I didn't hear from you earlier this morning."

"Sorry. I guess I slept good for a change."

"Well, I'm glad for that. But most of all, I'm glad you're okay. Did anything interesting happen last night?"

"You could say that," Layne answered. His tone was a mixture of smugness and mirth.

After hearing the whole story, Felina said, "Do you think Escribano will make you write a report explaining why you let the guy sit in the passenger seat instead of putting him in the back of your Kilo?" It was a question Layne hadn't even considered. *Surely, it will be obvious that this man was in desperate straits and represented no threat whatsoever,* he told himself.

"Shoot. I don't know," he finally said, the smugness and mirth gone from his voice.

"You had good reasons," Felina offered, sorry she had brought it up.

Changing the subject—to something even more troubling for Layne—

she asked when Layne could come to Tucson to meet Federico and Alba. "The sooner the better," she said, "so they don't think you're avoiding them."

At the Bisbee end of the call, Layne frowned. He wished that he and Felina could carry out their grand scheme and get married without him ever having to face her parents. He felt the way he had years before whenever he was starting a new job or, while he was still in grade school, when meeting adults who were parents of his classmates. He dreaded the questions they were likely to ask him and their ultimate disapproval. He was already dealing with Escribano's campaign to force him to quit the Border Patrol. He had been scorned by peers and their folks so many times he'd lost count. Or so he thought. Now, he was facing what he was sure would be the toughest, not to mention most important, crucible of his life: Felina's mother and father.

"I should go to support group Saturday night," he said, "but I can drive to Tucson Sunday morning." An idea had popped into his head. "What time is Mass? Maybe I could get there in time, and we could go to Mass with them."

"Oh, Layne! That's a great way for them to meet you," Felina said. Then she asked: "Have you been to Mass before? Are you Catholic?"

"I was baptized, and I made my First Communion," he said. "But it's been a while since I've been to Mass. I'll need The Lord's mercy, along with His divine assistance, if we do this."

"I think we should. He will understand. And they will be so pleased. They will look at you differently because of this; I just know they will."

Felina promised to set everything up with Federico and Alba and text the name and address of the church to Layne along with the time of the Mass. The summary of the 12 Steps that Layne read at his first support group meeting came to mind, and he thought: *Maybe this is what they mean about a Supreme Being giving strength.* Then Dr. Ballinger's words in Layne's first meeting with him echoed in his brain: "The Creator doesn't care if you go to church. He wants to see if you walk the walk." Meeting

Felina's parents, and winning them over if he could, was part of walking the walk.

* * * *

AGENTS WERE JUST STRAGGLING into the Muster Room when Felina's prediction about Escribano and the "Mexican in the Night" came true. Seated toward the front of the room, Layne heard someone call, "SHEPPARD!" He looked around and saw that the FOS was standing in the open doorway, pointing at him. "Please come here . . . And bring your stuff." Layne cringed. Hearing those words reminded him of all the stories he'd read about pro football players finding out they'd been cut from the team during summer training camp by being told: "The Turk wants to see you. And bring your playbook." *Is this it?* he wondered. *If so, why now?* Obediently, he gathered his backpack, notebook, and pen and headed for the door as the other agents gawked.

"Supervisor Escribano wants to see you," said the FOS, as if it were the executioner speaking. "He said you should bring union representation."

Layne shoulders sagged noticeably. He felt obliged to say, "Thank you, sir." Then he turned and started out to find Ortiz.

"What this time?" Ortiz said after Layne asked him to accompany him to yet another meeting with Escribano.

"I'm not sure," was all Layne could say.

Escribano was seated at his desk, as usual, when they walked into his office. And, also as usual, he made them stand there for a few minutes as he shuffled papers and looked busy before finally acknowledging them. "Please close the door," he said to Ortiz then motioned for him and Layne to be seated.

"How many weeks have you been in the field, Sheppard?" he began. "Three? Four?"

"Yessir. This is my fourth," Layne answered.

"And you went through all of the Field Training phases before that.

Correct?"

"Actually, sir, you had me repeat some, so I had more than the usual," Layne said. He tried to appear polite and respectful, but Escribano bristled, nonetheless. Ortiz frowned.

"Well, then, would you agree that you've had ample opportunity to learn and understand the reasons for our procedures?"

Layne wondered where this was headed. Then he recalled what Felina had said and knew she was right. "Yessir."

"Then why," thundered Escribano, "did you think it was just fine to bring that Tonk in last night in the front seat of your Kilo instead of putting him in the back where he belonged?"

"It was at the end of the shift," Layne defended. "I thought it was okay."

"Did you call in on your radio and ask anyone if that's what you should do?" Escribano knew Layne had not.

"He was a lost soul; he hadn't had water in two days. I placed him under arrest and told him I was taking him in."

"And so you loaded him in your holding cell?"

"No, sir."

"Then where did you put him?"

"I let him ride in the front seat, next to me."

"Are you aware of Border Patrol policy that prohibits agents from allowing civilians to ride in Border Patrol vehicles without advance permission?"

"Yessir."

"Was he not a civilian?"

"He was harmless and in custody. I secured him."

"Harmless!" Escribano exploded. "Did he tell you he was harmless?"

"He was half-dead."

Before continuing, Escribano gave Ortiz a look that seemed to ask if he could believe what he was hearing.

"Once again, Agent Sheppard, you leave me with no choice but to record another infraction in your file. I want you to write a memo that explains your actions of last night. And I want you to write a report that lists all Border Patrol policies and explains why each is necessary. Please—"

"He's not writing a report about Border Patrol policies," Ortiz interrupted. "That's like having him write 'I shall not talk in class' a hundred times."

Layne was surprised to hear Ortiz stand up to his friend in that manner and thankful he went to bat for the whipping boy. It was all the more surprising when Layne considered Escribano's past as a union rep.

"I think he needs to demonstrate that he has reviewed all Patrol policies and understands them," Escribano shot back.

"He's not writing that stupid report," Ortiz insisted. "You've gone too far. He'll write a memo about his decisions in the field last night, which all sound reasonable to me. And you can add it to the case you're trying to build against him. We'll deal with you second-guessing him when the time comes."

Layne thought Ortiz had landed the last punch of this round, but Escribano spoke up as the pair got up to leave. "Next week, Sheppard, plan on processing illegals," he said. "I'm not comfortable having you in the field right now."

* * * *

ORTIZ DIDN'T USUALLY HAVE anything more to say after a meeting with Escribano, but this time, he couldn't contain himself as Layne walked alongside him.

"What a crock!" he muttered. "An illegal riding in the passenger seat happens all the time. As long as you handcuff them and secure them so they can't cause you any problem, it's no big deal. A lot of times, it's the best way to go. It's a judgment call."

Layne didn't know what to say. He could tell Ortiz felt Escribano had gone too far by making an issue of Layne's handling of the situation. But as upset as Ortiz was, Layne realized Ortiz still felt Layne should learn something from the incident.

"Once you take a guy into custody," Ortiz said in an almost fatherly tone, "the safest place for him is in the back with his seatbelt on." The holding cell of a Kilo has eight seat belts, he reminded Layne. But just that quick, he was back to talking about agents letting illegals ride in the passenger seat.

"If an agent picks up a mom and a couple kids along with five to six guys, he's not going to put all those people in the same cage for a forty-minute ride where he can't actually watch what's going on. So, he'll put the mom and kids up front with him, no handcuffs. He'll say something like, 'Here's the deal. I'm putting you up here because I don't want you back there with them. So, don't do anything that makes me have an accident.'"

"Who would want little kids and a mom with guys like that?" Layne asked rhetorically.

"Supervisors understand," he assured Layne, adding derisively, "except, I guess, somebody like Salvador." At that moment, Ortiz sounded disappointed in his buddy.

* * * *

LAYNE COULDN'T BELIEVE WHAT was happening. He'd finally started down the road to conquering his drinking problem, or so it seemed. And he'd found the girl of his dreams, and they had come up with a way for her to become a legal resident and eventually a U. S. citizen, while also becoming his wife. For the first time in years, he was beginning to feel some semblance of self-worth and self-confidence. *I can't let that scumbag Escribano ruin everything,* he angrily told himself. *I have to find a way to beat this.*

Just then, a picture formed in his mind—a flashback. He was sitting in the auditorium of the hotel in Tucson where new Border Patrol recruits were going through orientation. EOD, they called it: entry on duty. A union rep, an agent named Esterline, was telling the recruits why they should join the union, and Layne was skeptical but listening intently.

"There's a hotline number in the information that was passed out to you," Esterline was saying, "in case you're having problems and need to talk to someone. That number is only for agents. I don't want you to hesitate to dial that number if you're struggling. There's no shame in it. That's what it's there for.

"No matter how tough you might think you are," he continued, "you're gonna run into emotional problems in this job. Some days you'll be angry, and other days you might feel pity for the aliens you're forced to deal with. It's natural. Just remember, you're doing what you're told. You don't make the rules. The higher-ups who make the rules don't have to be face to face with these people."

Some of that applied to Layne's current dilemma, he thought. Certainly, Escribano hadn't been face to face with that poor soul in the desert. And Layne was dealing with a slew of personal issues—from liquor's lure to Felina's predicament to the impending meeting with her parents—not to mention his ongoing problems with Escribano. Maybe it was time he followed Esterline's advice and saw for himself if the union really could help him.

"This is Brian Palmer from the Border Patrol Union," announced the male voice on the other end of the call.

"Do you work at Douglas Station?" Layne asked. He had never heard of the guy.

"No, I'm at Sector level. I work at headquarters in Tucson."

Layne recounted what he'd heard from Brian Esterline during orientation and asked Palmer if he had it right.

"Yes. You heard him right," Palmer confirmed.

"I'd like to see you in person if I could," Layne said. "Any chance of a meeting on a Sunday?"

"I'm off on weekends, but I come in if someone needs help. That's my job."

The call went silent, and Palmer wondered if the caller had hung up.

Then Layne brought it back to life. "I'll be in Tucson next Sunday. Could I meet you at four?"

Palmer agreed and told Layne where to find him.

11

"**YOU'RE NOT OUT OF THE WOODS** just because you've joined our support group," Anthony said after Layne told everyone that he hadn't even had to resist a temptation to have a beer in the past week. All heads in the circle nodded in agreement.

"Truth is," Anthony continued, "the urge can come over you at any time. Doesn't even matter how long you've been sober. That's why we all introduce ourselves as 'recovering' alcoholics . . ."

"There ain't a one of us that ain't fallen off the wagon at least once or twice," Seth said to more nods. "So, don't be surprised if it happens to you, too. I'm bettin' it does."

I've got too many other things to worry about right now, Layne wanted to say. But then he thought, *Maybe that's what will cause me to have a beer.*

"I'm pretty overwhelmed," he admitted. "I'm driving to Tucson in the morning—to go to Mass with Felina's parents! Can it get more intimidating than that? And later in the day, I'm meeting a Border Patrol Union guy to see if he can help me deal with everything that's going on at Douglas Station, as well as my drinking and Felina and everything."

"Son, you gotta take it one at a time," said Colonel Cal. "If you don't, you'll wake up starin' at the ceilin' agin."

"Sunday Mass?" puzzled Sylvia. "How early do you have to leave here to make it on time?

"I have to be on the road by seven," Layne said.

Instead of nods, this time most occupants of the circle whistled.

* * * *

THE RISING SUN LIT UP THE eastern sky by the time Layne hit the road the next morning. He tried to remember the last time he'd gone to Mass—had to be when he was still in middle school, twelve to fifteen years ago. *But it's like riding a bike,* he said to himself, confident that he could look and sound like a regular in the presence of Felina's mother and father. *After all,* he mused, *the Supreme Being is giving me strength.*

The long drive gave him time to reflect, as he so often did. He wasn't a bad guy, he concluded, just a guy with a drinking problem who lacked self-assuredness. Aside from that, his values were above-average—his parents had reared him well. If he could resist the urge—overcome the desire—to down that first beer, which inevitably led to another, then another, then many more, the real Layne Sheppard would show through. *At last,* he thought, *I'm going to do it.*

About two hours later Layne pulled up outside Santa Cruz Catholic Church, a striking all-white building with a multi-story bell tower—the last surviving public building constructed of adobe brick in Arizona. Santa Cruz, which translates to Holy Cross, was dedicated in 1919 and added to the National Register of Historic Places in 1994. *There's nothing like this in Denver,* Layne marveled as he viewed the historic church and waited for Felina and her parents to arrive. He wasn't sure why they chose this church; others were closer to where they lived.

Mass was as unique as the church itself, at least in Layne's opinion. Before the service began, the priest, Monsignor Apodaca, stood on the altar and asked who was visiting that day and had each person stand and say where he or she was from. And then he asked who was celebrating a birthday, then an anniversary. It took ten minutes before he'd involved as many in the congregation as possible. *He didn't ask who had been away from Mass the longest,* Layne thought then scolded himself for his cynicism.

Once Mass began, Layne was practically blasted out of his seat by the mariachi band to the right of the altar. The blaring horns and the boisterous singing were a far cry from the reserved strains of the adult choir he remembered from Sunday Mass in the Denver suburbs. Then he saw the movie screens descend from the ceiling. Words to the songs to be sung and the prayers of the Mass that the congregation was expected to say aloud were projected onto the screens—half the time in English and half the time in Spanish. *This is a true bilingual Mass,* Layne realized. He had no problem participating; it really *was* like riding a bike.

Msgr. Apodaca delivered a homily that again had Layne thinking a Supreme Being was at work behind the scenes. He spoke of dealing with adversity and trusting The Lord to show the way. He said that answers to life's most difficult questions weren't always apparent, and that, in the end, faith and trust in Him to provide inspiration were the surest way to find the light. "Too often," Msgr. Apodaca said, "we ask God to solve our problem, to send help, but when He responds, we don't recognize the solution He has sent us because we are not open to His way. We have a different answer in mind, and we aren't willing or able to shift gears. We must leave it in God's hands and follow His plan."

Layne again thought back to his first meeting with Dr. Ballinger and what he said about the role of a Supreme Being in a person's life. "Maybe He doesn't acknowledge you because you're not doing what He intended you to do," the counselor had told him. ". . . when you sacrifice to do the right thing, you'll notice that the things you need will start falling in your lap . . ."

Layne glanced at Felina sitting next to him. He leaned toward her and whispered in her ear: "See, it's God's plan." She blushed as everyone stood to recite the Creed.

* * * *

AFTER MASS, FELINA AND HER PARENTS agreed that she would ride home with Layne rather than with them. Layne had parked on the street near the church. As he pulled away from the curb, Felina was almost giddy. "Going to Mass with them was a great idea," she said excitedly. "You knew when to sit, when to stand, and when to kneel, and you knew most of the responses the congregation was expected to say during Mass. Even I was impressed! And you're right. Monignor's homily is something I can refer to the next time I discuss our plan with my mom and dad.

"This is going really well, better than I could have hoped."

So far, Layne wanted to say. He knew the hardest part lay ahead, talking with Alba and Federico in their home, face to face. How much should he tell them about himself? How much would they want to know? He certainly wasn't going to go into the way he enjoyed drinking on weekends. And considering that on his SF-86 application, he had admitted only trying marijuana a time or two and withheld any further mention of drugs during the background investigation and interview that followed, he sure wasn't going to volunteer anything about that subject with Felina's parents. He would stick to basics unless they asked for specifics.

As soon as Layne and Felina walked into her parents' home, he saw an ornate crucifix displayed prominently in their living room. It told him what a good idea, indeed, Mass had been, but it also heralded the coming two-on-one. *This is almost as bad as facing Edward* (the federal investigator) *when I was trying to get accepted into Border Patrol Academy,* he thought. *But I got through that; surely, I can talk my way past them.*

"So, tell us about yourself, Layne," Alba said cordially in English. Layne was surprised by her tone but reminded himself what was at stake and resisted the inclination to relax and let his guard down.

"Would it be better if our conversation was in Spanish?" he asked in Spanish. He suspected that Federico's English was limited and Alba's not that much better. The reaction from Felina's dad to Layne's question confirmed he was right.

"Sí, si puedes. Eso seria genial," answered Federico before Alba could even cast a questioning glance his way. (Yes, if you can. That would be great.)

"I was born and grew up in the Denver area," Layne began. "I don't have any brothers or sisters. I was an okay student in school, nothing great. I played sports and was pretty good, especially at baseball. I was a good batter. I got the chance to play in college and professionally. But I hurt my arm and had to quit." After telling them a little about his parents, he jumped to the subject of work and how he got here. "I had several jobs, but I never found one I really liked and wanted to stay with. I thought I might like being a Border Patrol agent, so I decided to give this a try. When I was offered Douglas Station, I accepted right away. I couldn't wait."

"Where did you learn to speak our language so well?" Federico inquired in Spanish.

OUR language! Layne hoped he hadn't winced visibly at what told him so clearly that, despite the cordiality that seemed to be developing, it was still "me and them" as he continued trying to win them over.

"I lived with a family in La Paz for four months a couple years ago," he explained, "and they spoke only Spanish. So, I became fluent pretty quickly. It really helped me become a Border Patrol agent." He immediately wondered if he should have withheld that last comment, but it was too late. *Think before you speak,* he chastised himself.

"You need to speak Spanish to be in the Border Patrol?" Alba asked with surprise.

"It's required, and it's necessary," Layne responded. He didn't really want to get into the details of patrolling the border, but since he had opened the door, he figured he should try to leave them with a positive impression. He assumed they looked at the Border Patrol negatively.

"By being able to speak Spanish, we are able to communicate with the people when we find them in the desert. Often, they need help but don't speak any English, so they can't tell us anything unless we can speak enough Spanish to understand them." *I don't need to go beyond that, to arresting them and what happens after that, unless they ask,* Layne told himself.

"Jesus teaches us in the Bible that we must be good to the hungry, the lonely, the stranger—the lost soul," Federico said. "Jesus said, 'I was a stranger, and you did not invite me in.' How do you feel about immigrants and immigration?" The preface and the tone of Federico's voice told Layne this was a loaded question. He hesitated, trying to decide if he should be diplomatic and vague. *I can't be anything but honest,* he concluded.

"I think immigration is important to the United States and a good thing," he began. "But people should come here legally instead of sneaking across the border." He knew that's exactly how Federico and Alba had come to the U.S., so he quickly added: "I'm talking about what's happening now. All those people coming into the U. S. from Central American countries are breaking the law. Our country is struggling with its budget. It can't handle the increased cost of educating and caring for the thousands of people coming across the border. And some are coming for bad reasons.

"I understand that people who came from Mexico a long time ago, like you and your family, have made a life here. I don't think the government should make you leave after all that time, and I don't think the system should make it harder for you to live here." Layne was walking a fine line and knew it. He pressed on. "Politicians have to work together to fix our immigration system and take care of those who have contributed to our society, obeyed our laws, and paid taxes even without being citizens. Blaming each other doesn't accomplish anything. They're not sincere when they say they want to fix things but never do anything to make it better."

Alba spoke before Federico could. "They talk a lot about the illegal alien but never about the illegal employer who hires them for low pay." She wanted to know more of Layne's feelings about immigration today.

"I think people sneaking across the border is unfair to those who follow the system and often have to wait several years before they can enter the United States from their home country," he said, avoiding the cheap labor issue. "When I was growing up, we called that 'jumping the line.' It's also not fair that citizens who break a law, like DUI, often go to jail, but an illegal immigrant who does the same thing goes free." Layne immediately caught himself. *I did it again! Why did I say DUI?*

Without mentioning Eduardo by name, Federico said: "What do you think about ICE?"

"They have a thankless job," Layne said. "They're responsible for enforcing a system that needs to be changed. But until politicians fix it, they have no choice. We have a saying in America: 'Don't blame the messenger.' I think that applies to ICE agents who are just doing their jobs."

Felina had been listening the whole time and spoke up before the inquisition went any further. "I'm getting hungry," she said. "Who wants to get some lunch?"

* * * *

LAYNE EXCUSED HIMSELF AT 3:30. His GPS told him it was only a fifteen-minute drive, but he wanted to allow plenty of time to find the Tucson Sector office and meet Agent Palmer. The time with Felina's parents had gone as well as he could have hoped, though he had no idea if it caused them to feel any better about their daughter placing her future in his hands. He kicked himself mentally, over and over again, for speaking before thinking with his comments about sneaking across the border and illegals getting picked up for DUI. He was sure Felina would tell him where things stood as soon as he could talk to her again. He planned to call her after his meeting with Palmer, maybe even try to see her before heading back to Bisbee.

Layne had been too preoccupied with the imminent Spanish Oral Board Exam the last time he'd been to Sector HQ—in survival mode and not expecting to ever see the place again. He didn't remember the exact route to it, what it looked like from the outside, or even that distinctive lettering near the entrance that read:

U.S. Customs and Border Protection
Tucson Sector Headquarters, Tucson Arizona.

He pressed the visitor buzzer, and a trim man, about six feet tall, who looked like a fighter pilot, came to the door to let him in.

"The office closes early on the weekend," he said pleasantly enough, then got right to the point as they moved to his office. "I'm Brian Palmer. How can I help you?"

"My supervisor at Douglas Station is doing everything he can to run me off," Layne said bluntly.

"Who is it?" Palmer asked.

"Salvador Escribano."

"What exactly is he doing?"

"He drags me into meetings in his office for every little thing—even whether or not I shaved that day—and makes me write a memo for my file after every meeting. And he keeps changing my schedule, so I don't get good sleep."

Palmer knew all of that from reports filed by Ramon Ortiz, the head union steward at Douglas Station, but wanted to see if Layne embellished his situation.

"Do you feel you've caused any of the discipline you've received?" Palmer was testing Layne again.

"I've done a few things that maybe deserved some kind of corrective action," Layne admitted, "but I think Escribano has overreacted to them because he wants to get rid of me."

"Like what?"

Layne related the stories of his lost notebook, the high-speed chase with Agent Tipton, and the "Mexican in the Night." He paused then added: "I've had a drinking problem and was hung over when I reported for some shifts. I had to call in sick two days right after I passed the Spanish Oral Board and was made a regular agent."

Palmer leaned back in his chair. He'd seen dozens of agents who were in some kind of hot water, and he had learned that the only ones he could help were those who were honest with him about their situations. He sensed that Layne was one of them.

"What about this drinking problem you mentioned?"

"I'm getting help," Layne said. "I've seen a really good counselor in

Sierra Vista, and he got me into a support group in Bisbee, where I live. I have a sponsor who is a lot of help. I feel I'm starting to get control of my problem. But the constant pressure I'm under from Escribano is making it harder. I'm always wondering what little thing he'll call me out on next."

Palmer knew a red flag when he saw one. "Who knows about your efforts to curb your drinking?"

"In the Border Patrol?" Layne responded. "Only you. I haven't brought it up at Douglas Station; I figured Escribano would use that against me, too. And I'm still pretty self-conscious, embarrassed, and ashamed. It's been very hard to face it. I couldn't have done it without the support group and my counselor. They've been great. I really feel that I can become a good agent. I'm getting myself together."

Palmer knew enough about Layne's situation to understand that turning it around would be an uphill struggle. In cases like this, he had to exhaust the alternative before getting the union involved in a lengthy fight.

"Have you considered submitting a letter of resignation right now?"

No way, thought Layne, voicing his feelings indignantly: "Why should I do that?"

"If you do, they won't be able to tarnish your SF-51 if you reapply."

"I think this was my only opportunity to work for the government," Layne said, and he knew it was true. "If I quit, I give them what they want."

After an awkward silence, Layne spoke again. "Does management tell you to try to convince agents in my situation to quit? Is that what they want you to do?"

Palmer cursed then said, "I couldn't care less what management wants. I'm just trying to help you."

There was another pause before Palmer said, "Why don't you make it easy on yourself?"

"Because I want to give Escribano as much of a headache as he has given me."

Palmer abruptly rose and moved from behind his desk. It was obvious the meeting was ending, and Layne wondered if that meant that Palmer and the union were going to abandon him.

Palmer shook hands with him. Then came the unexpected.

"I appreciate your honesty," he said. "Honesty and a good work ethic can go a long way."

Then he added: "I won't kid you. I think you're in a tough spot right now. But I, on behalf of our union, assure you we will do everything we can to help you. Just do your part by following procedures and doing a good job."

* * * *

LAYNE'S CALL TO FELINA WAS going through before he left the parking lot of Tucson Sector Headquarters. He wanted to see her for dinner, if possible, before he drove back to Bisbee. He wanted to believe that his visit to the union honcho was the right step to take and that he could put his faith in Brian Palmer even though he was a stranger that Layne had just met for the first time. But only time would tell.

"Hey," Felina said when she answered his call. "How did it go with Mr. Palmer?"

"Hey, yourself. How did it go with your mom and dad?"

They agreed it would be better to answer each other in person over a quick dinner. Layne let Felina pick the place—part of his continuing effort to impose self-control and avoid temptation—and she chose a casual restaurant on Congress known for its cheeseburgers. When they walked in, Layne immediately noticed the fully stocked bar with multiple beer taps. *Talk about temptation!* he thought as he followed Felina and the hostess to their table. Felina hadn't noticed or given it a thought.

"You first," Felina said, but Layne couldn't wait to hear how he'd done with Alba and Federico. "Mine will wait," he said.

"Actually, you did pretty well," Felina beamed. "Going to Mass impressed them. And speaking to them in fluent Spanish put them more at ease. You speak Spanish better than I do! They don't agree with anything you said about immigration, but I wouldn't expect them to. I think they could tell that you were sincere in what you said, and they appreciated that you didn't try to B-S them. They didn't come right out and say they approved of you or what we are planning, but they didn't object, either. That's huge, I think."

Layne wanted to feel encouraged, but he knew the difficulties that lie ahead, He resisted his usual inclination to expect the worst and told himself this glass was at least half-full. *Best I could hope for, I guess,* he concluded. He proceeded to report on his meeting at Tucson Sector Headquarters.

"Brian Palmer is a no-nonsense guy," he began. "I got the feeling that he's dealt with this sort of thing many times before. I was honest with him about almost everything."

"Almost?" Felina interrupted. "Did you tell him how drinking was affecting your performance and that you are getting help?"

"Yes."

"Then what do you mean by, 'almost'?"

"I didn't tell him about us, about our plan, or Eduardo and his predicament."

The waitress brought their food, and both began to eat in silence. Layne yearned to order a beer, or better yet, to head to the bar. But he stared, instead, at Felina and said: "I wasn't sure what to tell him about our situation, so I just didn't bring it up. In the end, he said the union would help me any way it could as long as I followed procedure and tried to do a good job. That was as much as I could expect from my first time meeting the guy."

Felina was in deep thought. "We're going to have to sit down and really figure out how this will work," she said, "and then I'll have to tell my grandma I'm going to come see her and my grandpa. And ask her if I can live with them for a while."

"Will she ask questions?" Layne said.

"I would think so. I'll have to tell her what's going on."

"Will she be okay with everything?"

"I expect so."

Layne realized he was pumping his leg as he always did when he was anxious. He wanted to make sure Felina believed that they were in this together. He put his credit card with the check the waitress had left at their table and motioned to her. As she took it and went to run the charge, Layne looked earnestly at Felina. He couldn't remember ever before being willing to risk everything for another person.

"I'll come back to Tucson as soon as I can," he promised. "We'll map it all out then."

LAYNE BEGAN HIS DRIVE BACK to Bisbee later than he had planned. And between the gauntlet Felina's parents represented—in his mind, at least—followed by that crucial meeting with Brian Palmer, and the prospect of planning a Hail Mary play for his future with Felina at stake, he was emotionally drained. When he turned off I-10 at Benson, he told himself he'd stop at his favorite little store and pick up a six-pack. Six instead of his usual twelve; *moderation,* he reassured himself, somewhat proudly.

As he drove eastward it got darker; dusk was in his rearview mirror. With the advancing night came drowsiness he wasn't prepared for. He rolled down his driver-side window and turned up the radio. He started singing the songs that played, and he shook his head vigorously. *Anything to stay awake,* he thought. He had forgotten how early the day had begun and the long drive with which it started, and he had underestimated how much nervous energy events of the day had consumed.

Replaying his meetings with Felina's parents and the union official as the music from the radio blared, Layne found his anxiety level rising. He began to worry that he'd told Brian Palmer too much, that he'd been too open with him about what was happening at Douglas Station. It occurred to Layne that Palmer probably already knew everything Layne told him. Well, almost everything. *I shouldn't have told him about my drinking.* Layne wondered what Escribano would do to him when he found out he had gone to see Brian Palmer in Tucson. Surely, he would find out; there were few secrets within Douglas Station.

Passing a sign that signaled Benson exits were fast-approaching, he mentally shifted gears to his time with Alba and Federico. He berated himself again for his thoughtless reference to illegals arrested for DUI. He wondered what would happen to Eduardo. *Will he make it back across the border? How? Where? When?* He realized that the Mexicans Alba and Federico knew were not criminals and only came to the U.S. in the hope of finding a decent-paying job and making a better life for their families. *Their pay for a whole day is what we're paid per hour,* Layne thought. *But that doesn't make it alright to cross the border illegally.* Turning onto the Benson exit ramp, Layne resigned himself to an irreconcilable difference with Felina's parents on that key point.

The gas pumps were vacant as Layne pulled up, but two other cars parked in front of the little convenience store told him he was not the only customer at the moment. He filled the tank of his Honda and went inside to get that six-pack and pay. He knew just where the beer cooler was; he'd opened that door many times. But just as he walked toward the refreshment he craved, his phone vibrated with a text message.

"Are you home yet?" Felina asked. "Thank you for a great day. Call me as soon as you get home. I love you!"

Timing is everything, Layne frowned. *I love you! Wow!* He reversed his path and went directly to the counter. "Pump number two," he said. He wondered if that Supreme Being was intervening at just the right moment.

Back in his car, Layne placed a call.

"Hey, bro!" Seth answered. "What's up on this Sunday night?"

For most of the forty-seven-mile drive to Bisbee, Layne related in detail the events of the day: Mass . . . jousting with Alba and Federico but not accomplishing much, at least in his view . . . baring his soul to Brian Palmer . . . second-guessing both . . . the realization of what was at stake with Felina . . . *and* the strongest urge to down a bunch of beers that he'd had since before his first session with Dr. Ballinger, his first support group meeting and getting to know Seth.

"Was only a matter of time, bro," said Seth. "I been wonderin' when you'd crash. We all do, at least once. Good news is you didn't give in."

"I would have if Felina's text hadn't come just in time. And if it hadn't said what it said."

"But you didn't," Seth emphasized. "That's what matters. We all need all the help we can get, wherever it comes from, whenever it comes, however it comes."

Seth proceeded to give Layne a pep talk, spiced with stories of his own struggles. Layne was wide-awake now and wide-eyed to learn that Seth had been through a lot worse than Layne's worst. As Bisbee grew nearer, their call wrapped up. Layne thanked Seth for being there for him, and Seth responded simply: "Anytime, bro."

* * * *

FELINA WAS INTERRUPTED IN MID-SENTENCE when Layne's cellphone lit up with the signal of another incoming call. "It's Douglas Station," he told her, then selected "Hold and Answer" on his phone.

"I was instructed to call you," said the caller, "and inform you that your schedule for the coming week has been changed. Instead of Processing, you are now Field, on Swings." No sooner than Layne said, "Thank you for calling," the voice blandly said, "Goodnight."

"Who was that?" Felina asked when Layne returned to their call.

"Someone from Douglas Station," Layne said, "but I didn't recognize the voice."

"What did they want?"

"He said he was told to call me and notify me that my schedule changed. I'm in the field now, and back on Swings."

"That's great!" Felina exclaimed. She knew how bored Layne was whenever he worked in Processing. She worried about him whenever he was alone in the field, but at least he wouldn't be out there in the dark virtually his whole shift the way he was whenever he worked Mids. "But why? How?"

Layne was pretty sure he knew. "Brian Palmer must have leaned on somebody, who in turn leaned on Escribano. I can't imagine any other explanation. I bet Escribano is miffed. He'll be laying for me even more."

Felina tried to reassure Layne. "Remember what Mr. Palmer told you," she said. "Just follow procedures and try to do a good job."

* * * *

THE WEEKS THAT FOLLOWED—weeks spent "following procedure and trying to do a good job"—were unusually uneventful for Layne. Even support group meetings had been pretty routine. As another Friday approached, he noted that after one more shift, he would be heading to Tucson to help Felina plan her move to Mexico and his subsequent application for her fiancée visa. As Layne drove his Kilo off the Douglas Station lot that afternoon, he hoped for a quiet end to what had been a relatively peaceful week. There had been a buzz in the Muster Room the last couple days. He wasn't sure what everyone was excited about, but clearly, something was up. *Maybe I'll find out before I leave for the weekend,* he thought.

It became obvious pretty quickly that the last day of Layne's workweek would not be like those before it. Radio traffic was more than usual that afternoon and got heavier with sensor calls as the day wore on. It was shaping up to be a busy start to the weekend, though thankfully, the activity so far was away from Layne's location.

Then it came.

"Ten-sixty, ten-sixty! 676, Port One for twelve," came the LECA's call for everyone in the field to pay attention—in effect, to "listen-up!"

That's near me, was Layne's immediate reaction. He knew that Port One meant northbound. He hadn't yet memorized the location of every sensor in the Douglas AOR, but he remembered 676 from a ride with Agent Ashlock, another nemesis. Ashlock had asked where 676 was when a call came in, and Chad Runyon, who would later flunk the Spanish Oral Board Exam, incorrectly guessed 6-Alpha. Another of Layne's fellow trainees, Carlos Dos Santos, had quickly checked his sensor list and correctly identified the area as 5-Charlie.

Follow procedure and try to do your job, Layne reminded himself.

"863, this is Delta-328. Ten-four on the 676; show me eight minutes out," Layne responded, followed quickly by "863, this is Delta-325. Show me responding, as well; I'm ten minutes out."

That's Carlos! Layne was buoyed to know that his buddy from the Academy was coming to help.

Coyotes, the common name for those who smuggled illegals for a price, typically sent a small group across the border ahead of the rest to determine if foot sensors were in the path that they had chosen that time and so they could find out how many agents were in the immediate area. These small groups didn't know they were being sacrificed for reconnaissance. All they were told was to scatter like desert quail at the first indication the Border Patrol was aware of their presence in the area. Their goal was to reach the pickup point, from which they would be driven to the safety of the Pirtleville maze.

Chasing "quail" in the desert was no fun even in broad daylight, which almost never happened anyway. At dusk, it was especially tricky—dangerous, actually. The ground is uneven; all types of cactus and bushes with thorns are everywhere; and, in the summer, rattlers curled up on the warm ground after the sun went down and were easily stepped on, kicked, or tripped over. In many places, barbed wire fencing was an additional obstacle. Hiding places were everywhere, or so it seemed.

Layne was first on the scene in this instance, which added to his tension. Apprehensively, he asked himself, *If I don't catch these guys, will I be in trouble with Escribano again?* As he exited his Kilo, he made sure he had all of his gear: radio, baton, handcuffs, gun, canteen, night goggles, Maglite. He set out in search of sign, not sure if he was even heading in the right direction. He trained his Maglite on the ground and plodded into the desert as his friend Carlos pulled up in his Kilo.

"I think they're gone," Layne said. "They scattered."

"We still should search the area," Carlos said. "If we don't make an effort to find them, or at least some of them, we'll have to explain why.

And no supervisor is going accept any rationalization for not trying." With that, they marched off together, Layne shining his Maglite and Carlos wearing his night vision goggles.

* * * *

AFTER PROBING THE DESERT for half an hour without finding anyone, Carlos was satisfied that searching further would be fruitless. He was disappointed; Layne was relieved. As much as it would have been a success for them to have apprehended at least some of the illegals, Layne wanted the shift to end quietly so he could get on the road to see Felina. They were going to spend the next two days planning her trip to Magdalena.

"Can we rest here for a couple minutes before we head back to the trucks?" Layne asked. The search on foot had left him a bit winded.

"Sure," Carlos replied.

Layne had felt comfortable around Carlos almost from the first day they met as recruits. There was something about him; he seemed naturally at ease in the Border Patrol environment. He decided to try to find out why that was.

"My dad was a Border Patrol agent back when nobody heard of or thought about the Patrol," Carlos explained.

Layne wasn't expecting that but quickly related it to what he knew best, baseball culture. "So, you were like the big leaguer's kid who grew up in the clubhouse and around the batting cage," he said. "And now you're in the majors, and you fit right in because you've been around it since you were a kid."

Carlos smiled. "I never thought about it that way, but I guess I did learn what's expected of an agent from my dad, may he rest in peace."

Layne wanted to know how Carlos's father got to the United States.

"He came across the border about forty years ago," Carlos said. "He was a factory worker, a reliable employee. But he couldn't support his family, no matter how hard he worked. He left three behind, my two brothers plus my mom. He walked and hitchhiked almost 500 miles—before there were caravans. At first, he worked in a restaurant, clearing tables and washing dishes. He sent money home to my mom every month. After a couple years, he went back then entered legally with all of them. I was born a year after he re-entered. It took a while, but he became a citizen. He joined the Border Patrol soon after gaining his citizenship."

All Layne could think about as he listened to Carlos was how Carlos felt about his role in the Border Patrol.

"My dad would tell me he didn't have a choice," Carlos said of the explanation for entering illegally. "He never had a childhood. All he knew was poverty and the hopelessness that comes with it. After he became a Border Patrol agent, he said it was like arresting his neighbors and friends. People would say, 'Aren't you one of us? Why are you doing this?' He said he would tell them, 'It's my job.'

"I tell myself, 'It's my job,' every time I search someone or take an illegal into custody."

Layne felt admiration for Carlos that he spoke so well of his father. It made Layne think of his own father and how his dad had worked with Layne from the time he was five to help him become a baseball player worthy of being drafted by a major league team. Almost sadly, Layne recalled the times when he came through with the clutch hit to win a big game and how his dad beamed with pride. He wanted that experience again, this time with Felina.

Layne felt bad for causing his friend to talk about such personal history, but Carlos assured him it wasn't a problem. "I'm proud of my dad and my heritage," he said. "Let's start back."

The two hadn't walked a hundred yards when they heard what sounded like a moan. They stopped and looked at each other quizzically, not sure if they'd actually heard anything. Then they heard it again, coming from a nearby cluster of mesquite trees.

"That sounds human," Layne said.

"*Si*," answered Carlos, lapsing instinctively into Spanish.

They moved forward, shining their Maglites into the brush and were startled to find a woman who seemed near death. She had been beaten and, it appeared, left to die in the desert. "Coyotes do this all the time," Carlos muttered. "She's in bad shape, but we might be able to save her if we can get help quickly. Call for backup."

For a second or two, Layne froze. *Call for backup?* He had never done that and wasn't sure what to do. Sensing Layne's uncertainty, Carlos told him how.

Much later, after the woman had been airlifted by a BORSTAR team—agents specially trained in operations in rugged terrain—Layne learned that the woman was from Guatemala and had been on the road—literally, traveling in tractor-trailers much of the way—for probably two weeks. She had fainted in the desert, so close to reaching the United States, and had been assaulted then abandoned. He wondered what would happen to her once she recovered. *What a job!* Layne reflected.

Back at headquarters and ready to start his weekend with Felina, Layne gave in to curiosity and delayed his departure. The dam had broken; gossip was flooding the halls. Some supervisors—no one seemed to know who or how many—had been busted for being part of some kind of kickback scheme. *Is it too much to hope for Escribano to be one of them?* Layne thought, then felt ashamed for wishing ill will on anyone, even his tormentor. There were few details so soon after the news broke, but it was pretty clear a bunch of guys were in serious trouble. *Maybe they'll forget about me for a while,* Layne hoped.

* * * *

THE IRONY OF A BORDER CROSSING in the opposite direction made Layne laugh out loud as he and Felina began planning her journey to Magdalena. He knew that almost anyone could go south whenever they wanted, with virtually no questions asked. "It's not quite a hundred kilometers from Nogales, about sixty miles," Layne said, studying a road map, "maybe an hour and a half to get there. Looks pretty straightforward. Once you get through the checkpoint and the city, go south on Route 15, *Heroica de Nogales – Imuris*. Will your car make it that far?"

Felina punched him in the shoulder, playfully. "Of course," she said. "I've had it serviced, and they fixed some things. Everything is fine now. But that raises a question in my mind. Won't they check records and see that I registered a motor vehicle in the United States and gave a Tucson address? Won't that make them suspicious of our story that we had a long-distance relationship while I've been living in Mexico? What about me going to school in Tucson and having a job here?"

Layne frowned. He needed to reassure Felina. "From what I know, they don't care about your history. They want to know how we met and if we're really getting married. They want to know if I'm a citizen, and if we're both old enough to tie the knot and not already hitched to someone else. I'll check out the points you raised, but I don't think questions like that come up during the review process." That sounded good; he hoped he was right. "To be safe," he added, "you should register your car in Mexico as soon as you can after you get there."

After a thoughtful pause, Layne changed the subject: "Have you contacted your grandparents and told them that you want to come and live with them for a while?"

"I called this week and talked to my grandmother," Felina answered. "It was obvious right away that my Spanish will have to improve, and I know it will if I'm living there. She was surprised, of course, and I don't think she fully understood. She wanted to know if Alba and Federico approved. I told her that, after they met you and talked that Sunday, they didn't object. Her house is not large, but she said she could make it work to have me stay with them. I told her I would help her make and sell her tortillas."

Felina's satisfaction shone on her face as Layne again shifted to another topic, one of the utmost importance to her.

"As soon as you're established in Magdalena—and that should only take a week or two—I'll submit the petition for the K-1," he said. "I should be able to do that from Bisbee. I can download it and fill it out on my computer, then just mail it to the Citizenship and Immigration Service. After that, we just wait for USCIS to do its thing. Then the application goes to the National Visa Center. They'll conduct a background check and send you some forms to fill out."

The words "background check" revived Felina's concerns about her life history in Tucson.

"No worries . . . as long as you don't have a criminal record," Layne assured. "When they do a background check, what they're really looking for is a police record." He tried to sound authoritative; once more, he hoped he was right.

Once again looking for a way to change the subject, Layne brought up what he had been thinking about for weeks.

"You know, when I file for a fiancée visa, we're supposed to be engaged to be married."

Before he could continue speaking, Felina threw her arms around his neck and said, "Aren't we?"

Layne was distracted by her sudden show of affection. He enjoyed the feel of her body tight against his, the smell of her hair, and the thought of having her as his wife.

"We are," he said, "but to make it official, you need a ring. Let's go shopping."

Layne assured her he had brought enough cash with him to make a down payment and said he figured he could put the rest on his credit card. It wasn't the most romantic of marriage proposals, but then, it wasn't a surprise, either. At least they weren't running off to a justice of the peace because Felina was already pregnant.

They went to the Tucson Mall and shopped four jewelry stores before picking out a ring that Felina liked and Layne told her he could afford. From the mall, they drove back to Mount Lemmon, where Layne had done the totally unexpected by describing the plan that they now were in the early stages of carrying out. Impatient to get there, both found the drive longer than any they'd ever taken. But it was where they both wanted to be for this momentous occasion.

Eventually they were back on the road they had driven only weeks earlier, when Layne had laid out his plan, which, Felina knew, was her plan, too. After pulling off at the same scenic overlook, with Tucson in the distance below them, Layne slipped the ring on Felina's finger and said:

"¿Te casarías conmigo?"

THE DISTRESSED WOMAN LAYNE AND Carlos had found in the desert had succumbed to her injuries by the time they reported to Escribano to explain their actions of the previous Friday. She was in bad shape when they had found her. She seemed doomed then. Still, it was upsetting to them; they were hoping they had saved her life. Now they would be expected to explain why they hadn't prevented the inevitable, a tragedy beyond their control.

The buzz in the building was all about what came down that Friday afternoon, but it would have to wait as far as Layne and Carlos were concerned. Layne wasn't particularly bothered by another command performance in front of Escribano, but for Carlos, it was another story. He'd never been questioned about anything he'd done since he first donned Border Patrol garb at the Academy. It concerned him to think he might suddenly have a blemish on his record. It was a matter of family honor to him.

"Good morning, Mr. Dos Santos," Escribano began. "I'm sorry you got dragged into this mess by Agent Sheppard. This shouldn't take long. I just need to know the facts of your Friday evening with him."

Carlos was stunned by the way Escribano talked about Layne as if he weren't even in the room and the implication that Layne had done anything wrong or caused him a problem. He hadn't seen enough of Layne since the Oral Board Exam to know about the harassment Layne was living with. He looked Layne's way, but his friend avoided any kind of acknowledgment that would cause Escribano to view Carlos as a sympathetic player in what was unfolding.

Escribano told Layne to wait outside his office while he interviewed Carlos. Layne knew what that meant. Escribano wanted to get the story then try to find differences or gaps in Layne's version. He paced for the first few minutes and wondered what Carlos was telling Escribano. Then he decided to find a chair that he could drag into the hallway and stop worrying about Carlos and what he'd tell their superior. He was sure he could count on his friend to avoid anything that might lead to more trouble with Escribano.

"Please relate how you became involved in what transpired after the initial report of a group on foot triggering Sensor 676," Escribano had said to Carlos after closing his office door to isolate him from Layne.

Carlos explained that he responded immediately to the call and proceeded to the location. "Agent Sheppard had already acknowledged the call and was about to begin cutting sign when I arrived," he quickly added. "We searched together." Carlos told Escribano they searched for about thirty minutes before concluding that the group had split up and escaped detection. He didn't reveal that Layne had suggested aborting the search sooner.

"What did you do then?" Escribano inquired.

"We rested for a few minutes and talked before heading back to our vehicles."

"May I ask what you talked about?" Carlos could sense that Escribano was looking for anything that he could hold against Layne. "Just family stuff. I told him about my father coming to this country and becoming a Border Patrol agent."

Escribano was familiar with the story of Felipe Dos Santos and knew better than to try to make any kind of issue out of what Carlos had just told him. So, he moved on.

"What happened next?"

We were on our way back to our Kilos when we heard a moan. At first, we weren't sure where it came from or if it was a person. Then we heard it again. We found a woman who was in bad shape, dumped in a mesquite thicket. We quickly realized that she needed medical attention as soon as possible. Layne . . . er . . . Agent Sheppard, called for backup, and we stayed with her until a BORSTAR team arrived."

"How is it that Agent Sheppard missed this woman's cries for help before you arrived?"

"I wouldn't call them cries for help, sir," Carlos corrected respectfully. "She was semi-conscious when we found her. We barely heard her moan. It wasn't continuous."

"Did you have to tell Agent Sheppard to call for backup?" Escribano probed.

"It was obvious," Carlos said, avoiding the specific question his interrogator had asked.

"Thank you, Agent Dos Santos," Escribano said politely. "I appreciate your candor. No need for you to linger here." He showed Carlos the door and summoned Layne from the hallway.

"Would you like me to call your union representative before I proceed?" Escribano asked.

"Why would I need a rep?" Layne responded. "Did I do something wrong? Am I in some kind of trouble for trying to help that poor woman?"

"I want you to write a report detailing events on your shift after you received the report of twelve aliens tripping Sensor 676. I need to understand how you failed to apprehend any of them and what more you could have done to help that alien. She died, you know."

"Stop talking," Layne blurted as he realized that Escribano was trying to set a trap. "I do want union representation. Right now. And I want you to say what you just said to me, to me and the union rep while he's present. I tried everything I could to save her."

It was obvious to Layne that the woman's death meant nothing to Escribano. That kind of unfortunate outcome occurred too frequently for it to affect him. This one merely presented an opportunity to skewer Layne Sheppard one more time.

"What this time?" Ortiz snapped as he entered Escribano's office.

"What a waste of time!" Ortiz shouted after hearing what Escribano wanted from Layne.

Escribano absorbed the abuse as he always did but didn't budge. Wondering if Ortiz and Escribano were still chummy, Layne walked out, miffed.

* * * *

CARLOS WAS CHECKING OUT his Kilo in preparation for heading to the field when Layne came from Escribano's office. "That was quick!" he said.

"I have to write a report on what we did Friday night. He's trying to nail me on inconsistencies with what he heard from you."

"That sucks," Carlos said. "Why is he doing that?"

"He's been trying to get me to quit almost since I got here. I don't know why. His way of pressuring me is to second-guess everything I do and make me write reports about everything he questions. It's a pain in the butt, but I've decided I can play that game until he gives up or moves on. I won't quit. He'll have to fire me, and I don't think he wants to go through the fight he'd have with the union if he tried that. In that way, he's a typical bully."

Carlos couldn't believe what he was hearing. He naively had no idea any agent faced that kind of scrutiny. Before leaving for the parking lot, he asked Layne if he'd heard the latest on the scandal that broke as they returned to the station the previous Friday.

"I'm not in the loop," Layne said. "What have you heard?"

"Apparently some supervisors had a side deal where they got some kind of a cut for getting new agents to rent rooms in motels and boarding houses around here. I don't know much more. The supervisors are accused of soliciting and accepting kickbacks, and a bunch of agents are in trouble for paying to get cheaper housing. Makes your situation seem not so bad."

"Escribano involved, by chance?"

"Not that I've heard."

They turned and headed for the lot as Escribano emerged from his office. Emboldened with growing self-assurance, Layne couldn't resist a chance to tweak his tormentor in return. And for the second time in less than an hour, Carlos couldn't believe what he was hearing.

"Did you hear about the supervisors being investigated for getting kickbacks for setting up new agents in temporary housing?" he taunted Escribano. "Remember when I first reported to Douglas Station for field training, and you offered to help me find a place to stay? You seemed annoyed when I told you I'd already lined up a house in Bisbee."

Escribano ignored him, but as he walked away, Layne fired one last shot.

"I sure hope you're not involved in this."

* * * *

RELOCATING TO MEXICO WAS proving to be more complicated than Felina had imagined it would be. It was going to take much longer than she expected to finally be ready to leave. For one thing, she had more "stuff" to pack than she had realized—and packing was the easiest part. She was down to five days left on her lease and still hadn't figured out what to do about her furniture. She didn't have a lot, and it wasn't in great condition. But she couldn't just leave it in her apartment. Should she try to make a few bucks with a "garage" sale, give it to The Salvation Army if they'd come and get it, or just set it at the curb for passersby to claim? In her neighborhood, she knew the latter was a realistic option.

And what about her job? She hadn't given Jabba her two weeks' notice yet. She suspected that he might tell her to just leave on the spot so she decided she'd wait until she was ready to go. But she was hoping to leave for Mexico with one more paycheck as a stake. If he allowed her to work out her notice, Marianne had told Felina she was welcome to stay at her house until she left for Mexico.

Felina excitedly showed off her new engagement ring and provided a word-for-word, mile-by-mile account of their ride to Mount Lemmon and Layne's actual proposal. Marianne hung on Felina's every word and was sincerely thrilled for Felina that Layne had taken the initiative. Her excitement, though, was tempered by the realities ahead.

"Are you uneasy about driving that far alone?" Marianne had asked. Felina assured her she would be fine; she planned to drive straight through, and her car, though older, would make it that far without trouble.

"Travel during the daylight," Marianne admonished.

"You sound like my mother," Felina had responded. The protestation was just for show; Felina appreciated Marianne's expressions of concern.

"I think you should have your car serviced before you go," Marianne continued. "Make sure you won't have a breakdown on the way. How are your tires?" Felina let out an exasperated sigh and said, "I have. The tires are good."

Later, as she filled the last of three suitcases, Felina recalled her most recent visit with Marianne and thought how lucky she was to have a friend who cared so much. She would miss her, she admitted to herself—miss their walks and talks . . . miss being able to call her almost anytime and to drop in when she needed a hug. "I hope we can talk on the phone," she said aloud to no one. She had forgotten, for a second, that she was alone with her thoughts.

Her cellphone interrupted the silence; from the Caller ID she knew it was Marianne. "What great timing," Felina said, skipping hello. "I was just thinking about you and how lonely I'll be without you."

"That's sweet," Marianne answered. "I'll miss you, too. But this is the right thing for you to do. It will be worth it, I promise." It didn't matter, at that moment, that Marianne couldn't promise anything about the outcome. "Are you all packed?" she went on. "Have you decided what you're going to do with your furniture? Have you talked to Layne lately?"

The questions were coming faster than Felina could answer them. When Marianne finally paused, Felina quickly responded. "Yes, I'm pretty much done packing. Deciding what to do with the furniture is next.

Layne's supposed to call me tonight. I want to discuss it with him.

"I'm nervous about telling Jabba I'm quitting," Felina continued. "I don't know what to say if he asks why or wants to know what I'm going to do instead of working for him. I don't think I should tell him I'm going to Mexico so I can come back and get married."

"Just tell him you've figured out a way to go to the U of A," Marianne said lightly. "That's true, sort of. If he asks how, just tell him it's too complicated to go into but you're confident it will work out the way you want. He'll just be trying to be polite, if he asks at all. He'll be relieved that you don't want to go into detail. Trust me."

"Do you think he'll tell me to just leave at the end of the day?"

"I doubt it. Who will do all the work that you do? He may not ever tell you, but he knows you're the one he can count on in that office. Trust me on that, too."

"Well, if he lets me stay, you'll have a boarder for a couple weeks. That still okay?"

"I'm expecting you," Marianne said. "Your room is all ready and waiting."

* * * *

IT WAS LATE EVENING WHEN Felina heard from Layne. She wanted him to help her decide what to do with her furniture, but before she could bring it up, he told her about the loss of the woman he and Carlos had tried to rescue. The woman's death obviously was weighing on him. Then he told her about the alleged kickback scandal. "Steer clear of that as much as you can," she advised. "Don't give Escribano the slightest excuse to question you about it." Hearing that, he decided he'd better not tell her how he'd challenged Escribano face to face about his possible involvement in the scheme.

Layne recounted the encounter with Escribano regarding the woman who died, and Felina said, "Well, I'm glad Carlos was with you and that he had the one-on-one with Escribano. I don't know what else you could have done. You've written plenty of reports by now; what's another one? Can you have Carlos look this one over before you submit it, to be sure it matches what he said?"

Layne felt like, for once, he was a step ahead. "I'm emailing it to him tonight, and he'll look at it right away and get back to me. I have to turn it in first thing in the morning."

The news that Layne had had another run-in with Escribano was unsettling to Felina, but it didn't sound like Layne had done anything wrong. *Just more harassment,* she told herself then moved on to her own current crisis. "I'm not sure what to do with my furniture," she blurted. The frustration was evident in her voice, and Layne realized immediately that he needed to put his concerns aside and help her think through the situation and reach a decision.

After listening to her describe the three options she was weighing, Layne said: "I don't think you want to leave stuff at the curb, even in that neighborhood. If somebody calls the police, you could wind up with some kind of charge that shows up later on your background check. And if you try to sell stuff, you have to get everything ready for the sale, and you have to be there the whole time. And you're bound to have some things left; then you have to figure out how to get rid of them. Besides that, it's one more thing you have to be responsible for. I think the best choice is to have The Salvation Army haul it all away. Let them deal with it."

"But I could use whatever money I might get from selling things," Felina said.

"Not worth it," Layne said firmly. "I've told you: I'll send you money regularly. If you need money to start, I'll come up with it."

Felina wished Layne were with her so she could give him a big hug and feel him hold her. "I love you," she said. It made Layne feel odd, at first; he wasn't accustomed to hearing a girl he cared about say that kind of thing. He thought about past relationships and realized he couldn't remember ever saying that to a girl he was dating. Right then, it dawned on him how different, how special, this relationship was.

"I love you, too," he answered.

After seconds of silence as two hearts communicated silently, Layne returned to the moment. "When will you know if you'll be able work for two more weeks?" he asked. He knew that serving out her notice and collecting another paycheck would make a big difference.

"I'm going to give notice at the end of the week. Marianne thinks Jabba will want me to stay for the two weeks because I do a lot in the office. She said he knows that, even if he never tells me."

"I think she's right."

They went over the plans for her drive to Magdalena and what each would do once she had settled in with her grandparents. Then Layne inquired about Eduardo.

"He's been staying in Magdalena," Felina reported, "but I don't know if he'll still be there by the time I arrive. I think he's going to try to sneak back into the States."

"Tell him to cross the border somewhere other than Douglas Sector," Layne cracked.

* * * *

SLEEPING HAD BEEN A CHALLENGE for Felina for the last few weeks as she anticipated the day when she'd tell Jabba she was quitting her job. By the time the eventful Friday morning finally arrived, she felt like Layne after one of his weekend binges. She had been living out of a suitcase for several days while at the same time, trying to project normalcy to her co-workers and Jabba, who probably wouldn't have noticed the difference even if it had been obvious. She couldn't remember ever feeling quite like she did as she dressed for what might be her last day at the job that she'd had for almost five years. *This is it,* she thought. The Salvation Army was coming the next morning; in an hour or so, she would give Jabba her two weeks' notice.

In a strange way, her long-term plan was starting to come together just as Layne's had when he was accepted into the Border Patrol. She could only hope that her journey would not be fraught with as many pitfalls as Layne's.

The day began like so many others, with the other women in the office crowded around Paul, Jabba's shiftless son, as he engaged in yet another game on the computer in his office. Jabba was on the phone, talking loud enough to be heard through his open door, sounding important. Felina debated when to go tell him, deciding that she'd wait until he ended his call rather than interrupting him. She wanted his undivided attention if at all possible.

Finally, he ended his call. Before he could pick up the phone to contact someone else, Felina hurried to his doorway and tapped on the doorframe. He looked up and, before she could speak, said impatiently, "What's up?"

Jabba's abruptness threw Felina off balance as she quickly took a seat. "I'm giving you my two weeks' notice," she blurted. It didn't come out the way she had rehearsed. She didn't get to lead up to it at all.

"What?" a startled Jabba said. It was his turn to be off-balance. "Why? Where are you going? Who will take your place?" Felina was unprepared for such obvious panic from the man she had thought was invulnerable. She recalled what Marianne had told her to say. She thought this was the perfect time to use it.

"It has been my goal, my dream, to attend the University of Arizona and become a doctor," she began. "I've figured out a way to do it so I'm going to go for it."

"Well, good for you," Jabba said, trying to sound supportive and enthusiastic. Actually, his mind was racing. He realized a big reason for his company's success was Felina's reliability. He was flailing like a drowning man trying to grasp the lifeline. "Can't you go to U of A and work here, too? I'm willing to be flexible to help you achieve your goal. It must be expensive. Would a raise help?"

Felina shifted uncomfortably in the chair across the desk from Jabba. She had never seen him like this—hadn't thought it possible. This was the same man who had never paid her the time of day, had never offered her a raise, and had cut her health benefits. Now, he was willing to be "flexible" and offering her a pay increase? She almost felt sorry for him. Almost.

"I'm sorry," she said, "but I can't attend U of A if I continue working here. This is my chance." Then she added, "But I would be happy to train someone during my two-week notice. May I finish out the next two weeks?"

"Of course. Of course," Jabba said, still flustered. "You can stay longer if you want." Then he began talking to himself. "What am I going to do? Where am I going to find someone to replace her? In two weeks!"

Felina did not expect the reaction she was getting from Jabba. Marianne had called it.

* * * *

FELINA REACHED LAYNE FIRST. "You won't believe it!" she exclaimed. "I've never seen Jabba like he was when I told him I was quitting and said I'd give him two weeks' notice if he wanted. He tried everything to get me to stay—even offered me a pay raise, which I kinda resent since he didn't ever consider one until he thought it might keep me from leaving." To Layne, only one thing really mattered: "Will he let you work your two weeks?" They talked for about fifteen minutes, then Felina reported in to Marianne.

"Leave the light on," is the way Felina began.

"I told you so," Marianne responded. "That guy Jabba has been taking advantage of you for years. He's either pacing the floor in his office right now or belting down drinks as fast they can serve them, wondering what he's going to do when you're gone. Serves him right."

"I'll need to move in this weekend," Felina said haltingly, concerned about imposing but with no viable alternative.

"I told you," Marianne reassured, "your room is ready and waiting for you to arrive. And if you need to stay longer than two weeks, it's no problem." Marianne understood the tremendous risk Felina was willing to take, and why, and wanted to support her friend in every way she could.

She nonetheless worried about all that could go wrong. She didn't want Felina to get hurt.

"Have you told Layne yet?" she asked without hinting at her concern about depending on him to make this work.

"Yes. I called him before I called you. He's pleased that Jabba not only is letting me work my two weeks' notice but also said I can stay until he finds my replacement. And he really appreciates it that you have a place for me to stay until I leave for Mexico. He continues to deal with that jerk, Escribano, but at least in the most recent instance, he was with his friend Carlos, who he said has a perfect reputation. His dad, in fact, was an agent, years ago. Layne's already researched the fiancée visa application process and is ready to go as soon as I get settled with my grandparents."

Marianne was glad to hear it all but not entirely reassured. It was time to change the subject.

"What's up with Eduardo," she asked. "How's he doing? It's already been four months. Hasn't he been staying with your grandparents? What's going to happen when you show up, too?"

"I think he'll be gone by the time I get there," Felina said. She wasn't sure of that, but she didn't want to deal with the issue until the time came—if it was still an issue then. "He's talking about trying to return to Tucson."

"Maybe you'll pass each other coming and going," Marianne cracked, trying to be funny.

"That's the last thing I need," Felina said, missing her friend's attempt at humor.

IT HAD BEEN ANOTHER RELATIVELY quiet stretch for Layne—as quiet as it can be when you're a Border Patrol agent chasing people who are trying to sneak into the United States, either to find work or smuggle drugs. He responded to sensor alerts and calls for assistance from other agents, tracked signs in the desert, and caught a few illegals. Nothing aroused the attention of Escribano so Layne wondered if he had maybe turned a corner. Or should he chalk it up to the intervention of Brian Palmer and the union? *The Palmer Effect,* he joked to himself. Or maybe Escribano really was in trouble. Layne didn't know and wasn't about to ask. All he knew was that things had calmed down some for him.

He was about to tackle something new. For the first time, he was going to drive Transport. That was usually one of the first straws a new agent drew. But in Layne's case it was delayed, probably because Escribano was trying to put him in situations that were more likely to sustain the ongoing pattern of harassment. Considering that he would be working Swings, Layne expected to be busy after nightfall. Daydreaming for a minute or two, he imagined coming to a posse's rescue and impressing everyone so much that they asked him if he had any experience riding and if he'd like to join their ranks. Once again, reality was quite different.

It was around 9:00 p.m. when the call came in. As soon as he heard that the Horse Patrol needed Transport, Layne had visions of a Wild West encounter. He was being called to help the most exclusive agents in the Border Patrol. Horse Patrol guys didn't muster with the field agents; they assembled among themselves and were pretty much left alone with their horses. They worked the more remote parts of the AOR and interacted with line agents mostly when they needed support.

The request was for a transport van to meet them on Highway 80 at a place called Paul Spur. Layne was expected to know just where it was, but he'd never heard of it. He drove Highway 80 from Bisbee to Douglas nearly every day, but he'd never noticed Paul Spur. He pulled off on the side of the road to do a quick online search on his cell phone. Paul Spur, he learned, was about twelve miles west of Douglas. It was called a "populated place" but didn't have a recorded population, which had to mean it was really small—a roadside sign and maybe a few shacks but little else. It was about two miles from the border with Mexico and near the western edge of Douglas Sector territory.

Why there? Layne wondered as he drove the lonely road through desolate country. It was obvious why the Horse Patrol and agents on ATVs were responsible for this stretch of desert. *Be alert for animals crossing the road in the dark,* he reminded himself. It was a little eerie but exciting, too. He felt like he was on his way to rendezvous with some Texas Rangers. *How exciting!* he thought. In less than twenty minutes, he came upon the "Paul Spur" sign and immediately realized that this was nothing more than the proverbial "dot on a state road map." He pulled onto the shoulder of the roadway and waited, aware that this adventure almost certainly would extend past the end of his shift. He was fine with that.

Bobbing small circles of light coming his way—Maglites in the distance, he realized—got his attention about ten minutes later. Three agents on horses were walking a group out of the desert.

Holy crap! Layne thought as they came closer. *This is a huge group! There must be twenty-five of them.*

"I'm Agent Carson," said the lead rider. "Thanks for coming. Hope you were able to drive straight to this spot. In case you're wondering, we specify this pickup point because there's a drop-down gate nearby. That's how we can get the horses to the road."

The agents herded the captives to the side of the road and directed them to sit next to the transport van. *I'm an agent now,* Layne was thinking. *I'm supposed to know what to do. They can tell by my star number that I'm new.*

Just that quick, the other two agents told Carson, "We'll go back and get the horse trailer and truck." Carson nodded, and off they went, their horses at a trot, even in the dark.

Layne was getting nervous as he surveyed the situation. "There's twenty-five of them and two of us," he said to Carson. "What do we do if any of them get up and start to run?"

"Don't worry," Carson assured. "We had everybody remove their shoelaces. They know if they try to run in shoes without laces, they're not going to make it very far. Your shoes just fall off."

Then Carson said, "I need you to search these people. Then we'll write 'em up."

Layne knew better than to search them within the group, where he would be easy prey for several to jump him. He looked quizzically at Carson, who either understood the look on Layne's face or anticipated his confusion.

"Search them at the back of the van, where you can have them put their hands on the doors and spread-eagle while you pat them down. I'll call them one at a time. These bodies were coming just to work, so they'll be very compliant. They know the drill. We caught them this time; they'll just try again tomorrow or in a couple days."

As Layne searched them one at a time, he recalled the night during field training when his group, led by FTO Tipton, had captured a group of twenty-five illegals, including a woman who tried to pass off her seven-year-old as eighteen in hopes that she wouldn't be separated from him. Transport had sent two vans that night; now he was thinking, *I have to have a seatbelt for each person I transport. This van won't hold them all.*

He voiced his concern to Carson and quickly learned how things worked in the middle of nowhere late at night.

"Nah," Carson said. "Welcome to Douglas. There's not enough vans; there's not enough Transport guys. This is how we get it done out here. Load 'em in and drive carefully."

Okay. I guess this is the way it is, Layne told himself. All the way back to Douglas Station, he worried that another round with Escribano was soon to unfold. But when he pulled onto the Douglas Station lot and marched all twenty-five bodies to the sally port, the last stop before the holding cells, no one seemed to think anything of it. He searched everyone in the group again before releasing them then turned in his write-ups and clocked out.

* * * *

FELINA GENEROUSLY DELAYED her departure to allow Jabba time to find someone who could fill her shoes in his company. And that was taking longer than Felina, Layne, or Marianne ever imagined that it would. So long, in fact, that they all had begun to wonder if Jabba actually was trying to find Felina's successor . . . or at least how hard he was trying.

"Anything new yet?" Layne asked as he and Felina began one of their calls that had become daily occurrences.

"He's being nice to me, nicer than he ever was before," Felina answered. "Maybe he's hoping he can get me to reconsider by being nicer to me. But that's not going to work; he just doesn't realize it yet or doesn't want to accept it."

Layne sensed that Felina was enjoying finally being appreciated for the job she did. He was concerned that Jabba had figured out that he could keep her indefinitely with flattery. It was time to counteract the developing sense of indispensability. "It's been almost two months since you gave him your two weeks' notice," Layne said with annoyance. "You might have to give him a definite date when you're leaving."

Felina realized Layne was right. She couldn't let this drag on forever; it was delaying their plan. "I'll tell him I have to leave by the end of September."

Satisfied that Felina was back on course, Layne dived into other topics. He had a lot to tell his fiancée on this call.

"I had the most amazing experience last night," he began, "unlike anything I've done since I entered the Border Patrol or became a regular agent."

Felina couldn't wait to hear about Layne's latest adventure. Apprehensive at first, she quickly was full of "Wows" and pertinent questions as he recounted his first night driving a transport van.

"Did the Horse Patrol meet you back at the station?" she asked.

"Nope," said Layne. "It was like they rode off into the sunset . . . or in this case, into the night. Last I saw of Carson was when I started the van's engine." Layne could tell he had impressed Felina and was happiest about that. A new feeling of self-confidence was building within Layne. He was taking charge, and it was a source of pride.

"My folks are coming next weekend," he continued. "I've convinced them to spend just three days with me. I don't plan to tell them about going to my support group or the issues I've had with Escribano. I'll show them around Bisbee, for what that's worth, and take them to Douglas Station. I got them a room at the Copper Queen."

"What about us?" Felina asked. "Don't you want them to meet me?"

Layne cringed at the question. He hadn't decided what to tell them about falling in love with an illegal and his plan for helping her become a U.S. citizen by marrying her. His parents were pretty conservative—especially his dad. They watched Fox News regularly, always Sean Hannity, and thought some left-wing plot had succeeded in ending Bill O'Reilly's nightly show. Could they possibly understand why he was willing to risk everything he'd worked so hard to achieve?

"I think it will be best if I play that by ear after they arrive," Layne said cautiously. He didn't want Felina to feel he was trying to hide her or their relationship. "I want them to share my excitement, and I think the best way to achieve that is to tell them while we're together, not before, so they can *see* how I feel. Then I can call you and tell you I'm bringing them to meet you."

Felina resisted the urge to break into tears and tell Layne he'd hurt her feelings. *I went through the same thing with having my parents meet him,* she reminded herself then said, "I understand. I think you're approaching it the right way. Just try to give me as much notice as you can."

* * * *

CHRISTY AND DUTCH SHEPPARD arrived in Tucson about noon on Friday, rented a car, and were in Bisbee right about the time Layne got home from the day shift he had requested, which, somewhat to his surprise, management had approved. They would have the whole weekend, with time to drive to Tucson on Sunday to meet Felina if things went the way Layne hoped they would.

"Hello, Agent Sheppard," Dutch said as he pumped his son's hand then gave him a bear hug greeting.

"Oh, Layne, you look so handsome in your uniform," said Christy, wiping away tears as she waited her turn to embrace her son. Standing in the lobby of the Copper Queen, Layne hoped no one he knew was watching.

"How was your flight and the drive over here?" he asked. That was a trite welcome, but Layne thought he should say it. "Isn't this place beautiful? It was built in 1902 for investors and executives of the Phelps Dodge mining company and has *never* closed. The entry doors don't have locks, so the hotel's literally been open for more than a century. When it opened, it had seventy-two rooms, with a *shared bath* on each floor. How's your room?"

"It's pretty modern now," Dutch answered. "It even has a private bath. You can tell they've remodeled more than once, the latest time fairly recently."

"It was a nice flight," his mother chimed in, "on time and smooth all the way. The drive from Tucson is very interesting, especially once you leave the interstate highway. I would like to visit that monastery in St. David sometime. And when we went through Tombstone on Highway

80, it reminded me of the old TV show, *Tombstone Territory*. Have you gone to Tombstone since you moved here to see where the Shootout at The OK Corral happened?"

Layne told his mother he hadn't stopped in Tombstone and wasn't aware of Holy Trinity Monastery. He invited his parents to see where he was living and suggested they return to the Copper Queen for dinner at The Spirit Room. "They say three ghosts live at the hotel," Layne said, "but they don't eat much. No one has ever reported seeing them in the dining room." Dutch roared while Christy made a face that indicated apprehension and discomfort.

The next day, Layne played tour guide, walking Main Street and driving to Lavender Pit and telling his parents the copper mining history of the area. "This huge hole—5,000 feet long and 850 feet deep—is named for Harrison Lavender," Layne, proud of his local knowledge, said as they viewed the gaping excavation from an overlook. "Some name, huh? He was general manager for Phelps Dodge for about twenty years starting in the '50s. His ideas and leadership kept copper mining profitable here until sometime in the '70s."

Dutch responded, "You mean they dug this out?"

And Christy marveled, "It looks like a mini-Grand Canyon."

From there they drove into Douglas, visiting Douglas Station along the way. Layne regaled them with stories of a few of his adventures—capturing the mules and dope with Darmody, the "Mexican in the Night," and his first shift as a Transport driver, hooking up with the Horse Patrol and bringing twenty-five illegals in for processing. He didn't mention Escribano and decided not to mention the unfortunate woman he and Carlos had tried unsuccessfully to save. They had dinner in Bisbee again then went to Layne's house to hang out.

"I have another piece of exciting news to share," Layne began as they sat on his small front porch.

"Don't tell us you're getting married," Dutch joked. Christy held her breath.

"Actually, I am," Layne said. "Eventually."

"What does that mean," his mother inquired, concern evident on her face.

Layne proceeded to relate the story of Felina and what he had in mind.

"So, she'll be leaving for Magdalena soon and moving in with her grandparents. As soon as she's an established resident, I'll start the fiancée visa process. By next spring, we should be able to have a wedding, and after that, she'll move back to Arizona with me." Layne hadn't planned to unload everything on them in one big dump, but once he started, there was no stopping. He hadn't realized just how excited he was about the prospect of having Felina for his wife until he started telling his parents. He virtually tingled.

"Oh, Layne, are you sure?" Christy asked almost in a whisper. "You're just getting established in the Border Patrol. What if she's just using you to become a citizen?"

Layne bristled at the suggestion. "It was my idea, not hers," he said sharply. "I thought of it, and I proposed it to her." He looked at Dutch and saw that he was about to be reprimanded by his father for speaking to his mother in such a tone. "Look," he said more softly, "this is the first girl I've ever wanted to share my life with, the first one I ever felt like I'd do anything for. It's not her fault that she was brought to this country as a two-year-old. It's not her fault she grew up illegal. She has been a good citizen, probably a better one than me, at least in some ways. She wants to be a doctor."

Then he added the punch line: "I want us to drive to Tucson tomorrow. I want you to meet her and see for yourself."

It was Dutch's turn to speak. "This is so unexpected, son. You have to understand that. You have to understand that your mother's concern—and mine—is that you not be hurt, not be taken advantage of. But you're an adult. I trust you to know when it's the real thing. We'll go to Tucson tomorrow and meet your future wife, our future daughter-in-law."

Layne hugged them both and said, "Thank you. I know you'll like her."

The next morning, they ate breakfast at the Copper Queen then hit the road by 9:30. While Dutch ate ham and eggs and Christy oatmeal with blueberries, Layne told them more about Felina, about her being so valuable in her job that Jabba tried everything to keep her and how much she tried to be there for her parents. Layne convinced them to spend the night in Tucson rather than driving back to Bisbee just to turn around the next morning to return to Tucson to meet their midday flight.

Layne had called Felina after he'd sprung the news on his parents. She was predictably apprehensive. It was Layne visiting her parents—*in reverse*. "It'll be fine," he assured her. "They'll love you. Just be yourself."

The two-car caravan arrived around lunchtime, which is the way Layne hoped it would work out. Felina joined them and they drove up in Layne's car to the resort hotel at Starr Pass where, at a table overlooking Tucson in the distance, Felina charmed them as Layne knew she would. They were the first group seated for lunch, and the last one to leave, which had the server shaking his head.

From there, Layne suggested going to the U of A campus. He considered it the equivalent, more or less, of him going to church with Felina's parents. He wanted his mom and dad to see her face light up as they walked among the buildings, the way it always did. Her desire to go to college and become a doctor was believable and her commitment to Layne apparent. The day ended with dinner, and then Layne's parents said goodbye with sincere hugs.

"She hot," whispered Dutch, ever the jock, making sure his wife didn't hear him.

"I can see why you are in love," said Christy. "Felina is very nice."

In their hotel room later that night, Layne's parents agreed that their son had chosen a challenging path to marital bliss, but they'd do everything they could to help him succeed. They wanted him happy.

* * * *

BY THE TIME LAYNE STARTED his next shift, his parents had landed in Denver. He was back on Swings, and after Muster, went to learn which Kilo was assigned to him. As usual, he was handed the vehicle's checkout folder along with the keys. Assuming the responsibility for a government vehicle was a lot like renting a car at an airport. The checkout folder contained an inspection sheet with an outline of the Kilo with every scratch and dent indicated by an *x* or a circle, initialed by the agent who caused the damage. The inspection sheet was cumulative and provided a running record of the condition of the vehicle it matched. When one inspection sheet was filled with notations, a new sheet was started. The older the vehicle, the more inspection sheets in its folder.

The agent assigned to the vehicle was expected to go over it with his supervisor before leaving for the field and to repeat the inspection with the supervisor on duty upon return, noting any new dings. A supervisor Layne was encountering for the first time, named Mathewson, met him in the lot. "Is the truck good?" Mathewson asked. Layne responded that he hadn't had time yet to walk around it and compare the inspection diagram with the damage visible on the Kilo. Mathewson shrugged and sent him on his way. "Looks good to me," he said.

Layne thought nothing of it; it wasn't the first time in his experience that a supervisor blew off the inspection. It wouldn't be a problem as long as Mathewson was there when Layne finished his shift.

After an uneventful eight hours mostly spent driving paved roads, Layne returned to the station lot. He turned in his keys and the checkout folder and was ready to head home when he heard the painfully familiar voice of Agent Ashlock, the anal troublemaker who started Layne's ordeal with Escribano months before by writing a report when Layne lost his notebook. Pressed into service as an FTO at that time, Ashlock now was filling in as a supervisor on Mids. "Hey, I need to see your vehicle. Let's go out to the parking lot."

Apprehension gripped Layne. *I hope nobody screwed me and didn't report damage on a previous shift,* he thought. Ashlock started going over the inspection diagram inch by inch, comparing it to the Kilo Layne had driven for the past eight hours. *He's looking for something, anything,* Layne told himself. A few minutes later Ashlock called to him from behind the truck. "Sheppard, please come here and tell me about this. I don't see anything on the diagram that matches these dents." Layne took one look and was sure the damage had not occurred on the shift he'd just worked. Somebody had jumped some boulders in the desert on a previous shift but didn't record the obvious result.

"Damaging government property and trying to hide it is a disciplinary offense," Ashlock said. "Is that what this is?"

What it is, Layne thought, *is a Hobson's Choice. If I say I didn't inspect the truck before I took it out, they'll say I'm not doing my job. But if I say my supervisor blew it off, I'll get him in trouble, and no one will ever trust me again. I'll be considered a snitch.*

"I wasn't trying to hide anything, sir," Layne answered after a prolonged silence. "I drove on paved roads all shift. I can't explain how that happened, when or where."

Many supervisors would have known what happened from experience, but Ashlock was not persuaded to let it drop. Just as he had started a paper trail on Layne when the notebook went missing, he intended to write a memo to the file about the botched inspection. "I'm sure Supervisor Escribano will want to see you before you go out tomorrow," he said.

Here we go again, Layne thought. He decided not to bother telling Felina about his latest problem until he met with Escribano and knew if he was really in trouble. He didn't want her worrying about it when she finally left for Magdalena.

15

FELINA'S WEARY COROLLA WAS packed like a college student's car leaving for her freshman year, which she hoped someday would be the case. Very soon she would be driving south on I-19 then, after passing through the Nogales Port of Entry, farther south on Federal Route 15 in Mexico. She'd be at her grandparents' house by early afternoon, maybe lunchtime. Layne was at Marianne's to see her off; Marianne, of course, too.

"More than two million cars go through the Nogales checkpoint every year," Layne said. All of a sudden, it hit him that Felina was venturing into the unknown, alone. He thought of how the Apollo astronauts and their families must have felt just before launch. "Even with Arizona plates, you should sail right through," he said, not entirely sure if he was trying to reassure her or himself. "Call me as soon as you get there."

"Call me, too, honey," Marianne said as she gave her a send-off hug.

It was a beautiful day for a drive. After a long embrace and an equally long kiss, Felina reluctantly pulled away from Layne and climbed behind the steering wheel. She thought back to the time Layne rode in the passenger seat and consoled herself that what she was doing eventually would mean he'd be next to her for more than a ride to Mount Lemmon.

As she drove away, Marianne turned to Layne and said, "Her whole life is at stake. If this doesn't work out the way it's supposed to, I may never see her again. Promise me you won't let her down."

Layne looked at Marianne with disbelief. She doubted him, just the way so many people had for so much of his life. His mind raced over all the times he'd been told he couldn't do whatever he was trying to do—and had ultimately proved them right because deep inside, he believed them.

He thought about why he chose to seek a career in the Border Patrol and how far he'd come—Escribano notwithstanding. And he thought about Seth and his support group. He was proud to finally be confronting his weakness for drinking. *I'm becoming a man,* he told himself.

"If you weren't her closest friend," he said to Marianne, "I'd be offended right now. But I get it that you want the best for her. I do, too. I love her."

Felina noticed the Border Patrol's northbound checkpoint south of Green Valley, an enclave created to appeal to retirees from Arizona and many other areas, and told herself, *One day I'll pass through there and not have to worry about being arrested.* She saw the signs for exits to Tubac, an art community with a fancy golf resort that was featured in the funny movie *Tin Cup.* She thought, *Some day, Layne and I will be able to come here as husband and wife and walk around the shops like we did in Bisbee.* Before she knew it, Nogales, Arizona was looming; on the other side of the Port of Entry was Nogales, Mexico. As she approached, the realization hit her, and she sort of shivered. *I'm really doing this.*

She arrived at the border and drove slowly toward signs that flashed *Alto* (STOP) and *Pase* (GO), aware that *Alto* meant she'd have to pull over to where an officer of the Mexican Border Patrol would question her. It might be as simple as, "What is your destination?" But, given her packed car and her Arizona license plates, she likely would face more detailed questioning. If confronted, she and Layne had decided, she would say she was on her way to meet a friend who was moving to San Carlos, and that she was driving the friend's car with her belongings because her friend had been required to fly into Guaymas to start a new job. Her natural reaction was to hold her breath as she watched the cars in front of her.

When the green *Pase* sign lit up for her, Felina exhaled and vamoosed. She kept her speed at 97 km/hr (60 mph north of the border) and tried to blend in with all of the traffic heading for Guaymas and San Carlos. After she paid the sixty-peso toll for the stretch of road to Magdalena, her next hurdle was the Tourist Visa Center, where visitors were required to show their passports and be issued temporary visas. She and Layne had agreed that she didn't need to stop because she wasn't an American citizen. Yes, her car lacked Mexico's plates, but foreign-registered vehicles were allowed in the northwest part of the state of Sonora without an importation permit. She had her Mexican birth certificate if she was stopped, and the story she was prepared to tell at the Port of Entry would suffice in this instance, too.

She didn't even slow down.

Forty-five minutes from Magdalena, Felina came upon clusters of people walking along a road visible from the highway. In any suburban area in America, such a sight would likely indicate some kind of a family walk or "fun run" sponsored by a parent-teacher organization as a fundraiser for a neighborhood school. But heading toward Magdalena, in the first week of October, there was no doubt what it signified: the annual *Mandas a Magdalena* pilgrimage.

Maybe it's an omen, Felina thought.

The fifty-mile, two-day walk attracted believers from the Mexican states of Sonora and Sinaloa, including from as far away as Agua Prieta and even a few from southern Arizona. All who made the trek—some years even in steady rain—walked with a *manda* or "reason to walk." A pilgrim's *manda* might be to seek health, recovery, or survival for a loved one; to offer penance for past sins; to make a promise of commitment to a cause or a life change, or to request assistance in dealing with any imaginable problem.

At the end of the journey, the *peregrinos* waited in line at the shrine of San Francisco Javier, sometimes for hours, to view a life-size statue of the saint lying in repose. Those strong enough would lift it and kiss its head; the rest would simply bend forward to venerate the likeness. Also at Plaza Monumental was the mausoleum of Padre Eusebio Francisco Kino, who founded Santa Maria Magdalena Mission in 1688. Eerily, a skeleton believed to be that of "Padre Kino" could be viewed from windows inside the mausoleum. (Padre Kino died in Magdalena in 1711.)

I wish driving my life's possessions along the route could count for walking it, Felina thought. *I certainly have a manda.*

Continuing southbound, Felina encountered a first, for her. As Highway 15 passed through the small town called Imuris, she was greeted by large speed bumps the Mexicans called *topes*. After the jolt of crossing the first one too fast, she nearly came to a full stop before traversing others. Something else very common in Mexico caught her attention: vendors hawking food and trinkets right in the middle of Highway 15 at each *tope,* hoping to engage drivers as they slowed for the humps. A little farther she saw small lots with dozens of stone carvings and beautiful copper pans of various shapes and sizes, all for sale. It reminded her of some artisan shops she had seen in Tubac.

* * * *

FIESTAS DE SAN FRANCISCO JAVIER, the days-long series of celebrations that coincided with the pilgrimage, was in full swing when Felina arrived in Magdalena. All around Plaza Monumental dozens of vendors—most local but some from elsewhere—were selling products and food. It was a peak time for the shops that bordered the plaza year-round, where visitors could buy religious figures, including statues of Saint Javier in repose, candles, rosaries, clothing, hats, shoes, jewelry, and glassware. It was as crowded as Times Square on New Year's Eve—many *peregrinos* had pitched their tents outside the shops and around the Plaza. Felina was sure her grandmother was there, offering her tortillas in the crowd. She hoped she'd be able to find her, though she realized the mass of people would make it difficult.

Plaza Monumental was the city's cultural and historic centerpiece, a place that local residents visited throughout the year. On the west side of the plaza stood the Temple of Santa Maria de Magdalena. Near the church was the shrine to San Francisco Javier, co-founder of the order of priests known as the Jesuits and patron saint of Padre Eusebio Francisco Kino. To the east was the mausoleum with Padre Kino's skeleton.

Driving the narrow brick streets on all sides of the plaza, she began to think that finding a parking space was hopeless. Just before giving up, though, a pickup truck with Arizona plates pulled away from the curb across from the Plaza. She squeezed into the space as cars behind her waiting impatiently, then began walking from booth to booth, searching for a small, older woman among the many merchants. A young girl, twelve years old at most, approached with tortillas in clear wrap. Felina declined politely. *Competition!* she thought. She passed areas where traditional dances were being performed, a staple of the *Fiestas*.

She had elbowed her way through the milling crowd for almost an hour and had just about decided that finding her grandma in such a festive atmosphere was hopeless when she spotted a small woman in her early seventies who had to be her. *"¡Abuelita!"* Felina shouted.

Surprised to see in-person for the first time a face she knew only from pictures, Isabella Rivera Serrano threw open her arms and exclaimed, *"Oh, cariña. ¡Eres tan hermosa! Estoy tan feliz de verte."* Then she began to cry tears of joy.

Felina was pretty sure her grandmother had called her sweetheart and told her she was pretty. No, beautiful. And that she was happy to see her. *I must improve my Spanish as fast as possible,* Felina told herself, then responded: *"Estoy tan feliz de estar aquí."* She was pretty sure she had said she was happy to be there. At least, that's what she intended to say.

"Estás aquí justo a tiempo," Isabella said. *"Esta noche es Las Mañanitas . . ."*

Felina had read about the tradition of singing Happy Birthday to San Francisco Javier during the *Fiestas de San Francisco Javier* so she knew for sure what her grandmother had just told her. *"Sí, justo a tiempo,"* she agreed, adding that she was glad she was not too late. *I'm usually in bed by midnight,* she mused.

Diego, Felina's grandfather, was waiting for them that evening when she and Isabella arrived after shutting down her tortilla stand. He was surprised to see his wife accompanied by their granddaughter, even though he knew she was coming. ¡Tú has llegado! *Mis oraciones han sido contestadas,"* he said happily. His prayers had been answered.

Isabella and Diego lived in a simple four-room stucco house. They had converted one of the rooms into a place that Felina could call her own. A kitchen, their bedroom, and a "social room" accounted for the others.

"*¿Todo de eso?*" Diego asked when he saw Felina's packed car. "*¡Tienes mucho!*"

"*Sí,*" Felina answered, confirming that she had brought everything and wanted to put it all in her room.

"*¡Ay, caramba!*" he said then began unloading.

Felina wanted to know about her brother. "*¿Eduardo, todavía está? ¿Ya se va?*"

The look on her grandfather's face told her she probably had said something incorrectly, but he seemed to grasp her intent and told her, yes, Eduardo had left Magdalena a few days ago. He told them he was going back home.

Ay, caramba, Felina thought. *Oh, no.*

* * * *

KNOWING THAT FELINA WAS at least on her way to Magdalena, and might already have arrived, Layne decided to go online and see what the application for a fiancée visa specifically required. He wanted to expedite the process if he could. This was a chance to show himself that he could be responsible for something important, follow through, and do it right. It didn't matter what Escribano thought of him, or anyone else, for that matter, including Marianne. What was important was showing Felina that she could count on him.

His cellphone buzzed with an incoming call, and he knew right away from the Caller ID that it was Felina.

"Hey," he said.

"Hi! I'm here," the voice on the call announced cheerily. Layne smiled, relaxed to hear Felina speak. "I sailed through the Nogales checkpoint. I thought they'd take one look at my car and stop me, but they didn't. I got here in the middle of the *Fiestas de San Francisco Javier*. I had forgotten that it was this time of year. I wanted to get out and walk with the pilgrims so my *manda* would be granted."

Layne was familiar with the tradition of the *manda* and the big annual celebration and asked, only half kiddingly, if Felina was going to participate in the festivities. "We're going to the church at midnight to sing Happy Birthday to the saint," she said, adding: "He was born in 1506 so he's getting up there in years."

Layne laughed out loud then told her he had been online when she called, checking out the fiancée visa application form. That made her smile. "How are your grandparents?" he asked. "I bet they were happy to see you. Are you moved in?"

It was Felina's turn to laugh out loud. "They're fine, and they are thrilled that I'm here," she said. "Their house is almost smaller than my apartment was in Tucson, but they've set up one little room to be mine. My grandpa was shocked to see how much stuff I had in my car, but it all fits!"

"I wouldn't say there's a language barrier," Felina continued, "but clearly my Spanish has to improve as fast as possible. I had to explain again why I came to live with them and what we are going to do. I had to go through it very slowly and repeat myself many times. Finding the right words in Spanish so they could follow what I was telling them was a challenge. But I think they get it now. And they seem pleased, actually. I wasn't sure how they'd feel, but I think they are happy for us."

The "us" part gave Layne a warm feeling inside. He'd never been part of an "us" before. He liked it a lot.

"Was Eduardo there when you arrived?" he asked. Noticeable silence followed.

"No," Felina finally said. "My grandparents told me he left a few days ago. They said he told them that, after six months, he was going home." She, of course, couldn't see Layne's frown at hearing that.

As Felina was telling Layne what her grandparents had told her, Eduardo was half an hour away in Imuris, dickering with someone who said he could get him back across the border. He had arrived in Imuris earlier in the day, about the time Felina was passing through on her way to Magdalena.

"Fifteen thousand pesos," the coyote had said then, speaking English because Eduardo did.

"Too much," Eduardo responded.

"Price has gone up," the man said. "More agents. More lights. Harder now."

"I'll do it myself," Eduardo answered with annoyance.

"Good luck, amigo."

* * * *

LAYNE SCROLLED THROUGH THE K-1 application after his call with Felina ended to get a better idea of what he'd need to do. He was a bit shaken to see that it was thirteen pages long. His first reaction was anxiety. It was going to be more work than he expected. He'd always avoided details like this. His next thought was that he'd be able to handle this better if he could have a couple of beers. That turned anxiety to panic. He called Seth.

"Yo, bro, what's up," the now familiar voice of his support group friend and sponsor said in greeting.

"I'm looking at the fiancée visa application form," Layne said, "and it's pretty daunting. I think I'd be able to do this better if I had a couple beers to relax first."

"You know you can't have just 'a couple' beers," Seth said. "You're doin' good so far; don't quit on me now."

Layne knew that's what he'd get from Seth. It's why he called.

"But this thing's THIRTEEN PAGES LONG," Layne fairly shouted. "This could take forever. And some of the questions—I'm afraid if I answer them truthfully, it'll kill our chances. It's worse than the SF-86 form I had to fill out to get into the Border Patrol."

"Like what do they want to know that's so bad?" Seth inquired.

"My employment history, for one thing. I've had a lot of jobs."

"They don't really care about that. They want to know if you've been in trouble with the law, and if you're already married to somebody else."

"I don't want to get her parents in trouble," Layne went on. "The form asks for information about them, like where they live. And it asks for her residence history, and if she has a Social Security Number."

"We can fill out that part together. I'll help you."

"They want proof of where and how we met, too."

"They're not going to question what you tell them, as long as it's plausible."

Layne persisted. "You should see the list of supporting documents they want."

"I'm tellin' you, there's nothin' we can't come up with to satisfy them. It looks worse than it is."

Layne felt the tension recede in his body. "Thanks for talking this through with me."

"Still need a beer?"

"I guess not."

* * * *

"IF IT WAS ME DOING IT," the old man with decades of wisdom said in Spanish, "I'd avoid Nogales."

He took a sip of his whiskey as the young man next to him responded, "Then where would you go?" Eduardo was planning his return.

"*Este*," the man said. "Somewhere between Naco and AP, or maybe even east of AP. You want an area where the Border Patrol is spread thin, where they're more interested in catching drug mules than people like you."

Eduardo took a draw from his longneck and thought about the advice he'd just received. "How do I get from here to there?" he parried. "It must be a hundred miles to Agua Prieta."

"A hundred and sixty-four kilometers," the man promptly informed, "two to two-and-a-half hours, straight through. If you hang around here long enough, you'll meet a farmer or a trucker going that way, and you'll be able to hitch a ride. Just don't say you want to go there so you can sneak across the border."

The conversation was taking place in a nondescript bar on Highway 15, the road to and from Nogales. Highway 2, which began on the Pacific Coast, west of Tijuana, intersected with Highway 15 nearby. The route went through the mining town of Cananea then Agua Prieta before eventually reaching Ciudad Juarez, which effectively meant goods could be transported from San Diego, California, to El Paso, Texas, through Mexico.

"Then what do I say?" Eduardo asked.

"Any fairy tale that comes to mind," answered the old man. "Visiting family. Looking for work. Meeting a girlfriend. You'll think of something."

Eduardo was still making up his story in his head when Alejandro, a regular on the road to AP, walked in and greeted the old man warmly.

"Good to see you again! And just in time," he said to the truck driver. "My young friend here needs a ride."

16

FELINA WAS ENJOYING THE sixty-five-degree morning cool as she luxuriated in the bed that nearly filled her cozy room. It was almost 9:00, later than she had arisen any day since she arrived; Isabella and Diego had been up for almost three hours already. The delicious smell of newly-made tortillas wafted through the air, reminding Felina of the past few days. She had helped her grandma sell her homemade tortillas at the *Fiestas*, and they'd sold out each day, which pleased Isabella. Even though it was October and Magdalena's elevation is about 2,500 feet above sea level, the afternoon high temperatures were near ninety. *I must get going,* Felina thought. *I have things I need to do now that the Fiestas celebration is over.*

Her room was crowded with everything she had stuffed into her car. The small chest—the only piece of furniture in the room besides the bed—and an equally small closet could not hold all of the clothes and belongings she had brought with her. Boxes were stacked in one corner, her empty suitcases on the floor alongside the chest. There was barely room for her to walk. But she was nonetheless grateful that her grandparents welcomed her into their tiny home. It made her feel good that they were so pleased to have her live with them for an extended time.

At the top of her list of things to do was register her car and her address in Mexico. *And I need to find out how Layne can send money to me here and where I can receive it,* she reminded herself. After that, she would see if she could find a job, even a part-time one. Helping Isabella wouldn't require all of her time, and any income would enable her to contribute to her grandparents' expenses. Every little bit helped.

Felina forced herself to leave the comfort of her bed and get dressed.

When she entered the kitchen, her grandmother greeted her cheerily.

"We wondered if you were going to sleep all day," she said with a smile. Already, Felina was improving her ability to translate Isabella's Spanish quickly and respond. "It felt sooo good," she replied.

"What will you do today, now that *Fiestas de San Francisco Javier* have ended?"

"I must tell Mexico I'm here!" Felina answered exuberantly. "I must get my Mexican driver's license and register my car and tell *Sepomex* my mailing address. And I must choose a place where Layne can send me money and learn how to do that." Inwardly, she was proud that she had done her homework and knew the name of the Mexican postal system.

"It's no longer *Sepomex*," Diego interjected. "A few years ago the government restructured the postal service to make it better, supposedly. It's now called *Correos de Mexico*."

"*Gracias,*" Felina said, disappointed that her research was outdated. She asked if Diego could tell her the address of the post office in Magdalena.

"*Oficina de Correos, Mariano Escobedo 109, Centro,*" her grandfather replied.

Magdalena had a population of more than 20,000 and was located in a high valley west of the Occidental Madre mountain range, with elevation and a climate almost identical to Tucson. Many residents were employed in *maquiladoras*, assembly plants that produced goods sold at lower prices in the U.S. because of lower taxes, or in the successful furniture industry there. Farmers and ranchers also populated the area. They grew more than 15,000 tons of vegetables, fruit, and grain annually and proudly claimed "the best in Mexico" Sonoran beef. The city wasn't large enough, though, to have an office of the national electoral organization, which issued the all-important voter registration card, nor an office of Transito, the transit police.

"You will need to go back to Nogales to get your voter registration card and driver's license and register your car," Diego added. "Magdalena is too small."

Felina understood and decided she'd go to Nogales *after* finding a place to have Layne send her money and learning what was involved in the transfers, and after establishing her residence for mail delivery. It also occurred to her that she needed to switch her cellphone to Telcel and, with that, get a Mexico phone number. She ate some fruit that Isabella had set out, declined anything else, and headed off to find *Mariano Escobedo 109, Centro.*

Setting up mail delivery in her name at her grandparents' address and switching her phone to Telcel were easier than she expected. She chose one of the nine OXXO convenience stores in Magdalena de Kino and schooled herself on Western Union's process for both sending and receiving money. On her end, she learned, in addition to the obvious—Layne's name and location and the amount expected—she would need her government-issued ID, that voter registration card she was going to get in Nogales, and Layne would need to provide her the tracking number for each transfer. Seemed simple enough.

Felina realized she'd left her birth certificate in her room so she swung back by her grandparents' house before heading to Nogales. She couldn't wait to update Layne on all that she was accomplishing. He would call when he was off his shift, she was thinking, but then it occurred to her that she didn't know what shift he was working this week. *I'll text him after I'm finished in Nogales,* she decided. Traffic moved well, and she arrived in the early afternoon—only to be disappointed.

* * * *

LAYNE SAT OUTSIDE ESCRIBANO'S OFFICE, nervously pumping his right leg, while Ortiz met with the supervisor behind closed doors. He expected to be called any minute to endure another tongue-lashing and be ordered to write a memo about "damaging government property and trying to hide it," as Ashlock characterized it in his report to Escribano. *I honestly don't know how that happened,* he said to himself in a barely audible tone. *Why am I always caught in the middle of these things?* He was beginning to lapse into one of his self-condemning thought-rants when the door opened and Ortiz walked out. "Go start your shift," he said. "No need for you to hang around here."

Stunned, Layne asked: "What? Why not? What happened?"

"He knows you didn't do anything wrong."

"But how?"

"That doesn't matter," Ortiz said firmly then added: "Just make sure you follow procedure when you check out your vehicle, no matter what the guy who's supposed to check you out says."

Dazed by the sudden turn of events, Layne did as he was told. He wondered if this was another instance of Brian Palmer's intervening then decided it didn't matter. It would be the last time he didn't walk his vehicle before leaving the lot. *Thank goodness,* he thought, *but I'd sure like to know what changed Escribano's mind.*

Checked out correctly this time, Layne drove his Kilo toward town and the border, wondering if anything could happen during his shift that would top the surprise he was still puzzling over—and if he'd ever find out why Escribano had a change of heart. Only a couple of hours later, he had his answer to the first part of his questions. An agent was tracking sign from the fence; a group of four, he concluded. Radio traffic picked up immediately.

"Just saw a body 300 yards from the highway," the agent said. "We have to pinch them off before they get to that road and get picked up."

Layne responded that he was en route. A canine unit and another agent were closing in, too.

"I saw a head looking my way over a cactus, then it popped back down," the agent on the scene reported. "So, I think they know I'm here. There's four of them and one of me. I'll hang tight until y'all arrive. They ain't running."

"Wait five minutes if you can," replied one of the converging units. "There'll be three of us to help you by then." To all, he added: "Be quiet. Sneak in."

Layne left his Kilo and approached the ditch where the group was believed to be hiding. He detected movement.

"They're starting to crawl," he reported. That usually meant the suspects were about to run for it.

"Everybody, GO!" the originating Agent directed.

Within ten minutes, all four migrants had been apprehended. *This will make a great story to tell Felina,* Layne mused.

* * * *

"IT TAKES AN APPOINTMENT to get a voter registration card," Felina told Layne in a raised tone of voice. Her frustration was apparent. "And you're supposed to make your reservation online. And you can't register your car without a voter registration card! So, I have to drive back there again tomorrow and try to do what I was there to do today."

"Welcome to Mexico is all I guess I can say," Layne responded, hoping a lighthearted touch would calm Felina. "It's a nice ride from Magdalena to Nogales, and you get to do it again! Sounds like you lucked out, in a way."

Felina didn't feel particularly lucky just then but moved on. "How was your day?"

"Eventful, to say the least." Layne wasn't sure where to start. He decided to save the funny stuff for last.

"Every day when you start your shift," he began, "you get your assignment then get keys to the Kilo you'll drive that day. There's an inspection sheet for every vehicle. The sheet is in a folder with those prongs on the top of the right side. The sheet has two holes in it so that it fits over those prongs. The inspection sheet has a diagram of the vehicle, and you're supposed to put an *x* everywhere there's a dent or a scratch on the vehicle. A supervisor is supposed to walk around the truck with you and make sure every dent and scratch has been entered on the diagram before you leave. And then they do the same thing when you come back, to see if you caused any further damage while you were driving it."

"So how does this affect you?" Felina asked, apprehensively.

"The other day the supervisor on duty waved me out without checking the Kilo against its diagram, and when I came back, that dork Ashlock was checking the returning vehicles instead of the guy who sent me out. He went over my Kilo like it was his personal car, and he found a couple dents in the back that weren't marked on the diagram. He accused me of damaging a government vehicle and trying to hide it. He reported it to Escribano."

"Oh, no!" Felina exclaimed, anxiety evident in her tone. Her future depended on Layne staying out of trouble in the Border Patrol, and this sounded ominous.

"It's okay," Layne quickly added. "I don't know why, but Escribano didn't even want to see me about it. Ortiz met with him, then told me to get going on my shift. I haven't been able to find out what happened yet, but I know I hadn't caused any damage; somebody before me must have done it and not reported it."

Layne waited for a reaction from Felina, but none came. She couldn't express the relief she was feeling. So, he continued.

"That's how my shift began. A couple hours in, we caught four guys trying to sneak across the border. It was pretty funny, actually."

Layne recounted the report from the agent who first picked up the group's sign and the convergence of the other agents.

"When he said, 'everybody go,' it was like the old silent movie *Keystone Kops*. The aliens started running, and two of them ran into each other and fell down. They were caught on the spot. Another guy got on one side of a mesquite tree and an agent was on the other. They danced around, trying to elude each other. But all they did was chase each other around the tree until the agent finally caught him.

"I ran after the fourth guy. He goes about fifty yards, and my legs are burning. I'm thinking, 'If he keeps going, I don't know if I'm going to be able to catch him.' I'm thinking it would be bad for me if he got away. Then I look up, and he's standing there with his hands up!"

Felina did relent and laugh at this tale. "That *would* make a funny silent movie," she agreed.

* * * *

LAYNE HAD SUCCEEDED IN lifting Felina's spirits. "My day wasn't a total waste," she admitted. "I was able to record my mailing address, which establishes my residency. I need that to get my voter registration card. And I switched my phone to Telcel and found out there are no more roaming charges for calls from the U.S., which means we can talk as much and for as long as we want without extra charges. And I picked out the place where you can send money to me and learned what I need to have to collect it. Have you looked into sending to me yet?" She didn't want it to sound like she didn't trust Layne to follow through, but it was, in a way, a test question.

"There are three Western Union places in Bisbee," Layne answered, "and six in Sierra Vista if I'm out that way sometime when I want to send you something."

"You can't just walk in and send me money," she said, "and I can't just walk in and get it. They have certain requirements."

Layne was proud of himself. He'd actually looked into how to send money using Western Union, and he was ready with a detailed response.

"Sending and receiving in person is just one way we can do this," he said. "I can also do it online through their website, and they even have a mobile app. I can send it to you for pickup or to your bank account or to what they call your mobile wallet, if you were to set that up. For us, I think the easiest way will be for you to pick it up. I'll usually send it in person, but it's nice to know there are ways I can do it electronically if I can't get to a physical location."

Then Layne reiterated what she already knew: "I need to be able to give them your full name as it appears on your government-issued ID and your residential address. You now have your address established, so all we need is for you to get that ID." Felina was pleased and reassured.

"I'm going back to Nogales tomorrow," she promised.

17

SETH SHOOK HIS HEAD AS HE studied the list of documents required by the U.S. Citizenship and Immigration Service to accompany the K-1 visa application. *I've got to keep my boy Layne feeling good about this,* he told himself, *even if it scares the bejeebers out of me.*

Just then Layne asked: "So, waddya think?" Seth smiled comfortably and said in a calm tone that belied his own concern, "You're right. There's a lot here. But we'll get through it."

They were meeting at Layne's little house in Bisbee. He had printed out all the forms and instructions and a few other articles about filing for the fiancée visa. "We can fill out these forms on the computer," Seth said, "but we have to print them and mail them with the required documentation. Or I guess you could hand-deliver them to the Tucson Field Office." Lacking confidence that he would be able to pull this off even though he desperately wanted to, Layne said, "Mail. I don't want to give anybody the chance to question me face to face."

"Okay, then," Seth replied, rubbing his hands together. "Let's get started."

They tackled the biographical questionnaires first, one for Layne and another for Felina.

"We can fill out her form," Seth said, "but it requires her signature. So, we'll have to get it to her and get it back before we can submit the application."

"I have her mailing address in Magdalena," Layne said. "That shouldn't be a problem."

Seth started through Form G-325A, Biographic Information. When he came to the Social Security Number box, he said, "We won't list one for Felina since the one she had was bogus." And at the section asking for residence information for the past five years, he proposed to use only her grandparents' address. "She just needs to tell them to say she's been living with them," he reasoned. "I doubt they'll even be asked. Same with employment; she's been selling her grandma's tortillas and just recently decided to supplement that because she's going to get married."

Layne was nervous. He imagined USCIS reviewers rejecting Felina's form as incomplete or vague, or investigators kicking in her grandparents' front door and hauling her away in handcuffs for misrepresenting herself. He feared that once the whole scheme was revealed, he'd be fired from the Border Patrol and probably prosecuted. Felina, he was sure, would be stuck in Mexico, at best, and he'd never see her again.

"You sure about this, Seth? I don't want to get anybody in trouble—most of all Felina."

"No worry, bro," Seth assured. "They're so busy, all they look for is to see if all the questions were answered and all the boxes filled in."

"How can you be so sure?"

"This ain't my first rodeo," is all Seth would say.

They moved on to the Petition for Alien Fiancée. The form itself was a relative breeze for Seth. It was as if he had done it before or was an immigration attorney, though neither was the case. He was simply brazen and certain he could bluff his way through the questions. Where he wasn't so confident was the list of required accompanying documents.

"I'll have to ask my mom for a copy of my birth certificate," Layne said. "I can have a passport photo taken here in town or in Sierra Vista, and I can tell Felina to have one made in Magdalena. She can mail it to me when she returns the signed G-325A. I'll have her send me a copy of her Mexican birth certificate to prove she's old enough to marry. Neither of us has been married before, and we don't have any kind of criminal record."

"That's really important," Seth said. "When they do the background check, that's the kind of stuff they'll be looking for. If your records are clean, you should sail through."

That sounded good to Layne, but he was worried about two other requirements: proof of intent to marry and proof of having met within the past two years.

"We don't have wedding announcements or a catering contract!" he said with indignation. "She has an engagement ring; that's it. We can't make more plans until we know she's going to get the K-1 visa. Maybe she can get her pastor, Monsignor Apodaca, to provide an affidavit saying she's going to marry me. But he's in Tucson! I guess she'll have to get a priest in Magdalena to vouch for us. Why I want to marry her will be easy."

Seth wanted to jump in, but Layne hardly paused to take a breath. His anxiety was pouring out.

"I can make up a story of meeting her in La Paz while I was living there and she was on vacation. And telling how our relationship developed won't be hard. But I don't have any photos of us—much less photos of us in Mexico—and the dates on my passport are older than two years ago. Are you sure this can work?"

Seth wanted to remind Layne that it was *his* idea, but he knew that wouldn't help the situation. He was amazed by the sudden realization that Layne had never conned anyone the way Seth was practiced at doing. "It's not so much *what* you tell them, but *how* you tell them," he finally said to his overwrought friend. "Think grey instead of black and white. What they're really trying to do is make sure this is a legitimate relationship, not some Green Card fraud or marriage broker deal. When we get finished, you'll be golden."

Layne had little choice but to believe Seth.

* * * *

THE K-1 VISA PROCESS moved much more slowly than Layne and Felina expected. He hadn't bothered to check into how long it took when he pitched his idea to her. And they hadn't inquired about the time it would take before they decided to try it or even when they went shopping for an engagement ring and Layne popped the question. As Felina finally left her job with Jabba and drove to Magdalena, she still had no idea it would be so long before she could return to Tucson for her wedding. Three months passed quickly after Layne submitted the K-1 application. In that time, Felina and Layne observed their first Christmas as an engaged couple via Skype, email, and the postal systems of two countries. It was also the first time she hadn't celebrated the holiday with her parents.

The USCIS review supposedly had begun more than a month ago, just after New Year's. She began to worry that the "grey areas" that Seth assured would not be a problem were actually red flags in the I-129F, and that any day, she or Layne would get bad news. *Then what?* she fretted.

Life in the Border Patrol had settled into a pattern, as most jobs inevitably do, though this pattern could hardly be called routine. Or boring. Layne was learning a lot about himself as he progressed from newbie to veteran, with the stories to prove it.

Felina, meanwhile, had managed to find a job in one of Magdalena's *maquiladoras*. Her office experience working for Jabba not only got her hired but also immediately set her apart from others doing similar work. She was an instant star. Her looks made her a star of another kind, as well. But the Layne wannabes were wasting their time. Felina viewed them as slightly older versions of the alpha males she had sworn to avoid, and besides, they couldn't help her achieve her goals of U.S. citizenship, a college degree, and a medical career. She decided it would only upset Layne needlessly if she mentioned their unwelcome advances.

It was during this seemingly endless stretch of waiting for action on the K-1 petition that Layne caught his first coyote. The man said his name was Alberto, but Layne never knew if that was his real name. When they ran his fingerprints in Processing, the results showed he had used a different name each of the five previous times he'd been picked up by the Border Patrol. Layne was disappointed that he'd only caught a repeat offender. *It's like catching the same dumb little trout over and over,* he thought with disappointment. *You keep throwing it back, and it keeps hitting your fly. I want to catch a big one.*

Layne nabbed Alberto, or whoever he really was, in a most unlikely way. His fellow field agents considered it dumb luck. Escribano dismissed it as a fluke.

Driving Highway 80 toward Bisbee, just after finishing his shift on Swings, he came upon a young woman frantically waving along the side of the road. This stretch of the highway was only a couple of miles outside Douglas and closer to the Mexico border than Paul Spur, where Layne had rendezvoused with the Horse Patrol a while back. Layne had changed into shorts, a t-shirt, and flip-flops before leaving Douglas Station; he looked like a young guy on his way to a bar, which until fairly recently, he might have been.

Layne drove past the woman, rationalizing that he was off duty, and stopping could put him in danger of being mugged or killed and having his car stolen. He was a trained law enforcement officer; he should know better. In the next instant, though, doubt pierced his thinking. *What if that was Felina? I'd want someone to help her.* Against his better judgment, he pulled to the shoulder and whipped a one-eighty.

The woman's father was injured, she explained in Spanish. How lucky for her that Layne was fluent in her only language. "Can you help me? she asked, pleading, "Please, help me."

Layne assumed the distraught woman and her father were illegals, but he felt sympathy for them. He agreed to see what he could do, and the woman turned immediately and started back into the desert, pausing for Layne to join her. Before he got out of his car, Layne decided to conceal his gun in his waistband and put his handcuffs in one pocket and his radio in another. *Precautions,* he thought, hoping he would not need them.

The injured man was in the desert, not far from the road. Layne followed the woman about fifty yards and found her father, lying on the ground with a broken ankle. Alberto was with him.

"*¿Hablas español?*" Alberto inquired.

"*Sí.*"

Alberto then asked Layne his name and who he was. Saying only that his name was Layne, he explained that he was driving along Highway 80 when the young woman stopped him and asked for help. Something about Alberto and his wariness made Layne wonder what he'd walked into. He decided he should ask a few questions, like "What's your name?" and "Where do you live?" and "Why are you out here in the desert at night?"

The woman's father was in obvious pain but was alert enough to follow the exchanges between Layne and Alberto. Finally, he started to tell his daughter to explain to Layne why they were there and what had happened to him. Alberto interrupted and told them to "shut up." But the woman went on anyway. She and her father had left Nuevo Casas Grandes, a town about 140 miles southwest of Agua Prieta in the state of Chihuahua the night before. They were dropped off on Mexico Highway 2 a little west of AP. Alberto was supposed to lead them to Highway 80, where a vehicle was to meet them and take them north. But her father stepped in a hole in the darkness of the desert. She couldn't leave him and somehow convinced Alberto not to, either.

I should have realized sooner what's going on, Layne thought, disappointed in himself once again. *I'm so gullible.* He pulled his gun from his waistband and said to Alberto, *"Soy agente de la frontera."* ("I'm a Border Patrol agent.") Then he told him to lie face down and not move.

To his surprise and relief, Alberto complied. Layne handcuffed him and told him to remain on the ground. The woman and her father were wide-eyed.

"I will radio for help," he told the woman. "Someone will come who can help your father."

As they waited for response, Layne struck up a conversation with Alberto, who was quite willing to tell Layne a story. Layne had no way of knowing whether or not it was true. Alberto had worked in Arizona, he said, in construction. "But the money wasn't that good, and it was hard work." He told Layne he had a wife and three children, two sons and a daughter. Even after paying the required bribes to the Mexican military and police, he could make thousands per week as a coyote. And until now, he'd been able to do it without getting caught. He said sympathy cost him this time.

Layne couldn't wait to tell Felina that he'd nabbed a coyote who had eluded capture until this moment. Maybe he wasn't so gullible after all. Maybe Escribano and his fellow agents would look at him differently in the future, knowing he had the wits to apprehend a coyote even when he was off-duty.

It never occurred to him that "Alberto" had played him for a fool or that his colleagues would do anything but admire him for his bravery and resourcefulness after finishing his shift.

* * * *

"ALBERTO" HAD BEEN EXPOSED for the fraud that he was and sent back to Mexico weeks ago, along with the woman and her injured father. Layne had just visited Seth and, after telling him about his most recent adventure, expressed frustration with the slow pace of the K-1 process. It was his day off, and he was heading to the post office to collect mail from his P.O. Box. It was sunny and warmer than usual for late February—nicer than the day a year ago when he nervously completed the Spanish Oral Exam to pass from trainee to agent. Layne had recently celebrated his first anniversary of that milestone, though he could share it with Felina only by phone. *So much has happened in the past twelve months,* he reflected.

Several letter-sized envelopes were in his accumulated mail, and one in particular caught his eye. The return address identified it as correspondence from the United States Citizenship and Immigration Services. Layne tore it open with trembling hands. Minutes later he called Felina.

"The petition for your K-1 visa has been approved by USCIS," Layne excitedly told her. He could hardly hold onto the phone. "It's been forwarded to the National Visa Center."

"So, what does that mean?" she asked. "What's next?"

"They'll send you some forms to fill out, and they'll conduct background checks on you and me."

"Background checks?" Felina said gravely. "Won't that be the end of us?"

"Not at all," Layne assured. "They'll be looking for previous or existing marriages, past criminal charges and convictions, and evidence of a marriage broker or matchmaker. They want to make sure we're truly in love and this isn't a fraud. And they want to know that we're not lawbreakers. We should pass without a sweat, though it will be a while from what I've read."

"Isn't there anything we can do now?" Felina sighed.

"Well, I don't think it's too early to start prepping for the interview at the U.S. Consulate. Once the Visa Center finishes the background checks and has reviewed the documents you send them, they'll send the file to the Consulate. They'll ask you for some more stuff and have you get a medical exam, then they'll schedule the in-person interview, which is the last step."

"Where is the Consulate?"

"There are three in Mexico. I think they'll have you go to either Monterrey or Guadalajara."

"But they're both so far away!" Felina exclaimed. "Where is the other one?"

"Mexico City."

"That's even farther!"

"Don't worry. We'll handle it when we know where you have to go. You'll be fine."

"What will the interview be about?"

"That's what we're going to rehearse."

"How long will this interview last?"

"I'm told only fifteen to thirty minutes."

"That's pretty long."

Layne had spent a lot of his free time surfing the Internet for information about the K-1 process and the consular interview. He felt confident—a new sensation for him—and he wanted to reassure Felina. For once, he actually felt like he was on top of a situation and could handle something important. The transformation was not lost on Felina, and her confidence and optimism grew as she saw Layne evolving.

"I realize the prospect of this interview is nerve-wracking," Layne began, "especially not knowing just when it will occur or how long you'll have to wait. But it won't be that bad if you're prepared, which you will be, and if this is legit, which we both know it is. Just relax and be yourself.

"Most of the personal questions are easy, like name, date, and place of birth; if you've been married before and have any children; if you've ever been convicted of a crime; and if you've been sponsored for a K-1 visa before. They'll probably ask if you've visited the U.S. and if so, when and why, and if you have relatives living in the States."

"Well, they'll get me right there," Felina said.

"No," Layne countered. "You don't have any legal record of your residence in the U.S. Just answer, 'No.' With no criminal record, no previous marriage and a bogus Social Security number and driver's license, it's like you were never there. Same for your parents."

"What about my car registration?"

"They won't dig that deep," Layne bluffed.

Felina was skeptical but wanted to believe Layne. She would really have to practice answering those questions convincingly.

"What else will they ask me about?"

"They'll probably ask you a lot of the same questions about me. They'll want to know where I live and if I have a job; if you've met my parents; if I have brothers or sisters; if I've been married before and have any children; and even what languages I speak." Layne paused then added: "Best of all, they'll ask you what you love about me. Feel free to give a lengthy answer."

"I'll have to think about that one," Felina teased. "I'm glad I have time."

Layne played along, secure for the first time in his life when it came to a relationship with a female. It provided the perfect segue to the last likely part of the interview.

"They'll want to know about our relationship," he said, "how and where we met; how long we dated before we got engaged; what we like to do together; when and where the wedding will be; how we are communicating while we're apart; if we have plans for a honeymoon . . ."

"Speaking of that," Felina interrupted, *"Where are we going* on our honeymoon?" She obviously had relaxed to some degree. On the other end of the call, Layne smiled.

"We have time to figure that out," he said. "For any wedding-related questions, it's okay to say you don't know yet. But if they ask you to describe the day that I proposed to you, I expect you to make it sound as romantic as I tried to make it—considering that I was in Arizona and you were in Mexico, of course."

"Don't worry," Felina assured pleasantly.

"Better tell me what you decide to tell them, in case they ask me so they can compare stories," Layne said.

"My pleasure. You'll love it, I'm sure."

Layne was grinning as he wrapped up their call. "We'll have time to go over any questions that concern you in the weeks to come," he concluded. "In the meantime, all we can do is wait."

$$\boxed{18}$$

IT HAD BEEN MONTHS SINCE Layne and his friend Carlos worked the same shift by the time they checked the schedule for the next pay period and found themselves both listed in Processing on Swings. The last time was when Carlos wound up in Supervisor Escribano's office, asked to recount events that included discovering a migrant woman who had been left to die in the desert. After Carlos finished, Layne was ordered to submit his version of that night in writing.

"How's it going with Escribano?" Carlos asked Layne. "Has he let up yet?"

"I don't know if it will last, but it's been going better ever since I had to write that memo about what happened when we found that woman in the desert, and I bullied Escribano about the kickback scandal," Layne said.

"Wow! That was quite a while ago," Carlos said.

"Yes, it was. I think it really made a difference that my account matched what you told him face to face. I truly appreciate you looking over my report before I turned it in to him."

"I didn't really do anything," Carlos said. "You told it exactly the way it happened. Your report matched my version because it was accurate and truthful."

"That may be, but you helped me a lot just by confirming that my version matched yours before I turned it in. I was able to be confident in front of Escribano because of you, and I think he sort of decided to move on after that. He sure had been trying to make my life miserable."

"Did Escribano ever get back at you for the way you talked to him that day about the kickbacks?" Carlos asked.

"No. I think he wanted to avoid that subject entirely. He hasn't been named so far, but the investigation's still going."

Carlos nodded. He didn't want to get drawn into that mess, either.

"I did have one other run-in, so to speak," Layne continued, "but he was half-hearted about it and hasn't pushed it further. I got crossways over one of those vehicle inspection sheets. The supervisor on duty when I started my shift blew off the checkout, and when I came back at the end of the shift, everybody's buddy Ashlock was filling in as a supervisor. He insisted on checking out my Kilo almost with a magnifying glass, and he found a couple dents in the rear that weren't on the inspection sheet. He said I tried to hide it and wrote a memo to Escribano.

"I didn't want to finger the other supervisor, so I was going to take whatever came. But you won't believe what happened. Darmody—the agent who's supposedly always looking for trouble—heard what was coming down and stepped up and said he'd driven that truck before me and had forgotten to report the new damage. Since they think a lot of him, they let him off and Escribano just let it drop."

Carlos shook his head in amazement. "You sure have been through it," he said. "Hopefully this will be a quiet week."

And it was, at least through the first four-and-a-half shifts.

"How many 826 forms have we processed this week?" Layne asked Carlos during the last shift of the week. They grabbed bites of their sack lunches before beginning to enter basic information for two more illegals.

"I lost count two days ago," Carlos responded. "It has to be hundreds."

The process was monotonous. Each agent at a processing terminal was given a stack of 826 forms, the sheets agents filled out in the field when migrants were apprehended. The name, date of birth, and other basic information on a form was entered into the ENFORCE system while the corresponding individual sat with the agent. Then the subject was "rolled"—the term used to describe taking a person's fingerprints.

Once fingerprints were entered, the system quickly determined if the individual had been detained and deported before, if he or she had been charged with any crime or crimes, and if the fingerprints matched aliases previously entered. If the newly entered data came back clean—that is, not associated with another identity and without pending charges—the person would be shipped back to Mexico, usually by the end of the shift.

"Only a few more hours of boredom to go," Layne said. He flipped through the remaining forms in his current stack to see how many there were and felt a chill as he saw the name on the bottom form: Eduardo Camarena Rivera.

* * * *

"CAN YOU TAKE A BATHROOM BREAK?" Layne nervously asked Carlos. "I need to tell you something in private. It shouldn't take long."

Carlos looked at Layne with a mixture of curiosity, confusion, and surprise. "Sure, I guess. But we shouldn't leave together. You go first, and I'll be thirty seconds behind you."

Layne checked the stalls to make sure he was alone. It reminded him of the times he had snuck into the men's room before the Spanish Oral Board to down a Valium. He had come far enough that he didn't wish for one in this instance. Carlos entered and said, "What's up?"

Layne proceeded to share with Carlos what he hadn't told anyone at Douglas Station. Quickly, he summarized meeting and falling in love with Felina, their plans to enable her to become a U.S. citizen, and the dilemma with Eduardo and that he apparently had been caught trying to sneak back into the U.S. somewhere within the Douglas AOR.

"I have a plan," Layne concluded. "I just thought it up, and it's farfetched. But it might work. I'll need your help."

He outlined it hastily, and Carlos said, "It's one-in-a-million, but if I see it coming together, I'll do my part for you. Now, we better get back to our stations. You've been gone the longest, so you go first."

"No. You go," Layne responded. "I have a reason I was gone so long, if anyone asks."

Within thirty seconds after Layne returned to his seat, Supervisor Calavera was at his side. And Layne was ready for him, as promised.

"Why were you gone so long, Sheppard?"

"Loose bowels, sir. It must have been something I ate. But I think I'm fine now. By the way, do you still need someone to drive the VR van tonight? If so, I'll volunteer."

Calavera was short-handed because three agents had called in sick. He still needed a driver for one of the Voluntary Return vans. As Layne suspected, Calavera not only would take him up on it, he was so relieved and pleased that he forgot about Layne's extended trip to the men's room. He didn't even hesitate to accept Layne's offer.

Overhearing the exchange, Carlos rolled his eyes. *His outlandish plan might work after all,* he thought. *But he needs a couple more longshots to come home.*

They resumed processing their 826 forms, and Layne watched for an opportunity to activate the next step in his scheme. He was sure Felina would be impressed—and appreciative—if he pulled this off. And he'd be proud of his resourcefulness.

"I've never driven VR," Carlos said. "How does that work?"

"It's pretty simple, really," Layne answered. "You drive down to this area by the Port of Entry that has two gates in the fencing. They open the gate on the U.S. side and the van pulls in. That gate closes, then a gate opens into Mexico. Everybody gets out and goes back into Mexico. Then the Mexico gate closes, and the U.S. gate opens again, and you drive away."

Carlos began to see how Layne's ruse might work. He had to get Eduardo into the "processed" cell then make sure he was one of the fifteen illegals who rode in his VR van. Once he got inside the U.S. gate, everyone but Eduardo would get out. And after Layne drove away, he could find a place to stop and let Eduardo free. *Ingenious but risky,* Carlos told himself. *Not something I'd ever try.*

* * * *

IT WAS GETTING LATE IN THE shift, and Carlos was beginning to think Layne might not pull it off when Layne got up from his terminal and walked to RED-1, the holding cell for migrants waiting to be processed, as he had done numerous times through the past seven hours. He called for Eduardo by surname as impersonally as he could, mirroring all of his previous calls. Carlos watched as Layne led a jaunty Hispanic to the chair next to his station. *How's he gonna do this?* Carlos mumbled.

Layne was counting on goodwill with his supervisor, earned by volunteering to drive a VR van. He leaned forward and began to speak in Spanish in a low voice. It caught Eduardo off guard, and he wanted to say, "Can you talk louder?" in a voice that surely would have been heard by others. But sensing that Eduardo was about to speak, Layne said in a commanding tone: "Don't say a word unless it's to answer a question that I ask. *We* do all the talking here." Carlos was mesmerized by Layne's audacity.

"*Soy Layne, el amigo de tu hermana,*" he began. Carlos understood that Layne had just told Eduardo he knew Felina. "*Voy a ayudarte. Solo haz lo que te digo que hagas.*" (I'm going to help you. Just do what I tell you to do.) Eduardo was astonished, but he would do just as this stranger ordered and see what happened.

Layne went through the motions of entering information from Eduardo's 826, curious why Felina's brother had been so forthcoming after he was rounded up but unable to ask him about it. Next, he pretended to "roll" Eduardo and hoped that no one—especially Calavera—was paying attention. Quickly, he announced, "*Bien, ¿estás listo para unirte a los demás que serán enviados a casa?*" (Okay, are you ready to join the rest being sent home?)

As Eduardo said "no" to the idea of going "home" to Mexico, Layne took him by the arm and started toward the BLUE-1 cell. As he looked for an opportunity to explain more of the plot to Eduardo, Carlos delivered the one piece of the puzzle over which Layne had no control—which Carlos could not control, either, except for the ruckus that would ensue if he did get a hit. And that's exactly what happened. He "rolled" a migrant after entering the information on his 826, and *voila!* the fingerprints revealed this man was not who he said he was.

"Your fingerprints come back as belonging to this guy, and this guy, and this guy!" Carlos roared in Spanish. "Who are you?"

It was enough of a scene to distract everyone in the room—an incident just like the one Layne recalled from the night months before when he was a trainee, learning at Agent Darmody's side. That night, a young woman had pitched a fit after her prints came back with multiple warrants.

It was just what Layne needed. He hastily explained the plan to Eduardo, who could barely take it in before order was restored. Unlike the woman that night, he did as he was told. Dazed, he compliantly entered BLUE-1, still not sure what exactly was happening, and stuck with seeing things through to the finish. What choice did he have?

* * * *

LAYNE MADE SURE THAT all fifteen illegals in his VR van had fastened their seatbelts, then drove away from Douglas Station. He'd be at the U.S. gate in about fifteen minutes. He was quite pleased with himself for having the ingenuity to conceive this plan on the spot then pull it off. Luck played a huge part in it, he knew. How else to explain Carlos rolling a guy with multiple aliases? But, "Hey, better lucky than good," the old saying goes. *Runyon should see me now,* Layne thought. Then, *screw Runyon; Felina should see me now!*

Layne pulled up to the U.S. gate, and it opened as if it were waiting for him. Once the van was inside, that gate closed and the Mexico gate opened, just as it was supposed to do. Layne got out of the van and started ushering out the illegals who had agreed to return voluntarily to Mexico. One by one they passed through the open gate back into their home country. Everyone knew they'd be back in the U.S. within forty-eight hours, probably sooner.

There was enough re-entry activity that no one counted heads. Layne was banking on that. He made sure Eduardo was laying low inside the van then closed the door. The U.S. gate opened, and Layne started back ostensibly to Douglas Station. On the way, he stopped at the Walmart in town. When he came back out of the store, he expected Eduardo to be gone.

"Estás por tu cuenta desde aquí. No te dejas atrapar otra vez y no se meta en problemas," Layne said to Eduardo.

It was late, so Layne waited until morning to call Felina and tell her what had transpired the night before. "I told him he's on his own, and he should stay out of trouble," he said. Felina was stunned.

"I can't believe he tried to re-enter way out there," she said. "Where was he picked up? How was he caught? Was he alone?"

"I don't know any of that," Layne answered. "I couldn't believe my eyes when I saw his name on an 826. My first thought was how to keep him from being deported again."

"You took a tremendous chance. What were you thinking?"

"I was thinking about you. I didn't want you to have to worry about your brother anymore if I could do anything to prevent it."

Felina's voice broke as she said, "I love you."

It was one of those times when he didn't have to respond in kind; what he had done for her brother told Felina all she needed to know. Layne swallowed hard and changed the subject.

"So, how's it going—life in Magdalena and living with your grandparents?"

"I miss you, and I'm anxious to hear something positive regarding the visa application. But I'm making the best of it."

Layne wanted to tell her it wouldn't be long, but he knew better. She probably would be stuck in Magdalena for at least a few more months. They wouldn't be spending weekends together for who knew how long. That would be the hardest part, figuring out how to see each other at least once in a while. Their phone calls would be their lifeline. He was committed to trying to survive in the Border Patrol at least long enough to bring her back, marry her, and help her become a citizen. After that, he hoped Felina could realize her dream of going to college and becoming a doctor and that he would still be her husband, whether he remained in the Patrol or not.

"It isn't as encouraging as I'd like it to sound, but 'hang in there' is the best I can say right now," Layne said. He mentally crossed his fingers. "I know this will work out the way we want it to if we can be patient. As Monsignor Apodaca said that day I went to Mass with your parents, we need to trust in God."

Layne felt a direction and purpose that had evaded him his entire adult life, and it left him with a feeling, mixed with a lingering touch of his usual apprehension, he hadn't experienced before. Being a Border Patrol agent had tested him in ways he never imagined, but he had stuck with it, even enduring what was obviously exaggerated harassment. He was proudest that he was addressing his drinking problem, and he knew he couldn't have done that without Felina. He realized, too, how important his support group and his friendship with Seth had become.

I have turned a corner of some kind, he thought. The gloom he was feeling dissipated, and the hair on his arms stood up.

His introspection triggered in him thoughts of one of his favorite songs, "Southern Cross," and he recalled within his mind some of the lyrics, which fit his mood and maybe, hopefully, brighter days ahead. The verse that came to mind alluded to the realization of why a certain route had been chosen and that the past wasn't nearly as intimidating as it seemed. It spoke of the future in optimistic ways. He saw in the words metaphors for his decision to join the Border Patrol and his plans for a life with Felina.

He thought, too, of passing the Exit sign as he drove south on I-25 on his way to Douglas Station after spending a week with his parents following Academy graduation. "Truth or Consequences," it read. *I've been there before,* he had thought at the time. But he never considered it a peculiar name for a town until now. The irony of the name led to a new awareness. *Consequences aren't always bad,* he reflected. *They can lead you toward a better path.*

"I can do it if you can do it," Felina assured, snapping Layne out of his momentary introspection and bringing their phone call back to life. "It's nice enough here, and I get to be with my grandparents and get to know them in ways I never thought I would. It's a special time in that way. I know it will be harder for you; you're alone. Please promise me that you'll continue to attend your support group meetings and rely on Seth. And do all you can to keep from winding up in Escribano's office. Maybe he'll get his promotion and leave you behind to start fresh with someone new."

"Or maybe he'll get busted as a result of that investigation that's still going on," Layne said defiantly.

"That's out of your control," Felina responded. "Actually, almost everything that will influence our future is out of our control, come to think of it. The whole visa process is in others' hands. All we can do is 'hang in there,' as you say."

After seconds of silence that seemed like minutes, Layne spoke. "I can, and I will."

"I'm proud of the courage and strength you've shown these last few months," Felina said. "You are my hero."

Layne was beaming. He wanted to be Felina's hero forever, and if things worked out the way he hoped, he'd have that chance.

ABOUT THE AUTHOR

Sherryl and Christopher LaGrone

Sherryl LaGrone is the mother of the late Christopher LaGrone and daughter Aimee Hestera. She is a retired high school teacher who now enjoys being a "snowbird" in Mesa, Arizona, which is a couple hundred miles to the north of the setting of *The Delta Tango Trilogy*. Sherryl and her life partner spend their summers in the mountain town of Grand Lake, Colorado.

For more information about *The Delta Tango Trilogy*, please go to www.deltatangotrilogy.com, email us at Deltatangotrilogy@gmail.com, or follow us on Instagram or Facebook, searching for Delta Tango Trilogy.

A free ebook edition is available with the purchase of this book.

To claim your free ebook edition:

1. Visit MorganJamesBOGO.com
2. Sign your name CLEARLY in the space
3. Complete the form and submit a photo of the entire copyright page
4. You or your friend can download the ebook to your preferred device

Morgan James BOGO™

A **FREE** ebook edition is available for you or a friend with the purchase of this print book.

CLEARLY SIGN YOUR NAME ABOVE

Instructions to claim your free ebook edition:
1. Visit MorganJamesBOGO.com
2. Sign your name CLEARLY in the space above
3. Complete the form and submit a photo of this entire page
4. You or your friend can download the ebook to your preferred device

Print & Digital Together Forever.

Snap a photo   Free ebook   Read anywhere

Printed in the USA
CPSIA information can be obtained
at www.ICGtesting.com
JSHW022331140824
68134JS00019B/1411